ZOMBIES · WEREWOLVES · ARMAGEDDON

PAVLOV'S DOGS

Permuted Press
The formula has been changed...
Shifted... Altered... Twisted.
www.permutedpress.com

ZOMBIES · WEREWOLVES · ARMAGEDDON

PAVLOV'S DOGS

D.L. SNELL
THOM BRANNAN

Permuted Press
The formula has been changed...
Shifted... Altered... Twisted.
www.permutedpress.com

ACKNOWLEDGMENTS

D.L. SNELL

Thanks to John Sunseri and Jacob Kier for their help brainstorming the original concept, and thanks to our awesome beta reader, author C. Dulaney. Also, I owe a debt of gratitude to my family: without you, none of this would be possible.

THOM BRANNAN

For Kitty, without whom my world would have no color, my sky, no sun or stars.

A PERMUTED PRESS book
Published by arrangement with the author
ISBN-13: 978-1-61868-021-1
ISBN-10: 1-61868-021-8

Turning and turning in the widening gyre
The falcon cannot hear the falconer;
Things fall apart...

W.B. YEATS

ZERO

THE SMELL OF SCORCHED OIL and metal came as a relief, considering the whole world was rotting under Paulo's nose. He and Marie hid behind the remains of an overturned Blazer, its trailer twisted around the hitch.

"I can no hear them," Marie said.

Normally at this point Paulo would have poked fun, lovingly, at her poor English. Normally.

He took in the dark, wavy hair framing her face, took in the strands of it stuck in her tears. Paulo decided to never make fun of her again, for as long as they lived.

Leaning down, he kissed Marie's forehead. "*Amorcita*, if we can't hear them, maybe they can't hear us." He took her hand and put it to his lips.

Marie smiled, knowing they were in bad trouble and he was going out of his way to comfort her, and loving him for it.

They moved together, stepping around the overturned Blazer.

Each of them had seen so much death in the past month. *In the past hour.* A whole world full of death and pain. So neither of them had paid any heed to the body pinned underneath the trailer, mainly because the corpse hadn't been of the variety that moved. But now it *was*.

The crushed woman looked at them without any eyes and moaned. It didn't take long for others to join in. They came out of nowhere and everywhere all at once: alleyways, shattered storefronts; one even jumped off a roof. Its legs shattered on impact, but even that was not enough to stop it.

At the sight and smell of the couple, arms shot up, jaws sprang open. Rheumy eyes zeroed in.

And the moaning.

The endless moaning.

Insistent. Tortured.

Like people dying at a hospital, groaning for help.

Paulo ran with short steps, giving himself shin splints so Marie could keep up. She could only run so fast. Not nearly fast enough.

He looked back, cursing their pursuers. Even the best horn players had to take breaths, yet these *things* could go on and on. Tireless. Ceaseless. Rolling out their monotonous one-note dirge.

Paulo steered them down an alleyway.

Suddenly Marie was falling down, dragging Paulo with her and crying out. She had rolled her ankle in a pothole.

No world, no public services. No DOT.

Marie sobbed as Paulo helped her up. He cringed and glanced down the alleyway. If any hungry corpses lurked ahead, they had just been called to dinner, certainly no thanks to the walking horn section behind them.

"*No puedo*, Paulo. I can't go on."

"No." Paulo hunched and pulled her arm over his shoulders. "We keep on moving, and we do it together."

Somewhere ahead, the forever moan was answered. By a single woman, from the sound of it. Otherwise, the alley seemed clear.

Paulo looked back, gauging the speed of the graveyard dragging itself along behind them.

Dead men ahead.

Dead women and children behind.

Paulo realized they didn't have much of a choice.

He and Marie hobbled forward together, and Paulo's eyes darted about, looking for *anything* they could call a shelter.

As if by some answered prayer, he saw a door ahead of them, slightly ajar. Paulo laughed once, and Marie lifted her head.

"What?"

He pointed out the door, and they altered their trajectory toward it.

Just ahead, a few dead men came around the corner. They instantly locked onto the couple.

"*Van a caer*," Marie said as Paulo moved faster, dragging her along. "If we fall..."

"Then we won't fall," Paulo said.

He and Marie moved almost as fast as the men. Judging by distance and speed, he worried they would reach the door at the same exact time.

Then what?

Die in the street?

As they drew in, the dead men lunged, snapped, then ran into the metal door just as Paulo slammed it shut behind him.

"I didn't hear it click." He bent down to study the moving parts. "Baby, there's no *latch*."

With a wave, Marie directed his attention to the room in which they now found themselves. She leaned against one wall, and the other three walls weren't far away. It was a small space, bare, completely empty: hall, tiled floor, a bit of debris that must have blown in with the wind.

"*¡Nada!*" she said. "No block, no nothing."

"We should go farther—"

Thump.

The door jumped against Paulo's shoulder. He jammed his foot against the base of it, into the crack, and pressed harder with his upper body. It felt as if he were holding back the pounding, swelling of the sea.

His cowboy boots slid. Not by a lot, but they slid.

"Marie, *por favor...*"

He didn't have to say the rest. They had been together so long—on the run for so long—some things could be left unspoken.

Marie nodded, then limped from one wall to the next. It had looked like such a small space, but crossing it felt like three hundred feet. She practically fell into the far wall.

Sweating, whimpering, favoring her one foot, Marie shuffled over to the hallway.

"Here!" she said. "*¡Una puerta!*"

The door stood at the end of the short hall, leading into an adjacent room.

"Keep going!" Paulo called, shouting over the constant drumming of bones and dead skin on hollow metal. "Find us something, Marie, *por favor!*"

She reached for the knob, but hesitated. How many times had they gone through one door only to turn back, chased by the dead?

It didn't matter though.

There was only one choice left.

Marie turned the knob.

Beyond, she saw another empty room, but the outer wall had crumbled to a pile of mortar and brick. She could see out into the alleyway, which was completely packed with the living dead, all trampling and climbing over each other like frenzied ants.

Marie put her hand over her mouth. So this was the force Paulo was holding back with a single metal door and a cowboy boot. And she knew the slightest sound would attract their wrath. Like *red* ants attacking a bug.

Luckily the dead didn't notice her as Marie quietly closed the wooden door. She noticed that the knob *could be* locked, if only they had the key.

Marie hobbled over to Paulo, who met her eyes briefly as she leaned back against his metal shield. He blinked and shook his head.

When would it ever end?

Even though they knew the answer to that, they sometimes wished to just get it over with. But then their common sense got the better of them because sometimes even death was not the end.

Paulo started to ask what Marie had found, but stopped. The fresh tears on her face answered his question.

She took a shuddering breath. "This is it, *mi vida*." She reached out and caressed the pocket of Paulo's jeans. "Do you still have them?"

He lowered his head and pushed harder on the door. A dark look had come over his face. "I wish we still had the gun."

Caressing his cheek, Marie smiled. "Do you still?"

"Yes," he said, "I have them."

Staring into his eyes, she dug into Paulo's pocket and pulled out the small cardboard sheath.

"I lost the other one," he said.

"But one is enough, no?"

He couldn't wipe the grave expression off his face. A gun would have been much quicker. Just two bullets and it would all be done. But a single razor blade? He imagined having to cut her, watching the light go out of her eyes as her life leaked onto the floor of this filthy little room.

Paulo blinked hard and swallowed. He thought about cutting himself after, but while he was still dying, and too weak to move, the dead would finally get to them.

Paulo caught Marie's hand and kissed her fingertips, tasting a bit of salt and grit.

"It is," he said. "It's enough."

They leaned in to share one last kiss, and as their lips parted, they heard it. Something *new*.

"Is that a... wolf?" Paulo said.

The hairs on the back of Marie's neck shivered on end. "*No se*, Paulo. It sounds like."

The single howl rose into a chorus, and the beating on the door ceased. They heard dead meat slump against the metal and slide down. The relentless weight was lifted from the door, as if the deadly invaders had simply ceased to exist.

Paulo reached to open it.

Marie slapped at his hand.

"Eh, stupid."

"I have to *see*."

She fidgeted, glanced back toward the hallway that led to nowhere. "Just a crack," she told him.

Paulo agreed.

He opened the door, just a crack, just enough to let in the light of some brand new nightmare.

Dark-skinned, hulking figures moved among the shambling dead, scything a path with their talons. Heads went flying, arms went flying. Corpses were launched into the air.

A large hairy beast, with fur like a golden retriever, leapt from car to car, homing in on the couple. Paulo's eyes widened as the figure lunged.

He slammed the door.

The day he first had seen a dead man get up and walk, Paulo had thought he had gone insane. Then after a while, the undead had become commonplace.

Now Paulo was *sure* he had gone insane.

He told Marie to run—hide!

There was no place but the hall.

She hid there, hoping it was deep enough, hoping Paulo would join her.

She heard the hollow boom of the metal door being pounded open, could hear Paulo cry out.

And then Paulo was *screaming*, his voice moving away, growing distant.

Marie whimpered.

Resisted the urge to peek.

Paulo.

He wouldn't stop screaming, somewhere out there. They had always hoped their deaths would be quick.

Marie couldn't help herself; she stuck her head around the corner, into the room.

One of the *wolves* was just stalking past the door, but then it stopped. Marie almost sobbed as she ducked back into the hall. She could hear it, sniffing.

She couldn't stand it anymore—she opened the door and stumbled into the adjacent room, toward the broken wall.

In the alley beyond, the dead lay in a common grave, twitching here and there, but overall silent and still.

Marie scrambled over the heap of brick, then tripped and fell face-first into the pile of corpses.

The wolf at the door whipped around, homed in again, and chased after her. It was a short chase.

Marie squealed as the beast tossed her over its shoulder. She clawed and kicked and screeched. It didn't seem to faze the monster in the least.

It carried her over the heaps of severed heads, jerking limbs, and slippery guts. They emerged into the street, and she saw a tractor clearing cars, and a bus behind it.

"Marie!" Paulo called.

The wolf with the golden coat was carrying him toward the bus—was loading him onto it.

From one of the bus's makeshift gun ports, he shouted again.

"Marie!"

And then he said something she didn't understand. "There's an island! They said there's an—!"

ONE MONTH AGO

ONE

THETA KAISER went for the throat. Samson sidestepped the attack, losing only a chunk of hairy flesh to his adversary's fangs. A canine tooth nicked his artery though, which spurted briefly before healing. Black skin grew back and new hair sprouted, softer than the rest.

"Their aggression," Donovan said. "Their loyalty to their Master. How is that all...?"

"Moderated?" Dr. Crispin said.

He and Donovan stood outside the chain-link fence of the arena, hands folded behind their backs.

"I was going to say 'controlled.'"

"How do you control any wild beast?" Crispin asked.

"Hmm?" Donovan had already stopped paying attention. "With obedience training, I'm sure. Or you just put the sorry mongrel out of its misery."

"Obedience training, correct. But also with a shock collar." Crispin held up some kind of papery web ensconced in a small case. "You've heard of BCI, yes?"

"Of course," Donovan said, not even attempting to hide his annoyance. He took great exception when someone insulted his intelligence. "That brain-computer interface is the shock collar, I presume."

Crispin smiled, yet cocked his head, as if he couldn't believe Donovan knew the answer. "Yes. Very astute."

Donovan took the BCI harness and looked it over. "Silk," he said, admiring the crinkly filaments; the strands of the web were each about 2.5 microns thick, so thin they looked as if they might fall apart if not supported by the case. Electrode arrays had been printed onto the grid.

"Indeed," Crispin replied. "Imagine a silk dress, the way it, ah, *clings* to a woman's hips. Now imagine the same principle here, only applied to the convolutions of the brain. One quick saline flush, and viola! Man's best friend."

"Fairly advanced BCI," Donovan said, and Crispin smiled with affected modesty. Then he and the new technician looked back into the arena as Kaiser spit out the chunk of neck meat and growled.

Samson growled back.

By going for the throat, Kaiser had changed a routine combat exercise into a power play. In front of their Master, no less. Samson was the Beta Dog, second in command. Kaiser was just a Theta. A grunt. If Samson were to lose to this *subordinate*, he would lose everything, including his rank.

And then the Dogs charged across the sparring cage, clawing at each other's arms and chests, nipping at each other's face. Blood and hair flew all over the concrete floor, and the combatants healed as they fought, their wounds scabbing over and sealing even as new ones opened up.

Kaiser slammed Samson against the chain link with a loud clash.

"Whoa," Dr. Crispin said, laughing and stepping back. "Rambunctious."

Donovan didn't shy away from the action. He stood so close he could smell the dog fur, could smell the coppery tang of blood.

Dr. Crispin laughed nervously. "You might want to step back. Just a small safety precaution."

Donovan ignored the advice. He reached out as the Dogs wrestled, and he touched Samson's Rottweiler fur, which was pressed through the diamond pattern of the fence.

"Dr. Donovan!" Crispin shouted. He went to pull the neurotech's hand back, but then the Dogs pushed away from the fence and circled each other deeper into the arena, crisis averted.

Donovan turned and noted the sweat on Crispin's brow. "They wouldn't have bitten me, would they? The chip."

"Well," Dr. Crispin began, "there's a reason we hired you." He let the statement linger and gazed out upon his Dogs.

Samson locked eyes with Kaiser, trying to anticipate his opponent's next strike.

Kaiser feinted and Samson fell for it. Ducking, rolling, swiping, Kaiser raked away both of his opponent's Achilles tendons. The Beta Dog fell and Kaiser again went for the throat. This time his teeth locked behind the esophagus, and when he shook his head and pulled back, he left a ragged hole that sucked for air and ejaculated blood.

Samson fell back, lying flat, dazed but regenerating, in utter disbelief.

Kaiser, panting heavily, spit out the mass of tissue and licked his bloody chops. Suddenly, he began to howl and transform. The bestial sound triggered something deep in Donovan's brain, and he felt a shiver run through his nervous system.

The neurotechnician squinted and leaned closer to the fence, studying the anatomy of the transformation. Beneath Kaiser's skin, bones shifted, and his snout sank into his face. The Dog's spine wrung an agonized cry from him, a uniquely human sound, as his vertebrae straightened and realigned.

Finally, after the Dog had shed all of his German shepherd fur, he was naked, muscular and sweating.

Shaved head. Cool blue eyes.

Human.

"The Change," Donovan said quietly. "I would have thought it was tied to the moon."

Crispin nodded. "Naturally, yes. And I honestly cannot tell you why, only that I know by observation that this is how it works; moonlight is its natural stimulus.

"But with the interface, I have managed to trick the brain. The Dogs simply have to *think* of the Change, and the BCI stimulates or inhibits the pituitary's very special growth hormones. From there, it's all a matter of proper enzymes and catalysts."

"Hmm." Donovan focused on Samson, who, with his reconstructed throat, gasped for breath.

The Beta, too, had reverted to human form, and he lay prone in a husk of dead cells and a pile of Rottweiler hair, some of which stuck to his dark, sweaty skin.

Donovan looked more closely at the two soldiers. He realized it wasn't sweat but liquefied fat and muscle shed from their fuller lupine forms. Then the smell hit him, and he stepped back, blinking away tears. It was acrid, a mix of rapid decay and something like burning plastic.

Kaiser, the triumphant, extended a hand to his opponent. When Samson went to accept it, Kaiser pulled back.

Grinning, he said, "On your feet, *Theta*. That's an order."

Not for the first time, Samson noticed Kaiser's human teeth, his canines just as sharp as his fangs. The fallen soldier struggled to his feet, still woozy from asphyxiation and shock and... loss.

"Excellent demonstration, boys!" Dr. Crispin shouted from the fence. For all he knew about lycanthropic behavior, he was oblivious to the shift in power that had just occurred. "I'll have you shower up and see Summer for therapy!"

The Dogs nodded and strode off toward the facility, a utilitarian building that housed the barracks, clinic, and cafeteria. The science labs were located in another building on the other side of the island.

Donovan turned to Crispin and raised an eyebrow. "Therapy?"

"Yes. Rather like bodybuilders. Without hormone therapy, the lower ranking Dogs would be stuck in their human phase for..." Crispin checked his watch, noting the lunar cycle. "Another three weeks, as their hormones waxed naturally with the moon."

Donovan raised his eyebrow even higher. "And what about the Alpha Dog? Is he akin to a bodybuilder?"

Crispin's grin grew very smug. "No, the Alpha is my crowning achievement. You'll meet him after your reception dinner."

Donovan smiled too, and Crispin realized he didn't like the man. He was clean-shaven, and his mouth looked like an infant's, accustomed to sucking and biting to meet its needs. But that wasn't it. Crispin couldn't quite put his finger on it.

The disobedience: maybe that accounted for his dislike. He saw the same rebellious spirit in Kaiser at times; the ability to resist commands despite the systems put in place to dictate it. Donovan excelled in his field though, was probably the best neurotechnician around, and not everyone was willing to work under such secrecy. Especially not for a privately-funded team operating under the government's radar.

Whatever aversion Crispin felt, he swallowed it, because Donovan was their last hope at emerging triumphant from the oppression of mainstream science.

"Well, sir," the project director said, clapping a hand on his new neurotechnician's shoulder. "Let us show you to your office."

Donovan nodded, thinking that he had a very ambitious ladder to climb here, and then he and Crispin headed toward the labs.

TWO

THE POP-TOP CRACKED open and foam came out of the beer can, but it didn't get anywhere. A black-mustached face came down and slurped up the overflow.

The man in the driver's seat looked over. "Come on, Jorge. You're gonna get us a ticket." He checked his mirrors. No cops, but traffic had been stop-and-go ever since he had merged onto the highway.

"Nah," Jorge said between gulps. "It's beer-thirty." He sat back and put his foot up on the dashboard of the Blazer. "And since when do you care about getting pulled over?"

The driver was a large man with sandy hair and a matching beard. Broad shoulders stretched the fabric of his chambray work shirt, and thick forearms kept the rolled-up sleeves tight and in place. He shot his friend a look, then one corner of his mouth came up. "Since I haven't registered the new gun. Check it out. It's under your seat. And at least keep the beer low, huh?"

Jorge, a slightly smaller, slightly rounder brown-skinned man, leaned down and rummaged under the seat. He held the beer up and steady on the dashboard.

Ken stared at the beer can, then stared at his friend.

Jorge smiled. "It's still beer-thirty."

"Whatever."

With a grunt, Jorge pulled a black case from under the seat. "Bitchin' eagle," he said, staring at the embossed motif on the case's lid. He put his beer in the cup-holder as he fiddled with the snaps. "Wedged in there good. How were you gonna—*¡a la madre!*" He brought up a re-volver from the case. It was large, with a blued finish and a rail along the five-inch barrel. "What is this, a fifty?"

Ken's smile returned. "Forty-four. I just picked it up off a guy. He—hey!"

He ducked and accidentally pulled on the steering wheel as Jorge swung the revolver around in the cab. The Blazer lurched to one side.

"Kidding! Kidding," Jorge said. He looked back through the rear window. "*Hijo de puta*, you gotta calm down, man. That trailer is heavy."

Ken looked over a moment at Jorge. His eyes went to the revolver in his friend's right hand, then flicked to the beer can now back in the other. Ken started laughing.

"What?" Jorge said. "I already told you, it's beer—"

"—thirty, yes, I heard you. Crazy ass." He laughed harder. Range safety had never been Jorge's "thing." He knew the gun wasn't loaded.

Smiling, Jorge put the revolver back into the case. "That is a nice gun. I hope you didn't spend *my* wages on it."

"Nope," Ken said. "Just half your paycheck. Didn't cost more than surgery or a new windshield, for instance."

Jorge ignored him. "What a day. I didn't think we were ever going to get out of there."

"Ah, that's how it is," Ken said, wiping his eyes. "I, ah, heh. You shit head. We get back to *la casa*, you want to shoot that thing?"

The beer can came up. "Why not? I got nothing else to do. And we'll get to shoot this, too." His left hand dug under his plaid work shirt and came back with a black square-looking pistol. "Eh?"

"Is that an automatic? What is that?"

Jorge laughed. "This, my Caucasian friend, is Mexican Judo."

"Oh, shut up," Ken said, chuckling again.

"It's a Glock."

"I can't believe you toted that thing around all day. You're mental." He looked out the windshield at all the traffic. "Is it a holiday or some-thing?"

Finishing the beer and chucking the can into the back seat, Jorge shook his head. "If it was a holiday, my ex would either be bitching be-cause I don't have the kids, or sending me pics of her having fun with them, rubbing her quality family time in my face." He burped. "Can't make up her mind." Jorge sank deeper into his seat and waved his hand at the traffic as it got denser and denser. "This is just how it is, I guess."

Ken's eyes slid over for a second, taking in the new expression on his friend's face. Sometimes there were reasons it was beer-thirty.

"Maybe this weekend we'll get out of town," Ken said. "Go camping or something."

Jorge snapped another beer open. "You chop the firewood."

"I always chop the firewood."

He shrugged. "You're good at it. Maybe you were a lumberjack in your previous life."

"Maybe you're a lazy ass in this one."

Jorge did his shrug again, which was so eloquent. Along with the look on his face, it said everything.

Around them, the stream of cars had thickened to a river and had slowed considerably. Ken looked over at the eastbound side of the highway, noting that the incoming lanes were mostly clear. The drive from downtown to the suburbs was usually a slow one, but *this*... and it wasn't even the weekend. He looked around at the cars, then checked his rearview mirrors. Stacked back there, too. And he was stuck in the center of it all, right in the middle lane.

Ken sucked in a breath and blew it out. He hated traffic—hated being hemmed-up in any way, really. And Jorge was right, work had been a bear. More than once that day he'd had to take his ten-step Anger Management card from his breast pocket and work through it. He hated the card, hated the class, but even though it was the dumbest thing in the world to him when he started, it had helped. Today was a tester. All paperwork and legalese.

Ken looked forward to shooting the new gun later. Hell, he even looked forward to shooting Jorge's automatic. His first experience with one was a Browning Hi-Power, and it had pinched the webbing between his thumb and forefinger so badly, he was converted to revolvers for the rest of his life. But it was one of those days.

And is it getting worse?

Traffic ground to a halt and he put the Blazer in park. "You've got to be kidding me."

Jorge nodded. "You're going to run out of beer by the time we get there." He popped a third can. "Better hope this clears up."

With a disdainful glance at the white can in Jorge's hand, Ken sniffed. "I'll be all right, thank you. That swill you're drinking is making you fat. Did you notice?"

Gasping, Jorge grabbed at the spare tire around his midsection. "*¡Ay ay ay!* When did this happen?"

They laughed, but it was short-lived. Ken started to tap his fingers on the steering wheel. "Come *on*."

He reached down and jabbed a blunt finger into the radio power button. It came on with a burst of static, and he cursed as he spun the volume knob down.

Even Jorge jumped. "You almost made me spill my beer," he said, looking cross.

Ken dialed the volume back up slowly. The station was on talk radio, so he hit the SCAN button. "You remember the AM station for traffic alerts?"

Jorge burped.

"Didn't think so," Ken said, turning the dial. Short snippets of songs came over the speakers as he sailed from station to station. "Whoop, got one."

"*... have erupted in New Orleans*," was all he heard before stabbing the SCAN button again.

"Fuck New Orleans," he said, and Jorge erupted in laughter.

He pointed at Ken. "You're still pissed about what happened at Harrah's! You got to get over that, bro. The house beat you fair and shquare."

"Fuck you, too," Ken said, smiling at Jorge's slurring. There was no way his buddy was already that drunk. "And I loved that truck."

"Sure you did," Jorge said. "But now you got Bertha the Blazer, who ain't never let you down." He patted the dashboard. "Ain't that right, baby? Aw, I know. Ken don't appreciate you the way he ought to. Let's say you and me, later, in the garage—"

"I have a gun."

"Under yo' *seat!*" Jorge slapped his own automatic, which still sat on the center console, close at hand; he had won.

"Under *your* seat," Ken said, laughing. "And it might as well be in Egypt. There's no way I'm venturing near your... hold on."

He stopped hitting the SCAN button and turned the volume up.

"*... wave of violence has—zzt!—National Guard have been deployed to—zzshht!—rumors of—*"

Jorge grunted. "Your radio sucks."

"Shut up."

Ken hit a button and swapped the radio to the FM stations, hoping for better reception. He immediately skipped the gospel station and stopped again.

"... has washed over Georgetown—zzt!—National Guard have been deployed to protect and defend—zzt!—rumors of walki—"

"We just heard that," Jorge said, putting his beer down. "Didn't we?"

Ken nodded and looked at his watch. "Yeah. Yeah, we did. Jesus, we've been sitting here for thirty minutes already."

"Doesn't seem that long to me."

"Says the guy with the beer." Ken stabbed the power button again; he had lost the station to static anyway. "We're going nowhere."

Shrugging, Jorge took off his seatbelt and opened the Blazer door, letting in the random shouts of frustrated motorists. He stood on the runner and looked out over the still ribbon of multi-colored metal. "I can't see anything," he said. "Cars are backed up all the way down. You think something's happening up that way?"

"Who knows?" Ken yelled over the horns that had joined the vocal cacophony. "Maybe it's still happening."

Jorge ducked his head back into the Blazer. "I'm gonna go take a look." He stepped down to the asphalt.

"If you're not back here by the time it starts moving..."

"I'll shoot your tires and we'll both walk out of here," Jorge said.

"Better take that then." Ken gestured to the 9mm. "Don't want an automatic in the car, anyway. Open alcohol's bad enough. I got binoculars, if you want. Check in the back seat."

Grunting, Jorge leaned the passenger seat forward and craned into the back. He paused for a moment and whistled. "You got a rifle in here, too?"

Ken turned to check, and yes, he had left his rifle in its case back there. "Huh," he said. "Forgot that was back there. I tried to sell it last weekend."

"What is it?"

Ken scowled. "Forget it. You'll just try to talk me down on price. Look for the—"

"I see 'em," Jorge said, snatching at a pair of black binoculars. "Gun me, bro."

Laughing, Ken handed the automatic over to Jorge. "Call me when you see what the hell it is." He pulled his cell phone from the center console and plugged it in.

"Sí, señor."

Ken chuckled at his friend and watched him amble up the shoulder of the road. A lot of people at work couldn't stand Jorge and his sense of humor, but Ken found him funny and refreshing, and after all, Ken was the contractor and could decide what was what and who was who. Jorge wasn't afraid to say what was on his mind, no matter how asinine it might sound to everybody else. Zero brain-to-mouth filter. Ken's ex-wife couldn't stand him. Neither could *Jorge's* ex-wife.

Then, realizing that he didn't have anybody to talk to now, Ken turned the radio back on. The first thing he heard was news of more insurgent activity (or whatever) in the Middle East.

"Whole world's falling apart."

THREE

SOFT, ANONYMOUS MUSIC filtered through the sounds of people at a meal; the clink of a fork on a plate, the murmur of conversation, the ringing chime of glass on glass. There was an occasional hiccup of restrained laughter.

The long, rectangular room played host to dozens of scattered oval tables, around which sat groups of people. The men and women were equally represented, and it was clear by their groupings which table was which.

Dr. Crispin, who had shed his lab coat, stepped into the room and waved his new neurotechnician forward. "This, Dr. Donovan, is the dining room. We like to call it Spago's Stepsister, but don't let the chef hear you."

Donovan nodded absently as he took in the various cliques in the dining room and the way they had arranged themselves. He didn't know who they were, not yet, but from how they sat with each other, and from their interactions, he had a good idea of who the linchpin personalities were for each department. He nodded to people as Dr. Crispin pulled him to the table nearest the doors at the end, the one with two empty seats.

He made a bet with himself as to which seat was Dr. Crispin's.

He won.

Crispin stood behind his chair, gripping the back of it tightly. He cleared his throat, then cleared it again, and the conversation dried up around the room.

"Thank you. I would like you all to meet Doctor Cornelius Donovan, our new neurotechnician. He comes highly recommended, and I would appreciate it if you all made him feel welcome."

Donovan, suddenly on the spot, turned and offered a half-hearted wave to the group. If Crispin wanted him to feel welcome, he would have skipped the part where he introduced Donovan by first name.

"Now then," Crispin said, taking his seat at the place setting. "Please, do introduce yourselves."

From table to table, people glanced at each other. Dr. Donovan shifted his weight from one foot to the other, but couldn't get comfortable in the spotlight.

For his part, Crispin was busily congratulating himself on making the new man the focus of this awkward situation. No, he didn't like Donovan, but it was more than that. The tech's resume had been impeccable, and combined with the lack of decorum (and fear) he had shown as they'd watched the Dogs spar and tear at each other's throats... the combination gnawed at Crispin. Donovan's youth was another point against him. Crispin knew what sort of single-minded and bloody determination it took to be acknowledged in any of the sciences, and for the new neurotechnician to have achieved that recognition already, well...

Keep your eyes off my job, Dr. Crispin thought.

Meanwhile, the head of another table stood up to begin the introductions. He was a man in his forties, with a wrinkled brow and a receding hairline. When he spoke, his voice carried with authority. "My name is Todd Sales, human resources. And this is Jenny Freis and Mauricio Tapia."

"Major General Mauricio Tapia," Jenny Freis interrupted. She looked at Donovan and said, "Mauricio's always reminding people that he was in the Air Force."

Everyone laughed, and Mauricio Tapia looked embarrassed but reserved. Then Todd Sales turned back to Donovan and said, "Ah, welcome." He cracked a smile as if it pained him to do so, and then he sat.

At the next table over stood a tall woman with hair like a dandelion. "Hello," she said brightly. "I'm Tracy Rivers, and this is Oscar and Homer Anders." She indicated a pair of curly-headed men, obviously brothers. "We're the admin team. If you need any materials for your work, just let us know!"

She sat and another woman on the other side of the room stood up. "Carmen, IT. This is Lucy, Lucy, and Pat—and don't worry about getting our names right."

"We know you won't," one of the Lucys said before knocking back her glass of wine.

Donovan's smile felt clammy on his lips, so he let it drop. The prospect of getting help from any of these people didn't appeal to him in the slightest.

From another table, a very fat man stood up with a wheeze. His red face gleamed with sweat, and Donovan felt uncomfortable looking at him.

"Ronald," the fat man said. "Ronald Michaels. I'm in charge of the medical facilities."

"He's not a doctor," Drinking Lucy chimed in, "but he plays one on an island."

"Lucy..." Dr. Crispin said, and Carmen put a hand on Lucy's, who promptly shook it off.

"As I was saying," Ronald continued, "the medical facilities are mine and my team's. Meet Alison Levenseller and Joshua Ericson, the nurses." He indicated a small, surly blonde who had a mouth full of food, and an equally surly dark-complected man, who desperately needed a meal.

Donovan felt a kick under the table, and he turned. Next to him sat another woman, a redhead with vibrant green eyes. "If you get hurt, come to me," she said quietly. Donovan looked back at Ronald Michaels' nursing staff and nodded.

A man was standing almost directly behind Donovan, and the neurotechnician had to turn so far to see him that his back popped loudly in the dining room. The other man, oblivious to Donovan's discomfort, pushed up his glasses and started talking.

"Doctor, I looked you up online as soon as I heard you were coming, and let me just say, I am thrilled to be working with you." He beamed at Donovan, waiting for a reply, until someone at the table smacked his wrist with a butter knife.

"Ow, what? Oh!" His pale skin flushed to the roots of his light brown hair, and he began to stammer. "I'm, ah, Gary Sims, and I'll be your lab assistant. And this is Summer Chan." He indicated his knife-wielding co-worker, a blond girl with a pert nose. "Also meet Scott Halstead."

Scott nodded his welcome.

Dr. Donovan looked back to the people sitting at his table, the red-head who had kicked him and a stern-looking older black man with a shaved head.

"Is this everyone?" Donovan asked.

"No, Doctor," the black man replied. "We eat in shifts, and I only gathered the people you see here because they're the ones you're most likely to interact with on a daily basis." He reached out a hand. "My name is Luke Jaden, head of security."

Donovan shook the man's hand and was immediately aware of the rough skin and strong grip.

"And my name is Holly Randall," said the redhead who had kicked him. "Maintenance is my department."

"Maintenance of what?"

She extended her arms to encompass the entire world. "Everything. I have an electrician, an electronics tech, a mechanic, and a welder. I'm the engineer. I dream it up, and they make it work." She smiled. "You're going to want to get to know me."

Gary Sims, Donovan's fanboy and cyberstalker, stood up and said, "Dr. Donovan—speech!" He started chanting it and looked around, hoping others would join in. His cheeks turned bright red when no one did.

Donovan started to stand up anyway, because he actually had pre-pared something. But Dr. Crispin put a hand on his shoulder and ges-tured for him to take his seat. Donovan remained standing. So Dr. Crispin threw his arm around the neurotechnician's shoulders, hoping to hide his inability to make this man do anything.

"I would just like to say a few words," the project director said, and Donovan caught Holly sinking in her chair.

"First, I would like to welcome Doctor Donovan to the compound. I know that with his credentials, he will very much be an asset to my team. With some guidance, he will become a great part of this well-oiled machine I have assembled, and together, we all will see the project through to fruition.

"Times have been tough, and we have suffered many setbacks, but please have no doubt that I will lead us into the annals of scientific and military history." His eyes widened a touch and he squeezed the neuro-technician heartily. "And Doctor Donovan's expertise will be the tip of the spear."

He let go of Donovan and struck up a light golf clap, which the rest of the room joined enthusiastically. Looking around, Donovan smiled and bowed, then took his seat.

"Don't let it go to your head," he heard Holly whisper. "We're all just happy he's shut up already."

"Long winded?" Donovan asked, not turning to look at her.

"Very," she said.

Luke Jaden, head of security, had already stopped his applause and was hungrily tearing into the chicken parmesan on his plate. Donovan looked down at his own meal; there was a dark-orange sauce between the cheese and the chicken.

He poked at it with his fork.

"It's good," Holly said around a mouthful of food. "Try to ignore the color."

Donovan's reply was interrupted by a newcomer in a blue jacket, walking briskly to the table and leaning down between Dr. Crispin and Luke Jaden. Donovan was barely able to make out the man's words.

"It's all over the airwaves, on every frequency. I'm not sure what to make of the reports, but... it's very odd. I need someone to check it out and make a decision."

Crispin's face wrinkled. When he answered, his voice was higher than Donovan had ever heard it.

"Why does it have to be me? It's like you people can't get anything done without approvals signed in triplicate. If I wanted that, I would have stayed with the government."

"Ah," the man said, shifting inside his blue jacket. "I meant I need Mr. Jaden, Doctor. This is definitely a security issue. Or at least, it could be."

Dr. Crispin threw his napkin to his plate. "I was done eating anyway. Mr. Jaden, if you please?"

As the lean, dark man stood, he nodded to Holly and Donovan. "Perhaps you should come also, Miss Randall."

Dr. Crispin shot the head of security an annoyed look, which went pointedly ignored.

"And you, Dr. Donovan," Jaden said. "If you're a part of the Command team, there's no time like the present."

Dr. Crispin started off without them. Neither Holly nor Luke hurried to keep up. Donovan noted this and lengthened his stride to measure up.

"Dr. Crispin," he said. "I would like to start as soon as possible. My predecessor must have left some notes behind, and the sooner I start on them, the better. I'm not unfamiliar with his work, but the Dogs intrigue me." He licked his lips. "How long will Beta Samson be in the recovery ward?"

The project director shook his head. "Not long, Doctor. The Dogs' healing processes are much faster than ours. But really, I must insist that you limit your exposure to the Dogs, at least for now." He turned a sharp eye to the neurotechnician. "We mustn't confuse them in any way."

This brought Donovan up short. "How do you mean?"

"We're here," Crispin said, punching in a four-digit access code to the radio room. The locking mechanism clicked and the door popped open an inch. The man in the blue jacket rushed forward to open it the rest of the way.

The radio room was a cold, dark office, jammed full of a dizzying array of equipment. Donovan turned to take it all in. He saw a radar screen, then another screen full of contoured static. The tech in the blue coat saw his gaze and said, "SONAR array in the waters off-island."

Donovan nodded absently, noting the name WINCHESTER stitched neatly on the jacket's right breast.

Several species of radio equipment shared space within a custom-built frame: a Thrane & Thrane cozied up next to a Furuno, their faces staring out at him. Under those sat an expansive JNC unit. Next to the radio frame squatted a set of screens; a control console of an AN/BQQ10 was mounted above, and Donovan recognized it as a piece of Army/Navy hardware. The other pieces... he was lost among it all.

A man sat in the room, wearing a pair of headphones and jotting on a piece of paper. Dr. Crispin and Luke Jaden stood patiently by, each with their hands clasped behind their backs. The head of security stood ramrod-straight, and Donovan knew he had to be ex-military.

"That's Morse," Holly said to Donovan as he watched the radioman translate and transcribe the beeps coming over his headphones. "Sometimes we catch messages on the Ham Radio. I think they're the only ones who still use it."

"It's the same message," the radioman said, putting his pen down. "Better get the old man and the n—"

"Ah, they're here," Winchester said.

The other tech stood, sending his chair spinning. "Sir!" he said.

24

"What's the same message?" Jaden asked, ignoring everything else. "What have we got here?"

The tech licked his lips. "You're not going to believe this, sir."

FOUR

"YOU'RE NOT GOING *to believe this,*" Jorge said over the phone. *"Pileup, man. And not just any garden-variety pileup. This is the mother of all—"*

"Will you just say it?"

"Whatever, grandma. Check it. There's a Greyhound on its back, and it looks like it's being humped by a big rig."

Ken snorted at the description. "Is there even a wrecker on the scene?"

"Well, yeah, but they're not moving anything yet. The paramedics are still dragging people out of the bus, which is lying on top of a motorcycle, I think. Jesus, it looks like an all-day thing."

Ken cursed under his breath, and his mind referred back to his Anger Management card. "There's nothing we can do about that. Is it really bad?"

"You should see this. I don't know how many dead there are, man. I haven't seen anything like this, not since the roller coaster went off-rail at—"

"I remember," Ken said. "I was there, too."

His fingers beat another quick tattoo on the steering wheel. Fatalities meant the road would be closed. And not just the part of the road where the crash had happened, either. The *whole* road, for a ways on either side of the accident. He was already thinking about an alternate route to take the next day, in case the investigation took that long.

Jorge whistled over the phone. *"Damn, bro. This is pretty gruesome. I think I can smell it."*

Ken wrinkled his nose. "Try not to breathe deep. You know what that is, right, when you smell something? Little particles of whatever it is, all up in your nose?"

Jorge *hurked* on the phone, and Ken smiled. The humor faded quickly as he remembered the reason for his friend's hurking, and he immediately felt bad for cracking a joke.

"How much longer, do you think?"

"They're not breaking any speed records, and... hang on. Well this guy is okay. You should see it, this guy's freaking out. I should be recording it, and... what the hell?"

"What?" Ken said. "What?!"

Farther up the highway, Jorge's hand came away from his ear, taking the cell phone with it.

"There's a fight," he said, lifting the phone to his mouth again. The last person out of the bus had wrapped bloodied arms around the neck of the paramedic and was *biting*. "One of the, uh, victims is freaking out and attacking the, uh..."

He stopped talking as all along the shoulder, figures with sheets draped over them started sitting up. On the overturned bus, the remaining windows broke as hands and fists came through, grasping at rescue workers.

"What's going on?" Ken said, sounding tinny over the phone.

"I think I drank too much."

"Jorge!"

"Right. Uh, people are getting themselves out of the bus, and, Jesus, one of them just tackled a cop. This is nuts! They're biting everybody!" He took a couple of steps forward. "Oh, sick. I think I... I think I see chewing."

"Get back to the car."

"Yeah, okay—"

One of the victims stood up and faced Jorge. Vacant eyes locked on his, and the phone fell from his numb fingers. Jorge's hearing went loopy, as if he were suddenly standing in a wind tunnel instead of the highway, and his vision narrowed drastically to include just the figure advancing on him. Motes danced around, colliding with each other to the mad music repeating in Jorge's head.

He. Has. No. Face.

He. Has. No. FACE.

Where the man's face should have been was just a red stain. Only shreds of pink skin remained in the crimson mess between chin and hairline. Most of it dangled like a torn mask from the man's neck. Deep runnels of black and dark red ringed the man's wide, staring eyes, and his jaw fell open as he took a step toward Jorge. An arm, bent backwards at the elbow, came up, its fingers hooked and twitching.

Screams from either side of him shook Jorge out of his daze. The people who had been lying on the shoulder were now up and leaning in through the windows of cars, heedless of their own gaping wounds as they attacked the motorists.

"Get me out of here!" Jorge yelled.

Back in the Blazer, Ken couldn't make out what Jorge had said, but from the sounds coming over the phone, he knew it wasn't good. He rolled down his window and put Big Bertha into gear, bumping the back fender of a car in the left lane. The driver, a bald-headed man, looked back with a what-the-hell set on his red face. Ken just leaned on his horn and bumped him again.

Of course I've got to be stuck in the middle, Ken thought.

The bald guy opened the driver-side door of his small brown coupe, and Ken dove across to Bertha's passenger side. He ripped the gun case out from under Jorge's seat. Glancing out the windshield, Ken fumbled the case open and grabbed the revolver, then sat up with it.

The bald man saw the gun, and his hands came up to his shoulders.

"No trouble," he said. Then he yelled it. The cacophony of honking horns and people shouting was almost deafening.

Ken waggled the gun at him to get back into his car, and then honked the horn again. The red-faced man, who had gone rather pale, fairly jumped back to his coupe and moved it forward three feet. Not a lot, but enough for the old Blazer to squeeze through without losing a whole lot of paint.

The van behind the coupe tried to immediately seal the gap, but Ken honked and pointed his gun at that guy too. Then, with a thank-you nod, which seemed ridiculous, Ken plowed the Blazer through the small gap and tore through the grassy median, his trailer bouncing and tools clanking behind.

After about forty yards, he saw he wasn't the only one with that idea; other drivers had seen something that spooked them, and were swerving out onto the grass, trying to get around the blockage in the road. Shapes hung onto the cars closer to the accident: some on the hood, some still leaning in through the windows. Feet kicked blindly for purchase, and the cars slalomed from side to side.

Jorge came running down the median, fleeing from another figure behind him. He wasn't watching where he was going, and didn't notice the old station wagon with a madman on its hood, heading right for him.

Stomping the gas, Ken sent Big Bertha surging forward. The heavy bumper of the Blazer clipped the rear end of the station wagon and sent it into a long, sideways skid. Its lead wheels hit a ditch and the station wagon rolled, missing Jorge by an inch. The hijacker on the hood went spiraling off into space, his arms and legs as loose as a rag doll's.

Ken watched it fly, and felt a thump as the Blazer hit something. He had a sick certainty that he hadn't hit a log. He stopped the Blazer and looked out; a man with twisted and crushed legs reached up toward the window, desperately pulling himself along on one arm. Ken groaned and opened the Blazer door.

He had stepped out to help the man when a terrific crunch of metal on metal pulled Ken's head up. On the highway, a huge passenger van had just collided with the wrecker, and they both were careening down the sloping median, right into another vehicle, this one a bright-red Jeep Cherokee.

A moan from the grass brought Ken's head back around.

I just hit a guy, he thought, and a cold sweat sprang from nothing on his brow. *Holy shit, I just hit a guy.*

"Hey!" Jorge yelled, scrambling for the door handle on the Blazer's passenger side. Behind him, aided by the peculiar slope of the median, the injured man staggered after, almost catching up. Ken was struck by the missing face.

And don't forget, a gleeful voice sang in the back of his head, *you just hit a guy.*

Jorge got into the car and slammed the door shut. Without even trying for the handle, the man without a face slapped his hands against the window and brought his mouth to it, jaws opening wide to bite at the smooth glass.

"Well?" Jorge yelled, and Ken snapped out of it.

With one last glance at the man he'd hit, Ken got into the Blazer, yelling, "I'm sorry!"

He eased onto the gas and spun the wheel, turning the heavy vehicle away from the carnage. Another car behind them flipped as it tried to do the same thing, and within seconds, staggering, shuffling figures descended on it like ants on a dead bird.

Ken goosed the accelerator, and the Blazer shot forward. "What the hell was that?" he yelled. His hands were shaking even as they squeezed the steering wheel.

Jorge shook his head. "I lost my phone."

"Your *phone?* That guy had no *face*. What the—Jesus!"

All four tires locked up as Ken slammed on the brakes, sending the Blazer into a skid. Big Bertha swayed, but held the road.

People who had run from the attackers now stood on the eastbound side of the highway, right where Ken was headed. There were maybe four pedestrians in all, and he made a snap decision.

"Let them in," he said.

"What? Did you *see* what was happening?"

Ken hit the steering wheel. "Hell yeah, I saw. And we can help them." *And you hit a guy!* his conscience screamed. "Let them in." He set his jaw, and Jorge had seen enough of that look at work to know he shouldn't even try to convince him otherwise.

"Whatever you say, boss. But I ain't getting out." He opened the door and shouted at the people. "Hey, free ride!"

Reaching down, Jorge leaned his seat forward for everyone to climb into the back, but he didn't make enough room. The first person to try, a young woman, had to blow out all of her breath to get through.

"Come on, Jorge," Ken said. "Really? Just get out, already. God *damn*, man, lay off the beer."

Shooting a black look at Ken, Jorge got out and stepped out of the way. As he did, several figures flocked to the open door, and soon the back seat was stuffed with four huddled people. Before Jorge could react, someone else, a sweaty fat man with a flat face and olive-hued skin, locked Jorge's seat in its upright position and jumped right in.

Jorge stared at him in disbelief, then his jaw dropped when yet another person jumped in the front, a slight girl holding a small dog.

"Ken..." he said.

"I don't know," Ken replied, realizing that it really wasn't an answer. The Blazer rocked, and he looked back, seeing people clambering onto the tool trailer, escaping the screams and gunshots behind them.

He blew out a breath, looked at Jorge, and cocked his head toward the trailer. "Just get on, man."

"Ken!"

"Just *do it*, will you? This isn't the time."

Jorge's face darkened, but he nodded. "There will be a time, you can bet your ass on that." He tromped to the back of the Blazer and got in.

FIVE

BY THE TIME DR. CRISPIN and the three team leaders made it back to the dining room, it was already full to capacity and beyond. All manner of men and women with worried looks lined the walls. Many of them Donovan didn't recognize from dinner, like the large man with dirty blond hair who stood at the front of the dining room. The man's thumbs were hooked in the belt loops of his dark-blue coveralls.

Donovan looked around and shook his head at the general atmosphere of anxiety. A glance at Jaden's face told him the head of security shared his feelings. Dr. Crispin's announcement over the loudspeakers had been poorly worded and frightening, but at least it had achieved the desired effect: everyone had gathered in one place as quickly as possible.

Ignoring all the pleading glances, Dr. Crispin marched to the front of the room. As he passed the large blond man in coveralls, he put his hand out, and the big man dropped his head once in quick acknowledgment.

"That's Alpha McLoughlin," Jaden told Donovan. "The rest of the Dogs are there behind him, minus Kaiser and Samson."

"They're still in therapy?" Donovan's sharp eyes roved over the band of homiform Dogs, wondering what they would look like after they changed.

At the head of the room, Dr. Crispin took to a podium that a member of the maintenance staff had set up. Two harried-looking technicians were hooking a sleek black microphone into an amplifier, which they had already attached to a pair of oversized speakers.

Dr. Crispin tapped the microphone, filling the room with a whine of feedback. The reaction was universal.

"Good, it works," he said. "I have an announcement. If any of you have already heard the rumors, it appears that they are true. As we dine, as we speak, the world outside our compound has been *set upon* by... well, I don't know how else to put it." He looked around the room. "The walking dead."

This was met with a mixture of gasps and guffaws. Those who were off-shift and had been watching the news, or those who were otherwise informed of the wide-scale rioting and upheaval, took the announcement with a resigned dignity—with a few exceptions. One lady (*The quiet Lucy*, Donovan thought) broke down into sobbing hysterics.

The laughter slowly died off as people around the room finally realized that, no, Dr. Crispin had not suddenly developed a sense of humor.

"I can't say what this will mean for us," Crispin said. "As far as we can tell, from the reports coming over the wireless and other sources, the phenomenon is widespread and universal. Communications—"

"What do you mean, you don't know what this means for us?" Joshua, the male nurse, said. His co-worker Alison tried to calm him down, but he recoiled from her as if she were holding a python. "This is serious."

"It is serious," Luke Jaden said, striding forward to join Dr. Crispin at the podium. "But we don't know what's being done. We can only assume that FEMA or Homeland Security is operating on a plan, and we may have to hold tight here for a couple of days."

Dr. Crispin nodded, placing his hand on the security man's shoulder. "Mr. Jaden is correct. We all know I've had my falling out with the military, but that was the upper brass. We need to have some kind of faith in the men and women on the ground."

Lucy spoke up through her tears. "What if it's longer than that? What if they just, I don't know, cordon the area off and leave us to rot?"

The other Lucy put a hand on the shuddering arm of her counterpart and patted it. At the same time, she stared over the rim of her glass at Dr. Crispin as she drank.

"Ah, that's one of the things I've gathered everyone for," Crispin answered. "As soon as we leave this room, each of the department heads will go immediately to your respective areas and obtain an inventory of supplies. Especially the medical personnel." He turned their way, spearing Ronald with a glare. "We need amounts, projected usage rates, expiration dates. And, maintenance..." He swiveled to take in Holly, who met his gaze coolly. "Inventory—"

"Spare parts and consumables, yes, Doctor." She tapped a tall, grimy man on the forearm to make sure he got it.

Donovan kept watching the Dogs. They couldn't keep still, as one would expect a paramilitary unit to hold themselves. Instead they were jittery, as if they could barely contain all of that mad energy he'd seen in the sparring cage.

"Effective immediately," Jaden said, "all watches on sonar and radar are doubled around the clock. Two bodies at all times. Coast patrol will venture no farther out than one nautical mile. Any and all trips from the main compound to any outlying buildings will be in groups of no less than three."

Other than the Alpha, Donovan thought, *they all look ready to split out of their skins and rend something.* He smiled at the thought. *Magnificent creatures.*

"The medical facilities will be guarded," Jaden concluded. Some of the looks shifted from frightened to insulted.

"You don't have a bunch of junkies here," someone behind Donovan said. The sentiment was met with grunts of agreement and more dirty looks.

"Now listen," Dr. Crispin said, holding up his hands. "Mr. Jaden is only doing his job. I'm certain there's nothing personal in the, ah, implementation of these security protocols—"

"Yes, there is," Jaden interrupted. "I know for a fact there have been thefts of hydrocodone and morphine from our medical stores."

Dr. Crispin's eyes shifted from Jaden to Ron Michaels. The sweaty medical man shook his head.

"We'll talk about it later," Crispin told Jaden, putting his hand over the microphone.

"In addition," Jaden continued as if he had never been interrupted, "the comms room will be locked and the satellite television system secured."

"You can't do that!" someone at the IT table cried.

"Hold on," Dr. Crispin said, finally raising his voice. "I didn't bring you here to debate the security measures demanded by protocol. I brought you here to apprise you of the situation, and to ask you a question."

Quiet fell over the entire room. Dr. Crispin was never one to poll for an opinion. On anything.

This was something different.

He looked around the cafeteria until he had each and every person's full attention. The silence grew, bloated and pregnant, until everyone was certain they had never been anywhere more still.

"We are in a unique position," he finally said. "The conventional authorities are undoubtedly overwhelmed by both the nature of this situation and its apparent, ah, vastness. Can you imagine it? Everywhere, all at once, there are dead people walking, moving, *attacking* the living." His voice fell off, and the silence remained, so thorough that everyone heard the rustle of fabric as Dr. Crispin shifted his neck inside its collar.

"Conventional methods will not work with this decidedly unconventional situation. And herein lies my dilemma. As mentioned before, I have a history with the heads of state and military leaders, and perhaps I'm too close to make a clear-headed decision." He stretched out his hand, indicating the Dogs, who stood now at perfect attention. "We have with us on the island the perfect rescue unit. This kind of situation is exactly what the Dogs were designed for! Dangerous extractions from behind enemy lines. Elite members of our military, recrafted, reforged into something entirely superior. So this is what I am asking. Should we deploy the Dogs to assist with search and rescue efforts?"

The dining room erupted with murmurs, and each table exploded with conversation.

Donovan struggled to overhear what everyone was saying. He found himself stricken with a sick fear at the thought of McLoughlin's pack leaving the island for any reason.

"Please," Dr. Crispin said into the microphone, his amplified voice cutting cleanly through the talk. "Please, deliberate amongst yourselves. Each department should tally your own votes and present them through your department head."

Donovan was already shaking his head, ready to veto any positive vote put forward by any member of his neurotech unit. He looked to the table he had sat at earlier during dinner, and saw his trio of assistants with their heads together, talking quickly.

At the podium, Dr. Crispin fiddled with the microphone until a loud click went through the improvised sound system. He was shaking his head and jabbering at Luke Jaden, who stood with his arms crossed, allowing the doctor's words to wash over him.

That kind of resolve would definitely be an asset, Donovan thought, taking in the silenced clash of wills. He thought furiously, trying to assimilate what little he knew of the security man, trying to figure out exactly what he could say to sway the man's vote.

"Are you okay?" Holly Randall said beside him. She gave him a small smile. "A lot is happening on your first day, Doc. I hope your entire time on the island won't be this way."

"As do I," Donovan said. "How will the maintenance department vote?"

Her smile grew. "We're going to vote yes. The Dogs were designed for military applications, and this kind of proving ground can't be manufactured." She nodded. "Dr. Crispin is right. It's time to let the Dogs off the leash."

Donovan's face paled even more. "But they're untested. Yes, yes, I understand that this scenario seems like an ideal method to shake everything up and see if anything comes loose, but..." His voice drifted off as he noted more than one face turned up to listen. He bit down on the smile that wanted to sprout on his lips.

"They're unproven in this application. I have no doubts as to the training of the men themselves, of course. Each of the Dogs is a top fighter. But the technology, as advanced a prototype as it is, is still just that. A prototype. I would love to see the Dogs pass this test with flying colors, and I feel absolutely horrible for all the people trapped on the mainland. But..." He ran his hands through his hair. "Do we really want to jeopardize all the years of hard work Dr. Crispin and my predecessor have put into the development of these Dogs?"

He turned to face the formation of genetically-enhanced soldiers. "Magnificent specimens, all of them. But if we send them out, and the technology fails any of them, in any way, that might invite disaster. The notion of a tightly-knit squad, or cohesive unit, is predicated on the principle that every member of the team will fulfill his or her job to the fullest."

Dr. Crispin, at the podium, had stopped talking at Jaden and was watching Donovan, mouth open.

"As much as I wish we could help people on the mainland, I can't imagine the potential loss we might incur if any aspect of the technology failed. People who have entrenched themselves, now brought out of hiding by the hope of rescue, might fall to these walking cadavers. We would lose all of them as well as the Dogs. *And*," he said, putting a finger in the air for emphasis, "if any phase of the rescue mission goes awry, surely the wrath of the Federal Government would be swift and furious."

He looked around the room.

"Think about that before you vote."

SIX

KEN GRIPPED THE STEERING WHEEL, and it was all he could do to keep his hands there. They were itching to wrap themselves around a neck, anyone's neck, just to make the questions stop. He stole a glance in the rearview mirror and wished he hadn't left Jorge to ride on the trailer.

Not long after he had turned the Blazer around and retreated from the chaos on the highway, a convoy had grown behind him. First one car, then two, then five. He found himself wondering how everyone else was getting along, but then rolled his eyes.

You got to leave that at work, he thought.

In the backseat of the Blazer, sitting in the middle, an older couple was praying quietly, and Ken could deal with that. The girl who had gotten in first, she was crying about her parents and her cat, and that, too, he could deal with.

The girl with the teeny-tiny dog, on the other hand, was starting to get under his skin.

Right. Under.

And the swarthy guy with the B.O. wasn't helping, either.

"Oh my God," the girl said again, petting her dog ferociously. "Where are you taking us? You can't just hold us prisoner, or whatever." Her eyes got big and her voice went up an octave. "Oh my God, are you taking us to be slaves in Mexico?"

"You never can tell," the sweaty guy said. "Desperate men do—"

"Stop," Ken interrupted. "Nobody forced you, any of you, into my car. If there's someplace you want to go, I'm all ears, lady."

She petted her dog even harder, and it began to yelp. "Sorry, Willow, I'm sorry." The girl turned her big eyes on Ken. "See what you made me do? And, my God, you can't just drop us off somewhere." She waved a hand at the world outside the Blazer. "We don't even know if it's safe in the city!"

"Where are we going, mister?" the crying girl in the back asked. Ken looked at her in the rearview and caught a glimpse of the older couple, who were looking up at him with some kind of hope in their eyes.

Taking a deep breath, he blew it out and tried to clear his mind. He had to calm down, or there would be an *incident*. At this stage of his life, he could not afford another one of those, as much as some people might richly deserve one.

"We've already called the police. City, county, state. Right?"

Most of the people in the Blazer nodded.

"We all know the story now. Things are out of their control, and they're waiting for backup."

They hit a straight stretch of road, and Ken closed his eyes for a second.

"Ladies and gentlemen, I am officially out of ideas. I welcome anything new."

The sweaty man threw his hands up. "I can't believe you. Just giving up."

Ken glared at the man, and part of his brain, the same part that had so gleefully harried him about the man he'd run over earlier, now goaded him to do some more damage.

Just one hit, it said. *He's right there. A glorious elbow would put a wonderful exclamation point on things, wouldn't it?*

Ken looked forward, then into the mirror again.

"We're pulling over," he said.

The girl with the dog protested, and the smelly man just sneered. But Ken knew if he didn't get off the road (and get them out of the car) an already bad day would get exponentially worse.

Putting his hazards on, he started slowing down and edging Big Bertha over to the right shoulder. A couple of cars from the procession zipped past him, but the rest slowed down with him and stopped on the side.

Taking care to turn the vehicle off and put the keys securely in his hip pocket, Ken got out and slammed the door behind him. A couple of other drivers got out of their cars, and Jorge, standing up in the tool trailer, was busily glaring daggers at him.

"Not right now," Ken said on the way past.

"What're we doing?" a voice yelled from three cars back, and that started a flood of questions.

Ken sighed, thinking that perhaps he would be better off being angry in the Blazer.

Another driver stuck her head out her window, frizzy brown hair pulled back in a sloppy ponytail. "I heard the riots or whatever are everywhere. It's all over the radio!"

"'Outbreak' is what they said," another man agreed. "But nobody's saying what *kind* of outbreak. No one really knows what the hell it is."

Ken put his hands up and opened his mouth to speak, but a sound caught his attention, faint at first, but getting louder. He looked up, and an angular helicopter buzzed by overhead. It was black and had short wings bristling with armaments.

"Military," Jorge said, showing up next to Ken. "Headed into the city."

"But we were just there. You saw. We drove all the way from downtown, no problems."

Jorge rocked his head at the rapidly shrinking chopper. "Oh, yeah. No problems." He put his head back and blew a raspberry. "Sometimes, man..."

"Well, it's what we know," Ken said, his face darkening a bit. "It was all right when we left, right? Come on! It's a nice place. There's no reason to think it's turned to anarchy or whatever in just over an hour."

Ken turned to the cars on the side of the road. "I'm headed into the city," he announced. "We might be able to find help or answers there. Who else is coming?"

Two cars edged onto the road and made neat turns, headed back the way they had come, except on the wrong side of the highway.

"They vote no," Jorge said, ignoring the black look from Ken.

Everyone else got back into their cars and rolled up their windows. A couple of them had traded phone numbers and were chirping each other to test. Jorge wished he hadn't dropped his phone earlier.

"You believe this?" he said. "I have no idea what my ex's number is."

"What do you want to call her for?" Ken asked, then felt stupid. *The kids.*

"Ah, don't worry about them," he added. "You said she lives in a nice place now, right? Some kind of gated community?"

Jorge nodded.

"See there? It'll be all right. Come on."

As Ken walked back to the Blazer, a woman got out of a yellow Volkswagen Beetle and waved him over.

Pursing his lips, he turned and went toward her.

"Yes?" he said, hoping that the fatigue in his voice would put her off, knowing that it probably wouldn't.

"I... think I might have a problem," she said.

He noticed that she kept her arm stiff and pressed up against her side. Her sleeve was darker than the rest of her blouse, and the sides of her white shoes were red.

"One of those p-people pulled me out of my car, and—" she broke off, crying.

Ken's stoic veneer cracked. "Hey, it's okay. Let me see. I'll help you."

She held out her arm and rolled her sleeve back to show him. It was a nasty wound: deep, leaking blood and pus, red around the edges. Her breath came faster at the sight of it, as if she had forgotten how bad it was.

"He was just *there*, clawing at me," she said through her teeth. "I went to hit him, and he just turned his head and... *bit* me. It hurts so *bad*."

"Okay," Ken said, frowning at how quickly the wound seemed to have become infected. "I have a first-aid kit in the Blazer. But don't let anybody else see that, okay?"

"I don't... think I can drive," she said, growing paler by the minute.

Ken's frown deepened. "Just stay right here," he said, and then he went to retrieve the first-aid kit.

Jorge intercepted him on the way. "What's her story?"

Ken threw a glance over his shoulder. The girl was just standing there, staring at her bloodstained shoes.

"Bite," he said quietly. "One of those crazy people bit her. And I know this is stupid, but... I don't want her to ride with us."

Jorge's eyes widened. "You can't just *leave* her."

"I won't," Ken said. "I'm not going to leave her. But, uh, I think she'll have to ride in the back. On the trailer." He grabbed the first-aid kit and turned to look at the girl. "Just in case."

Jorge stood by the trailer and watched as Ken wrapped the girl's injury and broke the news to her. There were some tears, but no more than were already flowing. She nodded and moved to the trailer.

Ken walked back to the Blazer, running his hands over his short hair and wondering when this day was planning on getting better. Jorge caught his eye and motioned him over.

"Two things," he said, keeping his voice low. "One, I think it's pretty messed up she's got to ride out back. It's like you're afraid of the swine flu or something, and I think it's stupid. We're men. We can take this kind of thing. Her? She should be riding in the front seat."

Ken started shaking his head before Jorge was done. "I know what you're saying, Jorge, but I can't take any chances." His face clouded over. "Just like work, right? Safety first."

"*Mierda*," Jorge said. But he let it go.

"What was the second thing?"

Jorge rocked on his heels for a second. He looked from the girl on the tool trailer and back to Ken. "Don't make me ride with her."

After a second of stunned silence, Ken's head went back and a terrific guffaw tore itself out of him. A few people glared at him, but he couldn't help it. There was just so much steam building up, it had to vent somehow.

"I can't believe you," he said to Jorge. "Hah! Yeah, man. You can ride shotgun, like you always do."

They turned back to the car, and Ken pointed at the sweaty man. "You," he said. "It's someone else's turn to ride up front." He hooked a thumb at the trailer. "Back there, big boy."

A cross look came over the man's face. "I'm not riding back there."

Ken put his arms out, looking up and down the highway at the other cars. A lot of them were already rolling, except for a few who wanted to follow the Blazer. "Well you either hit the trailer or you hit the bricks. I don't care, either way. Get out of my car."

Grumbling, the fat man bumped the skinny girl with the dog out of the way and stomped back to the trailer. The young man who had squeezed into the back with the older couple followed the sweaty man for some reason, and another guy from the trailer traded his spot for the back seat. Ken ignored the musical chairs and climbed in the passenger side, closing his door.

As Jorge was about to get in, another girl from the trailer ran up, thinking there was more room. Her face fell, and Jorge saw it.

"Go ahead," he told her. "I'll get in the, uh..." He was going to say "back seat" until he saw there was no more room.

He glanced at the trailer.

"The one lady who got injured," Ken said. "Why don't you take her car? I'm sure she'd rather not leave it behind."

"Yeah," Jorge said, staring out at the lady's yellow VW Beetle. "I guess I could... drive a girl's car."

Ken watched in his mirrors as Jorge went back to the trailer and spoke with the lady. She looked as spaced out as Jorge was acting. But she finally seemed to understand what he was asking and handed over her keys. Ken watched Jorge stare down at the keychain where the girl had affixed a big yellow daisy, same color as her car.

As Jorge got in the Beetle and tentatively put his hands on the fluffy white steering wheel, Ken couldn't help but chuckle.

"What's so goddamn funny?" the old man asked from the backseat.

"Nothing," Ken said, straightening up. "Just nervous laughter." He put Big Bertha in gear and took off, keeping one eye on the rearview mirror.

SEVEN

ALPHA MCLOUGHLIN, still in his workout coveralls, paced up and down the Dogs' barracks, listening to the chatter up and down the rows of bunks. The talk consisted mostly of the Thetas—along with the cluster of Sigmas—bouncing conjecture back and forth about the meaning of the radio reports.

The Alpha, though, found himself wondering whether he would ever get used to wearing topsiders instead of combat boots. At first it had rankled him to walk around in the flat-bottomed blue shoes, but he at least had gotten used to the feel of them, if not the idea. He knew why they were necessary, especially when it came to finances and the cost of replacing the boots versus replacing the canvas shoes when they tore during the Change. But at heart, he was a military man, and he wanted those trappings.

"God *damn*," Theta Rose said, "I don't care what those things are out there. They could be nuns on a 'roid rage, and I'd gladly wolf on them just to get some time off this rock." He laughed, showing off the gaps in his bottom teeth. "Can I get an amen?"

Rose put his fist out and several of the Sigmas bumped it.

Another Theta, a man with a skin tone somewhere between brown and red, spoke up. "That would be a good way to test ourselves: on the field of battle. My ancestors—"

Rolling his eyes, Rose said, "No one cares about that, chief. No one cares what your great grandpappy thought was a good way to die." He nudged one of the Sigmas with his foot. "I think he had to change his name to Runs-On-All-Fours, yeah?"

"My name is—"

"Knock it off," McLoughlin said, passing by them on yet another lap. "The name stitched on your uniform is Hayte."

"Theta Haytah," Rose said, sending the Sigmas into paroxysms of laughter. "He's right, though. We should be out there on the mainland, cleaning things up. We could be out saving people. Instead, we're what?" He slapped the bunk he was sitting on. "Chillin' on the island with old Doc Crispin."

Another man, reclining on his bed, laughed. "Yeah, what's up with that? He just rolled over and let the new guy call the shots?" He brushed one hand on the front of his coveralls, scattering imaginary dust off the name KRISTOS stitched there. "Ain't no way that flies with me."

Alpha McLoughlin pointed a blunt finger at Kristos. "Stow that shit, Theta. You know better than that."

Rose said, "Aw, come on, Mac. Don't tell me you're not itching to get out and sink your teeth into this. You know how many people we never got to help over in Afgha—"

"It doesn't matter what I want," the Alpha said. "That's not who we are. We are not a group of individuals. We are not freelance contractors. We are not civilians."

One of the Sigmas raised his hand, and Hayte smacked it down before the Alpha could see.

"We are a pack. We are the Dogs of War. And we do as we are told."

The barracks door opened, and McLoughlin turned to welcome Samson. But the greeting died on his lips.

"Kaiser? Where's your Beta?"

A sneer sprang up on one side of Kaiser's mouth. "*Theta* Samson is still in therapy."

Mac tilted his head to one side, like a dog hearing something it did not expect. He closed out everything else and focused on Kaiser, reading him.

It wasn't anything he had been able to communicate to the scientists; none of their instruments could pick up on certain aspects of the Dogs, but McLoughlin could. Were he of the New Age, he would have called it their auras; if he were an Oriental mystic, the chi. He didn't have a word for it, but something was different about Kaiser now, that indefinable thing by which McLoughlin had divided his men into ranks.

And certainly the fact that Kaiser had recovered more quickly than Samson indicated to everybody in the room that a shift in power had occurred. The hierarchy had changed.

But by how much?

"Does Crispin know about this?" McLoughlin found himself asking, just to fill the suddenly dead air.

Kaiser laughed. "Does Crispin know about *anything?*"

)

Donovan knocked on Dr. Crispin's door, unsure of his own intentions but wanting to talk to the man after the vote. Part of him relished in winning the majority, but another part, perhaps the side of him attuned to survival instincts, insisted that he talk to Crispin without delay. To smooth things over.

He knocked again.

Both Holly and Jaden had assured him that this was where he could find Crispin, but there didn't seem to be anybody home. He stood there looking at the door and deliberating.

Alpha McLoughlin, walking the corridors of the compound, ran the brief encounter with Kaiser over in his head. A few of the security men passing by gave him a look for crossing the open areas unescorted, but he was the top Dog. None of them met his eyes for long. When he caught a reflection of himself, he saw why.

"Jesus."

Samson's sudden demotion had upset him, but he hadn't expected it to show in his face so much. His cheekbones had taken on an angular aspect, and his sideburns seemed bushier than before; telltale signs that a transformation was imminent, if he lost control of himself.

With a conscious effort, McLoughlin calmed himself and continued toward Dr. Crispin's office. It would not do for the Alpha Dog to have the Change thrust upon him by circumstances.

He found Dr. Donovan standing there by the door, looking as if he couldn't make up his mind. McLoughlin gently shouldered him aside and knocked on the door, then entered, as was the norm. Donovan followed, and the pair found the project director sitting at his desk, a half-empty bottle of Crown Royal in front of him. Three empty purple bags lay strewn across the floor, and McLoughlin could smell it on him; Dr. Crispin was drunk.

The doctor ignored the open door and his guests, staring instead at the small radio set that was part of his in-office entertainment system. Over it hung a large silver sword, shining in the harsh fluorescent light.

"Dr. Crispin?" McLoughlin said. The sound of radio news came to him, a constant outpouring of speculation and reports of so-called un-dead activity. Every time the announcer used the word "zombie," Dr. Crispin flinched in his seat.

I've never heard that radio on before, McLoughlin thought.

"Doctor, I need to talk to you about an issue with the Dogs, sir." His eyes shifted over to Donovan, then back to the project director. "In private."

For several seconds, they waited for Crispin to respond.

"Sir?" McLoughlin said, and at that, Crispin waved his hand, beck-oning both men in.

Extremely conscious of Donovan's presence but helpless against his own nature, the Alpha Dog began to speak while the neurotechnician took a seat.

"It's Kaiser, sir. He's... well, he's more than a Theta Dog now. I know how you hate the, ah, unquantifiable aspects of the experiment, but I can tell, sir."

He paused, but Dr. Crispin said nothing. McLoughlin caught move-ment in the corner of his eye, and turned to see Dr. Donovan leaning forward in his chair, hand on fist and listening attentively. The Alpha shifted in his coveralls and cleared his throat.

"The thing is, sir, our hierarchy is established, but I know you mod-eled our behavior from wolves, and I'm concerned about the rest of the Dogs taking this path. I fear it may foster inter-pack aggression, when our focus should be on the enemy.

"I've been looking at our structure, and it would be wrong to keep Kaiser as a Theta, but I don't want him as the Beta, sir. He's wrong for it. He's not a leader. We could make Kaiser an Epsilon, an entirely new rank, but still subordinate to the Beta. Dr. Crispin? Sir?"

The news coming from the radio kept the room from falling into dead silence.

McLoughlin looked at Donovan, who raised his eyebrows.

"I don't know, Alpha McLoughlin. I just got here. You would know better than I the project director's moods."

The Alpha forced a smile and looked away. He didn't want to talk about the Dogs to this man, this outsider, but if he was the new neuro-tech leader, then...

Dr. Crispin dropped his glass to the floor and pointed up at the sword on the wall. "That thing," he said, enunciating carefully as people who know they're drunk do. "That sword up there. My father had it made for me, did you know that?"

Donovan, sure in his position—and Crispin's condition—turned his sharp gaze from the Alpha Dog to the project director.

McLoughlin felt even more uncomfortable than before. He didn't want to be in the office anymore, didn't want to see Dr. Crispin this way.

"He had it made for *me*," Crispin said, pounding the desk on the last word. "Always had a big imagination, my father. He said, heh, he said I was going to be a monster hunter." He put his hands up in the air, making a noise that would have been a giggle if it had sounded healthier. "Just like Beowulf. Heh. BAH."

Crispin reached for his glass and, seeing it on the floor, grabbed the bottle of Crown Royal instead.

"Me. A monster hunter. He said I was destined to slay them." He stared into the bottle. "If he could only see me now. I don't slay monsters. No, I... I only make them."

The tone of the radio report changed then, from insistent recitation of breaking news to something else. Crispin snatched up a remote control from his lap, fumbled it, and then used it to turn up the volume. The sound of breaking things and a low constant moaning filled the office.

"This station has... those things are inside," the male newscaster said. "I've locked the sound room door, but I don't know how long that will—"

The sound of shattering glass interrupted the man's last words, and the air was again full of moaning, then screams. The yells of the radio-man stopped abruptly, turning into a deep gurgle. There was another crashing sound, and then everything ceased.

"Dead air," Crispin said into his bottle. "Get out."

He powered off the radio and turned to Donovan and Alpha McLoughlin. "Didn't you hear me? Get the hell out of here! Out!"

He stood, raising the bottle as if to throw it, and Donovan stood too. His hands came up to protect his face as he and the Alpha Dog backed up to the office door. Crispin watched them go, then sat back in his chair.

"Monsters," he said as the door clicked shut.

EIGHT

A DARK SMUDGE OF GREY stained the horizon, and Ken felt his spirits sinking, way down into his boots.

"Are you seeing this?" he said into his cell phone.

"Yes, I am, jefe," Jorge replied. *"It doesn't look good. Unless it's a McDonald's on fire. That, I can live with."*

Ken sighed, wondering why he had expected a straight response from his friend. He checked the rearview mirror and could see Jorge on the road behind him, driving the yellow Beetle. Ken's eyes shifted to the people on his trailer. They were all hunkered down, shielding their faces from the wind. He couldn't blame them. He was only hitting forty, but that was quite enough when you were exposed.

"Any more texts from the trailer?" he asked the older couple sitting in the back seat.

The young man who had moved to the trailer was their kin, and for a short while, they had been communicating via cell phone. Ken had asked them several times to see how everyone back there was doing.

Looking to the trailer again, he found himself wondering about the girl who owned the Beetle, the one who had been bitten. She had been dressed nicely enough—a white silk blouse over a business skirt, and a pair of low heels. He grimaced, thinking of how cold she must be, out there in the wind-bitten trailer.

As the Blazer passed the first signs of civilization, it was easy to tell that civilization had fled. The Best Buy at the edge of town was a hive of activity, people running into the store empty-handed, others rushing out with armloads of electronics. It was much the same for the smaller stores on either side of the big blue box.

Ken fought the urge to spit.

Looting, pillaging, and rioting were all foreign to him. He saw it on television often enough, but had never understood it. How could people, normal everyday people, act so wrong? Never mind the law, what about what was right? He shook his head, glad he wasn't one of them. The mindless herd.

As the Blazer came around the bend, he saw the source of the smoke. Flames billowed from the hospital at either end, unchecked and uncontrolled. Through the smoke, it was impossible to see anything else at the foundation of the building, but Ken had a sick feeling in his gut that it might be similar to the scene back on the highway.

"Jesus," Jorge said. *"What do you think, the oxygen lines?"*

"Probably," Ken said. He tore his eyes from the merrily burning hospital and looked ahead. "What the hell happened here? We couldn't have been in traffic for more than an hour."

On the opposite side of the highway, a mob of people had converged on a small contingent of policemen and EMTs at the scene of a wreck. No one in the mob was moving with that awkward gait Ken had seen back at the bus wreck. This wasn't a crazed attack.

It was the beginning of a riot.

A quick flash of red in front of him made Ken step on the brakes. A fire engine roared up the ramp onto the highway, lights on but no siren.

"Firefighters do not wear white," one of the women in the passenger seat said.

Ken had to agree. It was also a completely foreign idea to him that someone would hijack a fire truck, but someone obviously had thought it was the right thing to do.

How badly have things broken down here?

Ken began to sweat. It was like a cold, clammy hand on the nape of his neck, and it made him feel unclean. His plan to make it into the city had been a poor choice. But at least they were still on the highway. If they stayed on it, it would take them through the city and out the other side. Besides, turning around wasn't really an option.

His eyes flicked to the mirror again. "You still got your iron?"

"Oh, yeah," Jorge said. *"It's digging a very nice hole for itself in my paunch."* In the mirror, Ken saw him look down at his figure. *"Maybe I should cut back on the beer."*

Ken nodded. That reassured him more than a little. Jorge might not be so much on range safety, but he hit what he shot at. Though just to be on the safe side...

He tapped the woman sitting next to him on the shoulder. "Do me a favor, will you? Reach down under your seat and hand me the case from under there."

He hated the idea of driving armed but it was the smart thing to do. If people were out and about and commandeering rescue vehicles, they wouldn't think twice about stealing Big Bertha right out from under him.

The woman plucked out the gun case and handed it over. Ken opened it up, and, driving with his knee, he loaded the gun.

The women in the front seat cast him a few furtive glances.

"Protection," he said with a nervous laugh. Then he dumped the rest of the bullets into his shirt pocket.

One of the women smiled; the other just looked away.

"Oh, come on," he said. "You wouldn't strap up if you had a gun?"

"Hey, it's the Army," Jorge said, and Ken's head whipped up to look.

Surely enough, two Humvees and a large covered flatbed truck sat off the side of the road. As Ken passed, he saw the man in the lead Hummer talking on a field radio. The soldier looked worried, and the gunners on the Humvee-mounted .50 cals looked alert.

"That doesn't bode well either, *compadre*," he said, meeting Jorge's eyes in the rearview. A blur of movement in the side of the glass caught his attention, and he turned the mirror so he could see into the trailer.

A red splash of blood arced away from the man with the bad B.O., and the man clutched at his neck. A second later, a scarecrow in a silk blouse was on him, tearing at his face with her teeth.

"Holy shit," Ken said.

It was the girl with the bite.

Jorge saw it too and shouted blasphemies in Spanish.

The girl had become a monster, completely numb to the blows raining down on her head from the other people in the trailer. She clawed back and forth between them, grabbing skin and pulling until it tore, lashing out with her teeth. She caught one man's nose and sheared it clean off. He fell back, holding the hole in his face, tumbling off the end of the trailer and taking another man with him. The old couple's kin.

In the Beetle, Jorge swerved and managed to miss them both as they tumbled along the road.

A woman in a T-shirt stepped up to defend herself, but the creature hooked two fingers inside the lady's cheek and tore her face wide open. The injured woman toppled over the side of the trailer, which jumped as the wheels rolled over her body. This time Jorge couldn't swerve because of oncoming traffic—a truck barreling out of the city with a deranged man hanging onto its rear bumper; the man's legs had been sanded down by the road.

With a feral look in her eyes, the she-monster swung to look into the Blazer, then swung the opposite way to glare at Jorge.

"I wonder if she wants her car back," Jorge said. *"Well you can't have it!"* Quieter, he said, *"The yellow's kind of grown on me."*

The woman snarled, as if she could hear his taunts. Then, like a stuntwoman, she got a running start and leapt off the back of the trailer.

Ken heard Jorge drop the phone, then heard his friend cry out in the background as the woman smashed into the windshield of her own car. The glass spiderwebbed and crumpled beneath her, and her elbow poked through.

She thrust her arm into the hole and swiped at Jorge, who glimpsed her face through the cracks and the splat of blood and snagged hair.

In the rearview, Ken watched helplessly as his friend swerved to throw the monster off. He heard a honking horn and looked forward into an oncoming motorcycle.

"Hold on!"

Ken jerked his wheel as the motorcyclist laid his bike down and slid, sparks flying, right under Ken's left tire; the combination of the motorcycle impacting and rolling under the Blazer, the twist of the steering wheel, and the shifting weight of the tool trailer was all too much for Big Bertha.

Ken jerked the wheel back, but he felt the vehicle tipping anyway, driven by velocity and mass. There was nothing else he could do.

The Blazer turned on its side, still hurtling down the highway at fifty miles per hour. It turned as it slid, and as it went perpendicular to the road, the whole thing began to turn, slowly at first, then with more speed as momentum took over.

Finally it stopped.

Ken, laying on his face and jammed up against the steering wheel, had one last vision before he blacked out.

Feet.

Feet and legs, shuffling toward the Blazer.

ONE MONTH LATER

NINE

"I CAN'T BELIEVE we're having rice again," Donovan said, staring down at his plate. "One month without a supply run, and we're living like poor Chinese farmers in the Han Dynasty."

Holly Randall laughed, earning a black look from the neurotechnician.

"Oh, lighten up," she said. "At least we're eating. At least we have electric lighting and armed guards." She looked at her forkful of rice. "Only a little while now before our crops pay off. Imagine the poor bastards out there in the *real* world. You know, we used to play a game, my friends and I, back in school." She stopped, looking over at Donovan.

He had put some soy sauce on his rice and was mixing it up. "Oh, go on. I'm enraptured with your story already."

Ignoring the tone of his voice, she continued. "This game, it was fostered by our instructors. The goal was to create the most realistic projection of a complete societal breakdown. The particulars of the precipitating event were left up to us. Any wild story we chose was acceptable, as long as the end result was the same."

She paused to wash down her rice with a swig of *horchata*. She looked at the cup. "Amazing. I'm eating rice and drinking rice milk. *Anyway...*" She turned to Donovan. "My scenario of choice was a Martian invasion. Wells is my favorite, you know."

"Mmm," Donovan said.

"We factored in weather and other conditions, but none of that had much of an impact. Especially not for this area, where the power grid is fed by a nuclear reactor. You know what the biggest contributor to loss of power and services was?"

"Mmm?"

"Leaks. That's it. Just stupid, simple leaks. With no one to replenish the water levels in the pressurized steam system... you know, the thing that turns the big power turbines? Eventually the water will run itself out. Then with no heat transfer media in the tubes, they break and let the primary coolant of the reactor leak out. Bada bing, bada boom, you have a meltdown in the course of days, if not hours."

Donovan continued to stare at his plate.

"Knock it off," Holly said, finally letting her irritation show. "The algae machine should be up and running in no time now. We'll have our Soylent Green by the end of the week."

"That's only halfway funny," Donovan said. "Do most people in the compound know what goes into the fertilizer for this rice?"

Holly crossed her forearms on the table and leaned over them. "Intellectually, yes. But we ignore that. I mean, you know what's in fertilizer that gets trucked out from farms, but that doesn't stop you from enjoying a hearty salad, does it?"

Donovan raised an eyebrow. "I suppose you have a point. But using the, the processed *ejecta* from the—"

"*Attention on the island,*" Crispin's voice blared over the PA system. "*Attention. There has been a new development on the mainland. All personnel not on watch are to report to the dining room in fifteen... no, ten minutes. Five—be there in five minutes!*"

Donovan put down his fork. "Well, *he* sounds happy."

"I wonder what it is," Holly said.

IT Lucy, the surly one, put down her tray at a table next to theirs. "Something on the radio," she said. "I was back and forth between his office and the communications room all last week, wiring his stereo and the Furunos and the satellite phone into his computer, and showing him how to record everything." She waved a fork in the air quickly, generating a breeze that stirred her fine brown hair. "He's been glued to it ever since."

"That's interesting," Donovan said.

Lucy shrugged. "Whatever. All the traffic about the hungry dead, I don't see how he can sleep at night listening to that shit. It's gruesome."

The doors to the dining room opened, and the Dogs came in, all eleven of them, with McLoughlin at their head. Kaiser and Samson flanked him, and the other eight Dogs followed behind. They had shaved their heads, and wherever exposed skin showed, there were swathes of pink skin, evidence of more bestial sparring matches.

Donovan, seeing the Dogs together like that, felt a chill run up his spine. In the past four weeks, he had come to marvel at the extensive work done by his predecessor, and of course at the marvelous specimens endowed with that work; the brain-computer interface tapped into just about every major area of the brain. One day the Dogs would be jovial, joking, and laughing human beings, and the next they'd be monsters lunging and tearing at each other in the cage.

Now when he saw them, he knew the action potential lurking within, and it thrilled him. He had come to watch them running drills on each other in human form, and even those moments of unarmed combat had set the neurotechnician's imagination aflame.

"Earth to Donovan," Holly said. "Do you have any theories about the hungry dead?"

"No. Barring some sort of supernatural involvement, there's nothing that springs to mind. Who knows what it is? Biological warfare or contaminated space probes from Venus. Does it really matter? The dead walk, and they eat." He pushed his plate away. "Now I'm not even hungry. I never should have let you talk me into watching the video broadcasts."

"I can't believe the man on watch let you in," Lucas Jaden said, coming up behind Donovan. "I docked Winchester's pay, but somehow I doubt that's going to make much of a difference anymore."

"Come on, Luke," Holly said, "Don't tell me you're out of hope, too."

He flashed a grin at her. "I'm a realist, Miss Randall. If you show me a glass, I see it as neither half-empty nor half-full. I see enough water to drown a man, if I can find a way to put it in his lungs."

Lucy stabbed her plate of rice. "You win for creepy sentence of the day." She looked over at Donovan, her tired eyes ringed with dark circles. "I've even been talking to Fatty Ron, learning about how meat breaks down." She jabbed her fork at Jaden. "You still win."

Dr. Crispin entered the dining room, his face full of manic energy that seemed to drift up into his unruly standing hair. He gave the impression of someone who just stuck a finger into an electrical socket and was eager to do it again.

Donovan turned to see the podium already set up and wired for sound. When had that happened? Surely, he hadn't been that captivated by the Dogs. Had he?

Crispin tapped the microphone twice, as was his custom. The maintenance tech standing by was ready this time, and he fiddled with a slider on his mixing panel. He looked up with a grin for the gathered island personnel. There was a smattering of applause.

"Thank you," Crispin said. "I know you're all eager to learn something about the situation, so I'll get right to it. Today, ladies and gentlemen, we have received a distress signal."

Immediately, the room was electrified. Donovan sat up in his chair, his early-warning synapses firing.

What does he mean, "we"?

Crispin put his hands up to fend off a sudden barrage of questions. "Now, now. Hold on. I have brought a sound bite for you all to hear."

He gestured to the sound guy, who nodded and then pressed a button on a little laptop he had set up. The crackling sound of airwaves came over the speakers.

"Mayday, mayday—please. We have been stranded here for exactly thirty and a half days. That's... 732 hours of trying to survive."

"Jesus," Holly breathed.

"Please, we are running out of food and water, and we have very little for protection. There are women, children. Please—"

Crispin motioned for the sound guy to stop the recording, and the room fell into silence.

"Fifty thousand minutes," Holly whispered. "Jesus."

Donovan noted that the distress signal had not divulged the survivors' exact location. *Smart*, he thought. Better to make contact first and build some form of trust or rapport.

"The communications men put the signal strength within reach of a search and rescue team," Crispin said.

Lucy wrinkled her nose. "Sounds fishy."

"The government has collapsed, people. There is no aid coming to these civilians. No comfort, no succor. The only hope they have of escaping their situation is the Dogs."

At this, the pack of men stood straighter, coming to attention. Alpha McLoughlin barked out, "Dog Pack, all present and accounted for. Ready for duty, Project Director, sir!"

Dr. Crispin smiled, beaming at his genetically-enhanced warriors. "Bravo, men!" Looking back at the assembled throng, he waved. "You see? The Dogs are ready."

"Just a minute," Donovan found himself saying. "Just one *minute*, Doctor. There are some unanswered questions on the table, and I think they should be addressed before we send the Dogs off on some mercy mission."

"Mercy mission," Crispin repeated. "I like the sound of that."

Frowning, Donovan waved that away. "I'm talking about the dead, Dr. Crispin. The *zombies*." He paused, looking to see whether the extra emphasis on the word had affected the project director at all. To his dismay, it had not. "The reports that we've received all agree; if one of us is bitten by one of them, an irreversible process begins, and then we die. We become... one of *them*."

Donovan had almost shouted the last word, silencing all other voices in the dining room. He lifted his head and looked around, then pointed at the Dogs, who still stood at attention.

"What happens, Doctor, if one of them bites one of our Dogs? Do we know? Hell no, we don't know."

Murmured assent blew through the room.

Donovan continued.

"Dr. Crispin, your humanitarian impulses do you credit. But, sir, we don't even have a specimen of the walking dead to examine. There is no way to know how the finely-tuned systems of the Dogs will react to whatever it is that turns perfectly normal people into ravening maniacs."

"He is correct," Ronald said. His medical team was nodding in unison. "We should wait until we have data."

Dr. Crispin's face changed, the smile crumpling to something unpleasant. "More data, Mr. Michaels? And where, pray tell, will we get this data if we don't send somebody to the mainland?"

Donovan panicked at the thoughtful look that passed over the medical team leader's face.

"Dr. Crispin—"

"No, Donovan—enough. It is my intention to send the Dogs on a combination rescue mission and specimen-collection run. As before, I feel that I'm too close for an objective view, so I ask you again, good people of the island. What should we do? All in favor of sending the Dogs, say aye."

A brief chorus of ayes came from scattered mouths around the room, but it was far less than half. Donovan sat back into his chair, blowing out a shaky breath. He had been worried there for a second, but it appeared as if common sense would prevail.

"Excellent," Dr. Crispin said. "The ayes have it. Thank you."

The rest of the room erupted in disbelief.

Crispin gestured imperiously to Alpha McLoughlin, who huffed out a short command: "March."

The Dogs moved as one, forming up behind Dr. Crispin and following him out of the dining room like an honor guard.

"Well, he finally got his way," Lucy said. She turned back to her plate of rice. "Crispy has flipped his lid."

TEN

A SMALL YACHT pulled into the deserted wharf, its presence announced by the thumping of the twin engines. Everything else in the night was quiet, save for the gentle rhythmic slapping of waves against the piers.

Then came the moaning.

From boathouses and offices they came, dead men and women dressed in rental company uniforms and grease-stained overalls, a few enterprising individuals who had tried but failed to get to their boats when the disaster first hit. One of the dead dragged behind him a small suitcase, strapped to his wrist.

As the yacht pulled up to one of the finger piers, the horde shambled faster in anticipation of a mouthful of flesh. Something to cool the furnaces in their guts. Clumsily but relentlessly, they moved forward, closing on the quiet yacht.

It bumped against the wooden pier as the waves pushed it around, and the noise drew more and more of them from inside the fenced-off shipyard.

Then a new sound split the night. At first, it was indistinguishable from the purr of the engines, but it rose steadily from a growl to a howl, ringing out into the dark.

The zombies, excited, hurried toward the boat.

A dark, furry shape shot up from the deck, landing heavily on all fours on the pier. The large, thickly muscled beast bared its wicked teeth, and, unwilling to wait for the rest of the pack, charged.

The creature hit the crowd of zombies at full speed, scattering them like ninepins into the water. Those that kept their feet reached for the Dog, only to draw back stumps of bone and flesh.

Clawing, slashing, the Dog rose up, scooping reams of bowels from bodies, letting thick blood from still veins spill, liberating heads from shoulders.

A short minute later, viscera, dismembered trunks, and rent limbs floated in the water, and the pier was clear of the undead, if a little slippery from the offal.

"Good job, Kaiser," McLoughlin said from the boat. "Come on, Dogs. Clear the rest of the boatyard. Keep your heads on. If you need to change, make it count. Because after you change back, you'll be stuck until we return to the therapy rooms."

The seven other Dogs put out a gangplank and crossed it, following in the wake of the hulking Kaiser.

)

The next morning, Thetas Hayte and Rose stood behind the gate, each holding a black bullpup submachine gun at the ready and sneering at the straggling dead in the street beyond. The sound of a heavy engine behind them signaled the beginning of the day's festivities.

Hayte turned and looked at the massive wrecker that Jaden's man had found. Last night, Dunne and Kristos had gone through the Change and had followed Kaiser out onto the street to clean out loads of walking corpses. The three of them were now sleeping it off in the hold of the yacht.

"Are we ready?" Rose asked, pointing at the driver, one of Jaden's men. Four of the security guards had come along to lend support. The man nodded and gave a thumbs-up, then wiped his forehead.

Rose grinned and stepped back, mouthing the same question to the driver in the school bus they had dragged in off the street. Holly Randall had raised hell about losing one of her welders for the job of fortifying the bus, but Dr. Crispin got his way.

The bus driver gave him an A-OK, and Rose whistled once, a high, piercing sound. An office door opened under a jet-ski rental banner, and Alpha McLoughlin strode out, with Theta Landis and one of his Sigmas in tow.

"When we get out there, Parker, you stick with Landis. Understood?" McLoughlin looked down at the Sigma.

Parker, a lithe man, redheaded and pale, nodded sharply. "Yes, sir."

McLoughlin clapped his hands together and looked over at Hayte and Rose. "Where's Samson?"

"Up here."

McLoughlin looked up and saw Samson already lounging atop the school bus, the trunk of his dark blue coveralls pulled down and tied around his waist. His dark skin shined with sweat in the warmth of the morning sun.

"Good," McLoughlin said. "We hit the ground running. The security team will drive and ride shotgun for each other. Samson, you and I will split off, looking for the survivors. Landis, you and Parker keep together, do the same. We have three directions to go. Remember," he said, tapping the side of his nostril.

Landis said, "Follow your nose—it always knows!"

He and Parker climbed atop the wrecker, and McLoughlin joined Samson on the school bus. Hayte and Rose pulled the gates open, and the wrecker rolled through.

After the bus was clear, the Thetas closed the gates and resumed their watch.

Rose already looked bored. "You think they'll find anybody?"

Hayte shrugged. "Only the Great Spirit knows."

The wrecker slowed, easing into the first entanglement of cars. Its engine revved up as the great, dirty machine pushed the vehicles apart.

"All right!" McLoughlin shouted. "Dogs deploy!"

The four men unzipped their coveralls and stepped out of them. Before the dark-blue garments had hit the ground, the Change had started. All four of them hunched over, dropping to their hands and knees as bone and sinew rearranged itself with popping, gristly sounds. Human cries and grunts dropped down to guttural depths, and then there were four Dogs on the vehicles, howling.

The Alpha leapt away to the north, his golden coat rippling as he ran. Dark-furred Samson followed suit, running south. Parker and Landis, in gold and patchwork brown-and-grey coats respectively, loped off to the west.

"I don't care how often I see that," the driver of the wrecker said, "I will never get used to it."

❦

"Did you see that? What the hell *was* that?"

The man at the door peeked out through the narrow glass slit, eyes wide. He wore a tattered red shirt over dark-blue jeans, and a green trucker's hat on his head. The back of his leather belt read BUCK in large letters, which was appropriate for the large man. He clutched a double-barreled shotgun that had seen better days.

"What did it look like?" a woman behind him asked.

"It looked like the devil."

The woman, who wore black motorcycle leathers, rolled her eyes. "Come *on*, Buck. Be serious."

"Screw you, Shayna. I saw what I saw. It was a... a... a *beast*. Fur, black as night. It ran by on all fours, big as a bear, maybe."

Shayna put her fists on her hips. "Oh, really."

Buck turned back to the door. "Not as wide. Thick through the shoulders, slimmer at the hips. Moving fast, too."

She walked forward, her square-toed boots clicking on the concrete floor. "You sure you haven't had a nip or two this morning? Let me see." She brushed Buck aside, and he let her.

"I saw what I saw."

Shayna put her face up to the safety glass, looking around. "Well, I don't doubt you saw something. If it was moving fast, maybe it was the rescue squad. But a beast-man?" She shook her head. "That doesn't sound—*oh, God!*"

A yellow eye in a black, furry face appeared in the window, and Shayna saw a mouth full of sharp teeth before she fell back.

"The Devil!" Buck shouted, lowering his shotgun and firing both barrels. The blast sheared away the window and a significant bit of wood around it. The face disappeared, and Buck hooted.

"I got it!" He put a hand out to help Shayna up. "And, no, I haven't had anything to drink this morning, thank you very much. Ran out two days ago."

Shayna's sharp reply was cut off as a thick arm, corded with muscle and covered in black fur, jammed through the broken window and slapped at the door handle.

"Oh, shit," Buck said, dropping Shayna and fumbling his shotgun open. "Shit, shit, shit." His hands shook as he dug shells out of his shirt pockets. He dropped four of them trying to reload his shotgun.

The claws hit the handle just right and the door popped open. The daylight from outside was eclipsed by the hulking, wolfish form. It looked up at Buck and snarled, pointing one black talon at the shotgun. Slowly, it shook its doggie head, flinging blood from its muzzle.

"Better put that down, Buck," a voice said from behind. Jorge came out of a stairwell. "I told you idiots the rescue squad was *lobos* or something." He cleared his throat and pointed at the Dog. "I didn't think that would be so literal, but... what the hell, right?"

The Dog grunted and licked its lips.

It turned to go.

"Come on," Jorge said. Then he yelled up the stairs, "*Vamanos*, we don't have all day!"

A line of people came down from the upper floor and followed Buck and Shayna, who were following the Dog. Outside, a tangle of dead limbs and torsos littered the street, and the survivors took care stepping over them. The Dog *woofed* once as a yellow school bus pulled into the intersection. Plate steel covered the windows, with crosses cut into them.

"Get to the bus!" Jorge yelled. He and the six other survivors jogged forward, but Jorge stopped as he got to the Dog. "Sorry about that. Buck's trigger-happy. It's why we love him."

The Dog growled, and Jorge took a step back.

"Yes, of course," he said. "Whatever you say."

He got on the bus and his legs went a little weak when the air conditioning hit him. "Oh, yeah," he said. "I could definitely... Marie?"

His ex-wife sat in one of the seats with another man. Jorge took him in, looking him over, eyes narrowing. Dark striped shirt, blue jeans, forearms and biceps powerful enough to crack nuts in between.

"Jorge?" Marie said. "*Ay, dios mio,* you're alive!"

"Yeah," Jorge said. "And who is this?"

The man's face hardened. "I am Paulo."

Jorge laughed once, an ugly sound. "Well, good luck with this one. *¿Y los niños?*"

Marie's face fell, and Jorge felt his guts turn to water.

"*N'ombre,*" he said. "Tell me they're okay."

"*No se,*" Marie said. "*No se. Estan con mi mama en Mexico, pero no se nada de ellos.*"

Paulo reached around Marie and rubbed her shoulders. He looked up at Jorge with clear eyes. "We tried calling. The kids have been with their grandmother for six weeks now, even before all this."

Jorge met the man's gaze and knew there was something he wasn't being told. "Shit," he said, turning away. As he did, a large man with a shaved head stepped onto the bus. He glistened as if he were covered in sweat, but the smell coming off his sheen was bitter and tangy.

"I'm McLoughlin," he said. "I realize my team must come as a shock, but everyone can relax. We're taking you someplace safe."

ELEVEN

DR. DONOVAN STOOD in front of a six-foot sculpture of a Dog, looking at it in the sharp fluorescent light of Crispin's Command Center. The statue was crafted in painstaking, loving detail, from the yellowish-black talons on the misshapen feet to the tufts of hair on the ends of the Dog's ears.

Donovan tilted his head. "So, this is... decoration?"

Crispin, who was sitting at a very large touchscreen above a bank of controls, took off his headphones and turned to the neurotechnician. "I'm sorry, what?"

Pointing at the model of the Dog, Donovan said, "What is this?"

"Oh!" Crispin smiled. His mood had much improved since the skewed vote, and it had only elevated with each positive report from McLoughlin's team. "There is a rectangle on the base of the statue. Step on it, please."

Turning away and rolling his eyes, Donovan did as the project director bid. A seam of light brightened down the center of the Dog, splitting it from crown to crotch. The two halves of the sculpture rotated outward, revealing a network of fiber optics and realistic viscera. The skeletal structure was exposed on the right, the musculature on the left, with all the organs suspended in between.

"That's... different." Donovan's eyes widened and took in everything. The fiber optics ran throughout the systems of the Dog, a fine line of pulsing light. "These are, what? The pathways monitored?"

Crispin grunted at the touchscreen. The monitor was tiled with little picture-in-picture video feeds of each Dog's vision. "Close, Dr. Donovan. Those are the neural pathways the Pavlovian Chip *controls*. I'll show you."

The doctor pinched his forefinger and thumb together on the touchscreen, then expanded them, zooming in on Samson's feed. The display was moving steadily and smoothly in hi-def, sweeping from side to side as the Dog searched the alleyway. The size of the monitor, combined with how close Donovan stood, induced a bit of vertigo. He put out a hand to steady himself.

"It takes a bit of getting used to," Crispin said. "The neural interface captures the image coming into Samson's eyes, even before it gets to his optic nerve. In fact..." He paused, raising one eyebrow at Donovan. "We can even intercept it. Would you like to see?"

Donovan nodded.

"Good. Let us see what our erstwhile Beta Samson is up to."

They watched as the view closed in on a stout wooden door with a lancet window of meshed security glass. Samson edged toward the door, bit by bit. Dr. Crispin's finger hovered over a button.

Samson moved, about to look in through the window, and then Crispin's finger came down. The image on the monitor erupted in a flash of light, and Crispin and Donovan jumped as the tinny sound of an explosion rocked the headphones. Vital signs spiked at the bottom of the display.

"Ah, damn it," Crispin whispered, taking his finger off the controls. He watched the screen in horror, grimacing and typing as Samson's pulse and respiration leapt.

Donovan stood back, knowing better than to ask questions as the project director typed in a string of commands. The motion on the screen stopped, and Crispin blew out a breath. He scratched at his chin for a second, then began typing again, fingers flying over the modified keyboard.

Onscreen, a black-furred arm came up and one talon pointed at the shotgun that had produced the burst of light. Crispin typed again, and the display swung from side-to-side. He pulled a microphone out of the console and spoke into it.

"Samson, this is Crispin. Stand down. I am returning control." He sat back and slapped at a glowing square button on the console. Looking up, he caught the sharp concentration on Donovan's face.

"As you probably have inferred, I can override one or all of the Dogs from here," he said. "The idea was to slow them down or stop them if one of their targets was deemed fit for interrogation instead of termination. But I also installed this quick release..." He pointed at the square button, which was no longer glowing. "The QR returns control to the Dogs in case they need to react independently."

Donovan indicated the keyboard, which had another full row above the function keys. "And this is the controller?"

Crispin nodded. "It is." He stroked his fingers over the extra row of keys. "These are the shortcuts, if you will. Each one has a string of commands tied to it to save time and facilitate ease of coordination between the Dog packs, if needed." He turned and pointed at the bookshelf that spanned from one wall to the next. It was crammed with two-inch binders and what looked like military manuals.

"You'll find all of this in there," he said. "I did the bulk of the programming myself, but every now and again, hah, I find the need to consult the Wall."

Donovan walked to the expansive bookshelf and plucked a binder from it. It was densely packed with folded papers, with a four-page table of contents at the front. He picked a folded sheet at random and pulled it out, revealing a three-foot, one-line diagram of system interconnections inside a panel labeled TxRx-3.

"What's TxRx-3?" he asked.

Absently, Crispin pointed at a spot on the far wall as he put the headphones back on. There, where he pointed, Donovan saw a small door built into the metal wall. The neurotech put the binder down and walked over, sure Crispin had made an error.

That access door can't be more than four inches square. Surely...

He got close enough to read the letters etched into the metal surface.

"TxRx-3," he said.

Twisting the little handle, he opened the access door and peered inside. Donovan sucked in a breath. There, in the space behind the door, was a circuit board ringed on all sides by filaments of wire. He closed the door and looked at the rest of the wall where he stood. From top to bottom, there were twenty such access doors, and another twenty next to those.

"Fascinating."

Looking back at the thick binder, Donovan saw that the cover said TRANSMIT/RECEIVE. He put it back on the shelf. "Is this how you get the commands to the Dogs? And how you get their readings?"

Crispin nodded.

"But there are only fourteen Dogs. You have forty modules. What are these, built-in spares?"

"Not exactly," Crispin said. "The... hold on. Yes!" He reached out and turned off the monitor. "Come with me, Dr. Donovan. We are going to have a celebratory drink."

"Celebratory? In celebration of what?"

"The Dogs have found survivors and are on their way back!"

❯

As the Dogs herded the two groups of civilians off the bus, Jorge split off and walked over to the big blond man who had called himself Mac. The big soldier had just turned off a radio of some sort.

"Hey. You the leader here?"

Mac turned to the smaller man, taking everything in quickly. "I am. You're the one who calmed things down when Buck shot Samson."

"Ah. Is he the, uh, what do we call you?"

Smiling, Mac put a large hand on Jorge's shoulder. "We're the Dogs. And that's all you need to remember for now. There'll be plenty of time on the island to play get-to-know-you."

Mac began to turn away, but Jorge caught his hand. "That's not why I came to talk to you. There are more of us out there."

Mac raised his chin. "Tell me about it."

The civilians milling around the bus stopped to listen.

"Okay," Jorge said. "About a month ago, when all this started..."

❯

The Blazer turned up on its side and rolled. In the VW behind Ken, Jorge slammed on his brakes. The other people in the convoy almost rear-ended him. A few other drivers did rear-end each other, and he heard the crunching of metal and the shattering of taillights.

Clawing at the door handle, Jorge undid his seat belt. He glanced in the rearview mirror and saw the crazy woman who had jumped into his windshield. She lay in the ditch, trying to get up, but the bones of her legs just kept buckling.

More walking corpses were coming up behind her.

Jorge jumped out and slammed the door behind him. Tearing his automatic from his waistband, he walked toward the zombies surrounding the Blazer, feeling his breath coming in great gulps. He tried to calm himself so he could shoot, but the twisted hulk of Ken's Blazer kept him from peace.

"Ken!" he shouted.

He took his stance and started shooting at the undead. The first one turned toward him and it got two in the chest, then one in the face for its attention. Another turned, and Jorge put a round in its lungs. It fell backwards, but got right back up. Jorge took another step closer and aimed, placing a round neatly in the middle of its face. It went down and stayed there.

"Ken!"

He kept firing, choosing his shots carefully, but there were more zombies than he had rounds, and behind him, another mass of undead was stepping onto the blacktop. He would get surrounded if he didn't *move*.

"Shit," Jorge said. He turned back toward the VW, and his eyes bugged out.

A burst of fire from behind the short caravan obliterated the first row of zombies to reach the highway. Then suddenly a Humvee raced up beside the line of cars, and a stern-looking man in a helmet shouted for them to follow.

Jorge opened his mouth to shout for help—his best friend was trapped in the wreckage—but the soldiers saw his gun and tackled him to the ground.

They carried him to the covered flatbed truck, even as he kicked and tried to wrestle away from them.

"Ken! *Ken!*"

"Jorge?!" his friend called back from inside the Blazer. "Jorge, I'm pinned!"

Then the military men threw Jorge into the truck and started moving again as the zombies closed in on Big Bertha.

❦

"Then, like, five miles away, we had to stop again for a car crash, and the dead were everywhere," Jorge said, finishing the story. "Only a couple of the soldiers got away, and of course, we used their gear to call you guys."

"Where are the soldiers now?" Mac asked.

Jorge shrugged. "Don't know. They heard you guys were coming, and they geared up and split. I think they went looking for my friend, Ken Bishop, the man in the Blazer."

Mac grinned crookedly. "You must have been very persuasive to get them to leave shelter like that. Especially to find a man who's in all likelihood dead."

"Well, these were the two jarheads who tackled me. I figure, I was about to use that lady's Bug to run the zombies away from the Blazer, then maybe, I don't know, somehow pull my friend out. But instead, I ended up with the jarheads. They owed me."

Mac nodded once and slapped Jorge's shoulder. "All right. We'll take you guys to the island. And then, after we regroup, we'll see if we can't find the soldiers. And your friend."

TWELVE

THE CALM OF THE AFTERNOON was infectious. Survivors stood in their groups at the pier, chatting and comparing stories. A problem with the boat's engine had slightly delayed their departure.

McLoughlin stood with Samson in an empty boathouse, checking the Beta's face and shoulder.

"Is it still sore?" McLoughlin asked.

"Nah, I'm all right. I got to tell you, it can't go on like this."

"Like what?" McLoughlin said, spraying his friend's wound with antiseptic. It was healing quickly, as the Dogs' wounds did, but this was the first gunshot wound they'd encountered since their upgrade. Dr. Crispin would want a full report on the recovery process.

"Doc Crispin was at the control panel."

McLoughlin looked up into Samson's eyes as he rewrapped the man's shoulder. "That's kind of what he does. If he's not watching us spar or do exercises, he's at the helm in Command."

"Yeah, well, he took my eyes." Samson grunted. "He took my eyes when I was about to check a room, and that fat, sweaty shithead got one off in my face."

Sighing, McLoughlin shrugged. "What do you want me to do? Dr. Crispin is the Master. He has been, and probably always will be." He finished bandaging the wound. "How's that? Too tight?"

Samson rotated his shoulder. "Very good, Nurse Macky. Is there a mirror in here? I want to check my face."

"It's terrible," McLoughlin said. "Horrible to look at. Probably give children nightmares."

"That bad?"

"Yeah. It healed right up, and you look just like before."

The men laughed. Samson stopped first, looking away from McLoughlin. "I'm serious. He listens to you, sometimes. If we're out in the field, he can't be—"

McLoughlin threw his hands up. "All right. Jesus. Better not tell the others about this. They get the idea they can get me to do stuff just by being annoying about it, I'll never get any sleep."

At the gate, Hayte and Rose were again posted as guards, carrying their MP5 submachine guns.

"This is horseshit," Rose said. "I didn't come along on this ride just to stand around and babysit a bunch of civvies." He shook his head. "We didn't even get our muzzles wet."

"We will," Hayte said. "When the time is right, we will have our moment in the sun."

Rose looked over at him. He waited. When it was apparent that Hayte was done, Rose smiled. "That's it? No native wisdom about the fullness of time or any of that?"

"No," Hayte said. "I believe I am done trying to impart the wisdom of the elders to you."

Eyes narrowing, Rose said, "Why? Is it because I'm not a Native American?"

Hayte turned to Rose, the hint of a smile on his lips. "If you know a cup has a hole in the bottom of it, do you keep trying to fill it with water?"

"Oh, ha ha. You should try open mic night. As a matter of fact, I..." He stopped talking and cocked his head to listen. "You hear that?"

Hayte and Rose turned toward the street beyond the fence. The sound, whatever Rose had heard, was growing.

And getting closer.

Moaning.

"Incoming!" Rose yelled. "A whole lot of them!"

He and Hayte flicked the safeties on their MP5s and stepped back from the gates.

"Come on!" Hayte yelled. "Get the bus over here! We need something to block the gates!"

He turned and saw there was nobody at the vehicles. A burst from Rose's gun turned him back.

A horde of undead, drawn to the marina by the sound of the engines, had found its way to the gates and was steadily advancing.

Hayte cursed. "Where the hell did the security goons go?"

Shrugging, Rose lowered his gun and spoke into his radio.

"Alpha McLoughlin, we have a situation here."

"I heard the shots. Keep 'em off the gate until I get there. Don't change until I do. We have more ammo aboard the yacht; use what you got until then."

"Light 'em up," Hayte said.

He and Rose switched their guns to full auto and swept the crowd, one Dog spraying the dead at head-level, the other taking out their ankles and shins. It wasn't good. The ones at the gate fell dead or disabled without feet, but the ones *behind* the ones behind them kept pushing. And as far as the Dogs had seen, the column of undead could support a coliseum.

A howl sounded behind them, followed by pounding paws. The hulking Alpha Dog flashed by, bounding into the air, easily clearing the twelve-foot fence.

"About time," Rose said, dropping his gun and working the zipper on his coveralls.

The Thetas began the Change, their muscles rippling and sprouting hair. Soon, a grey and reddish set of Dogs was ready to fight. They howled and charged after their Alpha, jumping to the top of the fence, then off.

Claws out, the Dogs came down in the midst of the zombie horde. They slashed and struck, the bizarre mix of canine and human physiology forming a perfect fighting machine. Senses sharpened by an evolutionary shortcut told the Dogs where their prey was, and human strategy took a backseat to primal fury. Each of the three Dogs became a tornado unleashed. Large, hairy fists pounded the tops of heads to mush. Claws unzipped bodies from sternum to throat. They heaved and turned, always a fraction of a second ahead of their enemy's teeth, always faster than their shambling foes.

They still weren't enough.

The zombie horde moved inexorably forward, flowing around the three islands of devastation as would a river. The street was too wide; there was no way the Dogs could hope to clog it with bodies. No way to create a bottleneck.

McLoughlin, seeing the dead reach the gates, snapped his jaws and put his head back, howling once. He bounded that way, flattening zombies left and right. He leapt up and back over the fence.

The gates started to open, and he was there, pushing against the iron framework of the gates, trying to hold them closed against the will and bottomless hunger of the living dead. The rotting tide ebbed and flowed as Hayte and Rose worked from the outside to gain the fence and lighten the pressure on McLoughlin.

There were too many of them.

Even the Alpha Dog's brute strength gave under the combined weight of the dead. He let go, loping back to regroup. Rose and Hayte scaled the fence and joined him, flexing and steeling themselves for the flood. Then they all turned toward the sound of gunfire.

Jaden's security men had climbed atop the bus and were picking away at the crowd. From the boat, Landis and Kristos took up their MP5s and joined the firing squad. McLoughlin shook his head, golden mane rippling.

The civilians were now lying on their faces between the bus and the pier, avoiding the crossfire. McLoughlin's fur bristled with frustration.

Zombies, not intimidated by the roar of gunfire or by the attrition rate of their cold brothers falling to either side, pressed forward. The first one reached the bus, and McLoughlin jumped at it, knocking the thing from its feet. He roared, and the survivors got up, screaming.

"Get on up!" Kaiser yelled at them from the deck. He, too, held a submachine gun. "Onto the boat, or we're leaving your worthless asses here!"

McLoughlin turned to herd the people up, but remembered the guardsmen on top of the bus. They were stranded there, having quickly run out of ammunition, surrounded now by a stream of rotting bodies. He turned back for them and waded into the dead, swinging his massive arms in great arcs, knocking the corpses around as if they were mannequins.

He barked once, and the security detail ran for the front of the bus, jumping onto the engine hood and down one by one. They joined the lagging survivors as they made their way to the gangplank.

Hayte and Rose joined them, but not quickly enough. A dead woman in a blue evening gown swept around the front of the bus and grabbed a shorter dark man in blue jeans, sinking her teeth into his shoulder.

Rose leapt forward and removed her head from the nose up. The woman's jaws released, and the Latino man she'd bitten fell facedown on the pavement, clutching his wound and screaming.

"*¡Chingas a tu pinche joto madre, cabron!*"

McLoughlin heard the cries and knew what they meant. His snout wrinkled as he herded the last of the survivors up the pier. Dunne slung the bite victim over his shoulder and hustled over the gangplank.

The dead kept coming, but Rose and Hayte were holding them off at the narrow entrance of the gangplank. McLoughlin closed his big eyes and the Change swept over him. Fur and cellular ejecta fell to the wooden planks and sifted through the cracks as his howl turned into a scream.

It was over quickly, and he stood, hairless.

"Kaiser! Where's the one who was bitten?"

Kaiser's teeth grew sharp, too large for his human face. "He's at the bow of the yacht. Why? You want to talk to him?"

"No. I just don't know what to do with him. The reports say he's going to turn, but until he's one of them, I don't want to just leave him here. Besides, the docs will want to see it happen, probably."

Kaiser reloaded his MP5. "Hold on a minute, Alpha. I have an idea."

The Theta walked to the front of the boat, and McLoughlin heard a scream. The bitten man flew through the air, arcing over the water and landing heavily on the marina lot. The Latino's screams continued, and the zombie horde, forgetting the gangplank, turned his way. Kaiser put one foot on the rail and he and Dunne picked off zombie after zombie, keeping them away from the screaming bait.

McLoughlin waved Hayte and Rose up to the gangplank, then followed them onto the yacht. Kristos undid the mooring line.

Face full of thunder, McLoughlin marched to the bow. He grabbed Kaiser and spun him around. "Get to the aft, Dunne."

The other man left McLoughlin and Kaiser alone.

"What the *hell* was that, Theta?"

The sweating Dog sneered, teeth still sharp. "You said you didn't know what to do, sir. And you didn't give me any orders. So I took some initiative, and look where we are." He put his MP5 down and spread his arms. "All the civilians and security loaded. The welder is back onboard. One casualty, if you don't count Samson's gunshot wound."

McLoughlin's jaw muscles bunched, and he stared into Kaiser's eyes, looking for the slightest sign of mockery or defiance.

For his part, Kaiser met the stare. Calm. Collected. Secure in the knowledge that he had done what he thought was right.

"As you were," McLoughlin said, turning away.

"Yes, sir, Alpha, sir." Kaiser threw a salute at McLoughlin's retreating form.

THIRTEEN

"TO THE DOGS!" Crispin said, holding aloft his glass of champagne. "This is a great day, Dr. Donovan, cheer up! We've had a successful field test of their abilities *and* we saved lives." He gestured with his glass, and Donovan finally tapped his against it. "That's the spirit."

Crispin sat back with a smile. Deciding to ignore Donovan until the man came around, he swiveled around in his chair to face the giant touchscreen. With a few quick taps, Crispin brought all eleven Dogs into view. He hummed to himself as he drained his glass and poured another one.

Behind him, Donovan kept a keen eye on the console, watching every move Crispin made. There was no limit to how much the system's intricacies fascinated the neurotechnician. He made a face when he realized the show was over. Whatever the project director had done, whatever series of commands he had entered to hijack Samson's system, he wasn't going to demonstrate it again. There was no reason for it now. Not even to show off.

Silently, Donovan went back to the Wall and plucked down another heavy manual from the shelf:

**BCI INSTALLATION
AND MAINTENANCE PROCEDURES
VOL I**

A serial number ran under the title.

Donovan flipped the binder open, revealing a series of full-color pictures. They showed in all its brilliance the brain-computer interface, a silk web embedded with circuitry. A few color photos illustrated the BCI's placement on a living brain. Donovan checked the table of contents and found half of the surgical procedures listed. They seemed straightforward enough, and he had done similar installs himself.

His eyes slid over to Crispin's anatomical model of a typical Dog.

Never on that scale, though. And the control scheme is extraordinary. I can't imagine the process for the specimen. That had to have been terrible.

"Dr. Crispin, if I may, how much fine control is wired into each Dog?"

Crispin, who was pouring himself a third glass of champagne, looked up to the ceiling in thought. "Each major limb, of course. The phalanges individually, but not the toes. The eyes, the ears, and some other... well, the sniffing mechanism, I should say."

Keeping his eyes on the model, Donovan said, "And the process? How long did it take to put in the implants?"

"The first Dog we did successfully—that would be Theta Kaiser—he took a good three months to get right." Crispin took a swig out of his glass and swallowed it. "Kaiser required a lot of recuperation time between surgeries. But once the kinks were ironed out, it was fairly easy."

Donovan put the book down. "And McLoughlin? He's got something the other Dogs don't, is that right?"

"Yes," Crispin said, putting his drink down. Then he reconsidered and drained it. "Mac is the only Dog to have successfully taken to the hormones. He doesn't require therapy after the Change, as the other Dogs do. His gland actually produces them now."

Finding his hands empty, Crispin poured himself another drink. "He is living proof that my procedure, my, uh, life's work, is, as they say, indistinguishable from magic."

The smug look on the project director's face was expectant, so Donovan gave him the satisfaction. The ego was the quickest way to a man's heart, and to his head.

"Genius," Donovan replied. "I suppose that accounts for the Alpha's large stature, as well." He turned back to the life-sized model. "All those nodes. Such a fine degree of control."

"Control," Crispin said. "Yes, it's all about control, isn't it? Or loss of it." He drained his glass and found the bottle empty. "Gah!"

The project director sat back and stared at Donovan, again in deep thought, brow furrowed. "Listen, have you ever seen footage of when those researchers poured cement into the ant hole? Ten tons of cement? They let it dry and then started digging?"

"No," Donovan said. "I can't say that I have."

"Well, what they unearthed was extraordinary. It looked rather like the air sacs in our lungs." He waved his hands around for emphasis. "And it all looked to have been masterminded by an architect, a single mind. But, no, it was built by the collective will of the hive. This is rather how the zombies behave, if you've been watching. In fact..." Crispin lowered his voice, "it's how they were designed."

The BCI manual fell to the tabletop. Donovan looked up at Crispin, his mouth open. "Designed, sir? Are you saying the zombies were *manufactured?*"

Crispin fiddled with the empty champagne bottle, a morose look on his face. "No, I've stopped saying those kinds of things a long time ago, Donovan. It's practically a clause." He blew his cheeks out and said, "We're out of bubbly."

Donovan grabbed his still-full glass and thrust it in Crispin's face, which lit up.

"Oh, there's more!" He took the glass, drank from it and put it aside. He looked up at the monitor, but his eyes were unfocused, staring at something else.

Donovan waited until he couldn't stand it anymore. "Sir, if you have something you need to get off your chest, perhaps about this outbreak..."

Crispin glanced at him, and the look on his face was so naked, so vulnerable, Donovan almost didn't need an answer, even though he desperately wanted one.

Oh. Oh, my sweet Jesus, Donovan thought. *Doctor, this is all you, isn't it?* His eyes widened. *Of course you have to try to save them. You killed them.*

Your father was wrong.

The burring ring of the comms unit interrupted the silence, and Crispin's hand slapped down on it. "What is it, Winchester?"

"Good news, sir! The Dogs are back with civilians. Right now, they're in quarantine until Ron and the med team finish screening them for bites and illness."

"Excelsior!" Crispin shouted. "Good work, Winchester. When your shift is over, get yourself a drink. Tell them I authorized it, if you're already at ration."

He swiveled his seat to face Donovan. For all the champagne he had put down, Crispin's eyes were bright and focused.

"You see that, Doctor? For all the mistakes I've made, for all the hurt, I now believe I have achieved some modicum of atonement. And this is only the beginning! Shall we?"

Donovan nodded, hoping the project director didn't want to walk arm-in-arm to meet the survivors.

"Where is the quarantine?"

"Oh," Crispin said, waving his hand. "I had Miss Randall fabricate some cages outside just for this reason."

A short walk later—accompanied by a pair of Jaden's security detail—the two doctors were in the presence of the survivors.

"This is it?" Donovan asked, looking over the huddled masses. He felt his face warming as he did so. Twelve—no, fifteen new mouths to feed. "Where are their belongings?"

Lucas Jaden, who had beaten the doctors there, turned to Donovan. "They brought none. There were a few firearms, but we've confiscated those." He looked over at Crispin. "And don't worry, sir. Everything was bagged and tagged. We're keeping a very careful inventory."

Crispin, overjoyed at the mass of people, just nodded.

"They have no supplies," Donovan said to Crispin quietly. "They have nothing. No food, no seeds. I doubt if any one of them has any skills we could put to good use. They are, in short, dead weight, Doctor. We could give them one of the boats from the marina and—"

"Enough," Crispin said, placing a hand on Donovan's shoulder. "They're here now. And if this is indicative of the Dogs' performance, there will be more." He smiled. "We're heroes now, Donovan! Saviors!"

He stepped forward and began to introduce himself and Mr. Jaden to the survivors, and as a cheer went up, Donovan backed away. He caught the eye of one of the security guards and snapped his fingers.

"I'm headed back to Command. Come on."

He stalked back to the central building, a black mood following him like a cloud.

Old fool. Doddering, incompetent. I cannot believe he's willing to endanger all of our lives, my *life, for these squalling civilians whom we've never met. People* his work *put in harm's way.*

Donovan stopped at the door to Command, staring at the retinal scan. He turned to the guard. "The door, please."

"Sorry, sir, only Crispin is authorized to enter Command."

"Well then we will need to change that, won't we? I will need *equal* access if I'm to—"

"Sir, I'm sorry, but I meant to say that Dr. Crispin is the only one who *can*. Not even security can get in there."

"Ah," Donovan said, backing down. "Yes, of course." After staring at the door for a second, he turned back to the guard. "Take me to my quarters then."

"Yes, sir."

After the guard had left him in his room, Donovan paced back and forth in front of his bed.

"Can't work for him. Can't do it. He's the antichrist, ushering in the apocalypse. *Shit!*" He had a sudden, childish impulse to sweep all of the orientation binders off of his desk. His hand had actually moved back to do so.

An idea stopped him.

Can't work for him, he thought. And like every other time he had ever felt that way about a previous boss, Donovan wondered what it would be like to work for himself.

FOURTEEN

"MAC! I THINK they found something!"

Alpha McLoughlin scowled at the shortening of his name. Theta Rose should have known better to address him that way in the field.

On the other hand, the Dogs were all eager and happy to be *doing* something instead of just running drills on the island. Still, a breakdown in discipline, left unchecked...

"It's Alpha," he said, cuffing Rose's ear. The smaller man reeled for a second.

"Yes, sir," he said as he found his legs. "Samson reports that Hayte's on point. I don't know what kind of scent he's found, but he's very eager about it."

From his position atop an overturned Hummer, Kaiser grunted. "All the money and time they spent making us into the apex predator, you'd think they would've left our voice boxes alone so we could *talk* when we're all fuzzy."

Mac pointed back the way Rose had come. "Theta Kaiser, I want you changed and on backup with Theta Hayte. Rose, you hold back. Tell Dunne to radio the base, let them know we're chasing a lead."

"Chasing our tails," Kaiser muttered, dropping to all fours as the Change swept over him. Shortly after, his German shepherd form went loping away. Mac stared after him as the Theta bounded over upside-down cars and mounds of rotting corpses left in the scout teams' wake.

"Of all the special forces units in all the world," he said.

"What was that, sir?" Rose asked.

Nothing, he thought. "After Dunne reports to base, recall Kristos and Landis if they haven't found anything."

Theta Rose nodded and jogged back toward their temporary headquarters in the marina boathouse.

McLoughlin stood at the closed gate, looking out at the ruins of the city. In only a month, the whole world had tipped on its ear. Intellectually he was sure there were pockets of survivors everywhere, just like in this city. Perhaps even more in rural areas. But looking at the husk of civilization that lay before him, it was hard to believe.

He rubbed his hand over the stubble on his head. After hearing the one survivor's story about an overturned Blazer and the devastated regular army, Mac really hadn't expected to find too many survivors. Not after seeing the way the zombies *swarmed* anything living. The city wasn't especially large, which factored into his estimate; low population density and a relatively unburdened infrastructure had allowed for the one group. A second group would be a welcome find. There shouldn't be too many of them.

❧

Samson watched Kaiser approach with a flutter of anxiety in his gut. On paper, Samson was still his superior, but after Kaiser's power play in the sparring cage, the new Epsilon carried himself as if it were the other way around. Never around Mac, but that was only a matter of time.

Kaiser padded up next to Hayte and sniffed the air. His black-lined jaws snapped a couple of times, and he turned in place on all fours.

Looking back to the building, Samson nodded and picked up his radio. "Samson to base."

"Go ahead."

"Base, confirmed survivors in the North Regional building. Establishing contact now, will have numbers soon, over."

"North Regional, copy. Base out."

Samson clipped the radio to his belt and whistled. Kaiser and Hayte turned their large, shaggy heads to look at him.

"I'm going in," he said. "First contact. Stand by for back-up in case they prove to be... non-compliant."

Kaiser snorted a doggy laugh, leaning over to dig a shoulder into Hayte.

Walking up the steps to the building, Samson checked the clear plastic magazine in his bullpup submachine gun. Loaded. He let the P90 hang by its strap from his shoulder.

The last time he'd made first contact, he had gotten a face-full of buckshot. He'd also been a large hairy monster. So the new protocol had been established. He patted the gun. *Still.*

The glass of the double doors leading into the foyer was shattered and scattered over the marble floor. He saw a reception desk. Clearly the area was meant to double as a waiting room, but there was no furniture.

And no walking dead.

Ah-hah, Samson thought. *Whoever you are, you're very sneaky. And clean. Good for you.*

Samson walked to the back of the lobby to the elevators, looking to either side for the stairwell sign. A place like this, with six stories and dozens of business suites, would definitely have a stairwell, maybe two. Broken glass crunched underfoot as he walked down the west side. He turned a corner and found the lobby furniture.

The Beta grunted. Easy chairs, end tables, and small couches were piled and interlocked in such a way that, in order to be moved, the barricade would have to be simultaneously pushed and pulled, as well as lifted. None of the living corpses would just wander through.

Not that way, then.

Samson turned back to the lobby and crossed to the east wing. He saw a clear marble floor this way, no glass, so he knew he was on the right track. He came to a turn in the corridor, and Samson slipped around it with his P90 at the ready. The door to the stairwell stood closed.

Tilting his head to one side, Samson considered this. He could understand keeping at least one route upstairs unobstructed; if there were people here, they had to at least go on food runs. But why block up the one door so thoroughly and leave this one so exposed?

He looked around the wall and ceiling. He got down and peered at the floor closely. He looked at the door, at the hinges, at the handle.

Nothing.

Shrugging, he reached out and pulled the handle. The door didn't move. He pulled harder. Still, the door refused to budge. Pursing his lips, Samson backed out of the corridor and went to the front of the building.

"Hayte!" he called.

The Dog bounded upstairs and came to a skidding halt in front of Samson, tongue lolling out one side of his mouth.

"Come open this."

Theta Hayte followed him into the building to the recalcitrant door. The Theta sniffed at it, checking for booby traps, detecting none. Turning back to Samson, he chuffed out an interrogative.

"Go ahead," Samson said.

Hayte turned back and worked his thick paw into the handle of the door. He set himself, and then gave a tremendous yank. The doorjamb splintered and gave way with a loud crack, and Hayte had to take a hasty step back to keep from falling on his ass.

"Excellent," Samson said. "Back to your post."

As the Dog padded away, Samson squared his shoulders and checked the safety inside the trigger guard of his gun. Clearing a building this size, room by room, floor by floor, and without his enhanced senses, would take some time.

Just another day in the Army.

He stepped into the stairwell and went up the first flight to the landing, then stopped dead. He started to laugh. On the wall he saw a message.

3RD FLOOR
INVITATION-ONLY
PIZZAS WELCOME

With a light step, Samson jogged up the two flights of stairs to the third landing. He tried the door, but it was better than locked. He didn't even find a handle on the stairwell side. Samson briefly considered working on the hinges of the door, but discarded that idea.

Instead, he knocked.

)

The young man in the hallway picked his head up off his forearms and blinked sleep out of his eyes. He shook his head once for good measure, and a lock of red hair fell down over his face. Had he been dreaming?

The knock came again.

"Holy shit."

He fumbled with a piece of twine on the tiled floor, failing to pick it up three times before finally getting a good hold on it. He gave it a strong yank, twice. He couldn't hear the bell ring on the other end.

From the front pocket of his hoodie, he pulled out a short revolver, a snub-nose .38 Police Special: the Door Guard Gun. The whole time he had been holed up in this place and on door duty, he never once thought he'd be so glad to have the gun in his hands.

Straining his ears, the kid anticipated footsteps from down the corridor. He was vaguely aware of a trickle of sweat that had started somewhere on his head and was now soaking the collar of his T-shirt.

"Come on, come on, come on."

As if summoned by his panicky utterances, a pair of soft footfalls rounded the corner, and following them was the large leader of this pocket of survivors.

"What's up, Jimmy?"

Jimmy pointed a pale hand at the door. "There was a knock." He dropped his hand. "Twice."

The large man brushed his beard. "All right then. Stand back and cover me. We should see—"

"Cover you?"

The beard-scratching hand fell to the man's waist, bringing up a big revolver. "You're my backup, Jimmy."

"Jesus Christ," the kid muttered, settling his grip on the gun.

"Good man. Just don't shoot me."

The leader turned to the door and put his left hand on the push bar, then paused for a moment to take a steadying breath.

He blew it out.

"Here goes."

The door opened silently on a submachine gun.

"Hi," said the man who was holding the gun. "My name is Samson. I brought pizza—"

A gunshot boomed in the hallway, right next to Ken's head. The man named Samson tumbled back down the stairs.

"Christ, Jimmy!" Ken shouted, covering his ringing ear. "He was about to crack a joke!"

Jimmy wasn't listening. He was staring down the stairwell, eyes growing wider.

"What're you...?" Ken began, but then he saw it too.

The man named Samson was *changing*.

Changing into some kind of... human dog.

Unsteadily, the shapeshifter pushed himself up onto one knee. He shook his head and flung blood from the hole in his cheek.

Both Ken and Jimmy's eyes bulged as they watched the hole patch itself up, as the hair grew back into place, softer, more lustrous.

Then Samson morphed back into a man and stood up, regaining his strength and his consciousness.

His voice sounded a bit congested but he managed to say, "Found your friends."

Ken thought about that for a second. He had a more pressing question.

"What the hell are you?"

Samson said, "Pizza man."

Ken actually found himself laughing. And he had to admit, he had never met a man in his life who could take a shot to the face and still be honest-to-God good-humored about it.

Ken would have admired the Dog even more if he'd known this was the second time that day Samson had been shot in the face.

"Nice to meet you," Ken said. Then he wiped the smile off his mouth because the next part wasn't a joke. "Don't go expecting a tip. This pizza is *so* fucking late."

❦

"We keep some semblance of privacy here," Ken said as he and Samson toured the third-floor hallway. "The eight families with us have the large offices to themselves, and the rest of us have our pick of the other offices."

Taking in the layout, Samson let out a low whistle. "What have you been doing for food?"

Ken dipped his head. "For the first week or two, we rationed out the contents of the snack machines and whatever else was left in the mini-fridges. After that ran out, we started going on scavenging runs." Ken then raised his eyebrows at Samson, "What do *you* guys do for food?"

"The island has a farm. We grow stuff, and the engineer has built up some kind of algae machine, to help feed the new arrivals."

"Yeah, so, like you said, you found our friends. Are you sure you haven't run across a guy named Jorge? Stands about yea high, black hair, bad sense of humor?"

Samson put his hands up. "Easy. There was a big group. I don't know any of their names. Just that some of them came from your Blazer."

"Right."

Samson looked around. "Speaking of big group, how many people do you have here?"

"Sixty," Ken said, lying by just a few.

"Six... *sixty?*" The Dog strode to a window and looked out. "I'd better get on the horn."

"Horn?"

"Yeah, there's too many."

Ken's face clouded over. "Too many for what?"

Samson looked at him as if he just realized they were having two separate conversations. "Too many to fit into the boat back to the island. Let me talk to my Alpha." He unclipped his radio, and took a step back to give himself some space.

"Now wait just a minute," Ken said.

A voice came over the radio. *"Go ahead, Beta leader."*

Samson waited to answer them until he heard what Ken had to say.

It had been one thing letting this stranger into the building, one thing to show him around. For one, Ken had feared they would've had a fight on their hands if they hadn't cooperated. And Ken didn't want to have a fight on his hands. At least not with something that could survive a fatal gunshot wound to the face.

He had to admit it, he was scared. Because if he didn't admit it, he wouldn't be able to hide it.

He stared right into Samson's face as he replied, "No one ever said we were leaving."

"This is base to Beta Samson," the radio crackled, *"go ahead."*

"So what should I tell them?" Samson asked Ken.

Ken couldn't figure out whether that was a threat. He kept getting mixed signals from this guy. On one hand, he kind of liked him. But on the other, how could he trust a shapeshifting killing machine?

Guess it's no different than owning a wolf for a dog, Ken thought. *Could kill you at any time.* The more disturbing thought, however, was that he'd never been bitten by any dog, but had certainly been bitten by a man.

This guy was both.

"Uh, Ken..." Jimmy said.

The kid had just been hanging out in the background. Ken had almost forgotten he was there. The redhead had been profusely apologetic and then very quiet after shooting Beta Samson in the face.

"What if they found my mom, Ken? What if she's on their island, eating... whatever kind of algae? Don't I get a say in this?"

"Don't they all?" Samson asked.

Ken wanted so badly to say *And what if it's a trap?* Just to see how Samson would react. And to get Jimmy to use some common sense. But at the same time, he couldn't forfeit any element of surprise he might hope to gain, just in case things went presently south.

"Base," Samson finally said into the radio, before Ken could decide what to do. "We have survivors." And what was Ken going to do about it? Shoot him? Hah!

"First contact made, numbers are sixty, six-zero."

"Actually," Ken said, "it's more like fifty-two."

Samson cocked his head as if asking him to explain.

"I was factoring in the force multiplier when I quoted you that first number."

Samson nodded as if Ken's excuse made perfect sense. "Please advise the Alpha," he said into the radio. "Awaiting instructions, over."

"Holy shit," said Base. *"Sixty, copy. Base out."*

Samson put the radio down and turned to Ken. What he said next was enough to trump any of Ken's fallback plans. Because Ken didn't have *that* kind of force multiplier.

"Before we go any further," Samson said, "perhaps I should introduce you to the rest of the Dogs."

FIFTEEN

THE SURVIVORS FILED onto the bus with a mixture of relief, awe, and fear etched into their faces. Fear and awe of the Dogs themselves, relief they were being rescued, and an extra dose of fear for the families who were splitting up.

Alpha McLoughlin shook Ken's hand. "You sure you want to stay?"

Ken nodded. "Absolutely. But do you think you could leave a radio for us or something? So the families can keep in touch."

"Better than that," Mac said. "Two of my finest will be staying with you for the couple of days it'll take to get everybody settled on the is-land." He turned away. "Dunne! Landis! Front and center!"

A pair of men ran up, both clad in matching black coveralls, their names stitched on the right breasts. Dunne had a shotgun, Landis a submachine gun just like the one Samson carried. He also wore a back-pack with a protruding antenna.

Mac said, "Samson told me you guys have gone on successful food runs." He waved a hand at the bus. "The sound of this will bring them around, I'm afraid. I'd be remiss if I didn't leave you with a little extra protection."

Ken nodded, watching the people board the bus. The process of choosing who would go and who would stay had been difficult, espe-cially for the families. For the most part, the men had insisted their wives and daughters go first, in most cases their sons, too. Ken had heard a variation of the same speech being given several times, words designed to bolster young men's sense of familial duty, underscoring the importance of keeping their mothers and sisters protected in this new place among strangers.

Mac saw the object of Ken's attention and smiled.

He cares about his people.

"Don't worry about them," Mac said. "A couple days in quarantine, then we'll be back out to pick up the rest of you. All right?"

They shook hands again, and Ken headed back inside with Dunne and Landis. Samson approached Mac.

"We'd better hit the road, Alpha. The engine noise..."

"I know," Mac said. "Get us moving."

Ken watched all this from the entrance. He looked to the bus and caught Jimmy's eye through one of the portholes. They exchanged a nod, which was all that was required. As happy as Ken was to have his people "rescued," he wanted to go into this eyes wide open.

Jimmy would be those eyes.

꜖

Two hours later, the yacht was tying up to the island dock and people were unloading into the newly-renovated quarantine area. People from the previous batch of survivors had gathered to see the newcomers, some out of plain curiosity, others looking for friends and family.

Donovan counted heads with something close to alarm; the reports had said these were only *half* of the survivors. "Huddled masses," he said, spitting afterward. "I am the one yearning to breathe free here. Bah!"

He turned on his heel and walked away, hands clasped behind his back, brow furrowed in thought. He almost collided with Alpha McLoughlin. "Excuse me," he said. "You must be very happy."

The Alpha exhaled noisily through his nose. "I am, Dr. Donovan, but I'm also very... I don't know the right word. Kaiser has crossed a line, and Dr. Crispin was in no state to hear it. Is he...?"

"Sober?" Donovan finished for him. "Yes. Sober and jovial."

"Well," McLoughlin said, "I'm fixing to ruin his mood."

He stomped off toward Crispin's office, and Donovan found himself tagging along. He was interested by this bit of intrigue with the Dogs, and if nothing else, it might get his mind off the boatload of survivors that had just showed up to eat Donovan out of house and home.

McLoughlin noticed that the neurotech was following him when he knocked on Crispin's door. "You're here."

"I am," Donovan said. "As before. Dr. Crispin has taken me into his confidence, and if I'm to fully understand your enhancements and how they affect you, then I should have a better understanding of the Dogs as individuals, don't you agree?"

The look on the Alpha's face told Donovan that Mac certainly did not agree, but the weight of his Master's authority overrode the Dog's misgivings.

"Enter!" Crispin yelled.

McLoughlin opened the door and waved the neurotechnician through. They found Dr. Crispin in a jovial mood indeed, playing the *1812 Overture* on his stereo system and banging along in time on his desk.

"Excellent work today, Alpha," he said, turning the volume down with the remote. "Excellent work. And of course, with zero casualties."

"Actually, sir," McLoughlin said. "I have a report on Theta Kaiser. I believe he might be unstable, sir."

Dr. Crispin put his palms flat on the desk. "Explain."

McLoughlin shifted his wide shoulders inside his coveralls. "On the previous rescue operation, in order to distract a mass of the undead, Kaiser purposefully and willfully sacrificed a civilian by tossing him off the yacht to the wharf."

Donovan's eyebrows went up.

"He threw a man off the boat? Bodily hurled someone to the zombies? Someone whom your group had gone to rescue?"

"Yes, sir."

Crispin drummed his fingers on the desk. "Well. This is certainly a situation. Had the man done anything to anger or insult Kaiser?"

Face reddening, McLoughlin shook his head. "No, sir. The man had been bitten, though."

"Ah," Crispin said, sitting back in his chair and steepling his fingers before his face. "That does change things, you understand?"

Muscles bunched on either side of McLoughlin's eyes. "It shouldn't, sir."

Crispin sat quietly for a moment. "The world has changed, Alpha. You should know this better than I. You've been out to see what the world has become."

"That doesn't excuse—"

"No, of course not. But if the reports are correct, and we have every reason to believe that they are, then the morbidity rate is one hundred percent. As is the mortality."

Donovan cleared his throat. "I might go so far as to thank Kaiser."

McLoughlin's head turned to the neurotech. "I'm sorry?"

"The bite is fatal," Donovan said. "Transmission is a certainty, as is everything that follows. If you had brought this bitten man to the island, well, I don't know what the protocol would have been. For certain, we would have liked to study him before he died and turned."

Crispin put a hand out. "While I disagree with the callous way Dr. Donovan has put it, he is, in essence, correct."

"Yes, sir."

The Alpha stood to leave. Crispin looked as if he had more to say, but only stared at McLoughlin's back with a slight expression of regret. Donovan, on the other hand, was taking great pains to hide his sudden glee.

Kaiser, he thought. *I need Kaiser.*

)

He found him an hour later in the Dogs' private gym, working out with free weights. Donovan noted with interest the number of plates on the bar Kaiser was preparing to bench-press. He wondered whether the Theta was already as strong as the larger Alpha Dog.

"Excuse me," he said, interrupting Kaiser's lift. "I'm sorry, but that is just under three hundred pounds on that bar. Shouldn't you have a, ah... "

"Spotter, Doc," Kaiser said with a snort. "And, no. Nobody spots for me, and I don't spot for anybody."

He put his hands on the bar in a wide grip, opening and closing his fingers on it several times before grabbing and pushing the bar off the stops. There was nary a tremor in his arms as the weight came down smoothly to his chest, nor as he pushed it back up, exhaling loudly. He did that seven more times and replaced the bar.

"Look, can I help you, Doc? Or are you here to get some kind of kicks?" He flashed his canines in a smile, seeing the flush of pink on Donovan's cheeks.

"I'm here, Kaiser, to see if you're happy with your lot in life. And to talk to you about the program. To get a new perspective."

Kaiser sat up on the bench. "How do you mean?"

Donovan suppressed a smile.

"I mean, *Epsilon* Kaiser, don't you have any ideas for how things should be run around here? With the Dogs and the missions? Or Jaden's ludicrous security dictates? Or the living conditions, or—"

Kaiser put up a hand. "Right, right. Why me?"

This time, Donovan's smile made it out. "You're different. I can see that. You don't follow the *herd*. You understand the harsh realities of the new world in which we've found ourselves, and you can do the hard things. Things that need to be done. I heard about the dock and your... decoy."

"Hunh. I wouldn't expect someone like you to get any of that, Doc." Kaiser stood, smiling. "I guess I was fooled by your skinny neck."

Donovan nodded. "You're underappreciated, Kaiser. I could tell right away, when I saw you and the Beta in the sparring cage. That was a very clean, very clever victory. And yet, do they treat you any differently?"

Kaiser crossed his arms, and Donovan felt something inside him go *whoop!* He knew he had him then.

"They don't even call you by your new rank! You are Epsilon Kaiser! Someone like you should be the leader of the pack. And the Alpha can't see that." Donovan lowered his voice. "Neither can Crispin."

"You got that right."

Nodding, Donovan said, "But I see your true potential, Kaiser. I see more than a Theta, more than an Epsilon. I see the Alpha Dog in you. There's a reason I understand your situation." He tapped his own breastbone. "I'm in the same boat. Unappreciated. Underutilized. I say that if things don't change for the better, then maybe we ought to make the changes ourselves."

Kaiser listened, eyeing the neurotech silently.

"No more fucking hind tit," Donovan said, and his sudden vehemence surprised both of them.

"Well, Doc," Kaiser said, "pleased to finally meet you."

SIXTEEN

TWO DAYS PASSED as the initial group of survivors was removed from quarantine and housed in the hastily-erected quarters designed by the engineer, Holly. In that time, the Communications and IT teams had worked together to rig up a radio line out to the quarantine, so the newcomers could speak with their families and the people they had left behind. Each day, Dr. Crispin went out to the short hill overlooking the sprawl of survivors, and he stood there, watching them.

They noticed. At first, they thanked him often, and he took it as his due, but as the hours wore on with no communication, the looks his way became a little more wary. Especially from one young man in particular, a tall, gangly twenty-something with flaming red hair.

Crispin had already made a note to the security chief to keep an eye on that one. If there was something they couldn't afford, it was a troublemaker. A rabble-rouser.

On the third day, Donovan found Crispin making his visit to the survivor camp.

"The Dogs are on their way out," the neurotech said. "I couldn't help but notice Theta Kaiser is not along for the ride."

Crispin nodded. "That is correct. Disciplinary action."

Donovan pulled a face. "Is that so? I was under the impression that you had sanctioned his actions at the pier. Once all the facts were known, of course."

"Of course," Crispin said. "I'm not going to lie to you, Dr. Donovan. I'm as happy as the next person that we haven't had to deal with any, ah, *infected specimens.* But Alpha McLoughlin is correct that Kaiser is a callous person. Very little thought went into the Theta's decision to throw a survivor overboard to a horde of the walking dead. As much as I would like to, we can't save everybody.

"No, this disciplinary action has more to do with placating Alpha McLoughlin than punishing Kaiser. I'm not a people person, Dr. Donovan, but I know enough about human behavior to keep my team leaders happy."

Given that Crispin had missed the power play between Samson and Kaiser on Donovan's first day on the island, the neurotech found his statement to be highly amusing. But he nodded anyway and said, "Very astute, sir."

The project director tipped his head, missing the flash of satisfaction that passed over Donovan's face. Kaiser's exclusion from this rescue mission just gave the neurotech more time alone with the Theta Dog. More time to strengthen the alliance.

As they walked away from quarantine, Donovan was already rehearsing the important points he wanted to make to Kaiser. He would need the Dog on his side if he was to supplant Crispin and his pet Alpha, McLoughlin.

*

Across the water, tensions on the mainland were running just as high. Twice a day, Ken had taken advantage of the Dogs' radio equipment to get a status report on Jimmy's group, as well as an update on the progress of the radio line installation. When the report came that the lines of communication were open, he breathed a sigh of thanks and went to break the good news to his people.

Theta Dunne stopped him as the other Dog, Landis, carried the setup to the roof, where the reception would be better. "Don't you want to be the one to talk to someone first? No one will fault you."

Ken shook his head. "I can't. There are fathers downstairs, and they deserve it more."

Dunne nodded, his estimation of Ken Bishop climbing even further, as it had been for the past three days. Ken was a capable man, and the sheer number of survivors he had gathered in this building and had kept fed (and calm) was staggering. Dunne had tried to talk to Landis about it, but the other Dog was unimpressed.

"Will you ask him on a date, already?" Landis had asked the day before, and that was the last time Dunne had said anything about it.

Ken went from room to room, letting the remnants of the sundered families know the radio link was up. Word got around quickly, and soon there was a prodigious line in the stairwell to the roof. Once everyone knew, Ken made his way up as well.

"St. John," he said, tapping an ex-cop on the shoulder as he passed, "you're too far up. Families first, you know that. You, too, Sammy. And Marly."

Ken made it to the pebbled roof and watched as people came up to use the radio unit. He couldn't keep himself from tapping his foot as report after report came in, all very similar: family members in safe and semi-comfortable surroundings. A thought struck him, and he was immediately upset it hadn't occurred to him before this.

"Dunne?"

"What's up?"

Ken cracked his knuckles. "Is there a roster or something? A list of the survivors maybe? I'm interested to know if someone in particular has already made it to the island."

Dunne scrunched up his face. "To tell you the truth, we're not really involved on the administrative side of things. We're more of the 'hit and bite stuff if shooting it doesn't work' end." He shrugged apologetically. "I can ask."

Ken looked at the line. Already, the survivors were separated into two groups: those who got to speak with someone, and those looking for someone they couldn't find.

The girl with the dog stood apart, petting the small animal. Ken winced. Nobody had said anything to her about it yet, since she kept to herself, but he was pretty sure the dog hadn't survived the crash. He wondered briefly who she was looking for.

"No," Ken finally said to Dunne. "I'll just wait my turn."

He paced the roof, watching the men walking from the radio with tears of relief in their eyes. Even more closely, he watched people walking from the radio with a different kind of tears. Especially those people who drifted toward the ledge.

He walked that way, looking down. Mac, the leader of the Dogs, had been correct: all the activity of the first evac had drawn attention. Ken grunted. If anyone jumped off the roof now but survived the fall, they wouldn't wait long for death.

The radio line got shorter. Slowly.

Ken looked at his wrist furtively, even though he knew his watch wasn't there. His entire adulthood, he'd been a slave to the thing, particularly after he'd started his own construction business. Instead of coming and going as he pleased, he was suddenly responsible for everyone working for him. Like Jorge.

He looked at the line.

The only one who seemed to notice Ken's anxiety was the girl who had jacked Jorge's seat in the Blazer. She looked away, keeping her head low. Her hair blew around in the breeze, and she hugged herself, clutching at her shabby brown sweater.

Dunne threw one of the roof pebbles at Ken. He looked up when it hit his chest, and Dunne pointed at the girl.

Sighing, Ken recognized her. He tried to remember her name, and finally came up with it. "Kelly! Hey, Kelly."

The girl stopped and looked up at him. "Hey."

He pointed to the line. "You waiting to use the radio?"

She shook her head. "No. No, I just came up to get some fresh air. You know, and to see if, uh, if your friend was okay."

Kelly's head dropped again.

"I'm sure Jorge is fine," Ken said, looking away. "He's too stubborn to die. And that's something you should know about him. Are you listening to me?"

Faintly, she nodded her head.

"Good. Jorge was—*is* one stubborn son of a bitch, and if he didn't want to do something, he didn't do it. Do you see what I'm saying here?"

Kelly sniffed.

Ken reached out and touched her shoulder. "What I'm saying is, Jorge had a choice. And he chose to give you his seat. It wasn't anybody's fault." A hint of a grin crept onto his face. "If you're looking to blame somebody, you should probably blame me. I was driving, right?"

The girl looked up at him. "Thank you," she said.

He watched her walk away. He hadn't lied to her, but he hadn't told her everything. She blamed herself, and so had he, at least at first. Not anymore, of course, but it wouldn't do Kelly any harm if he kept that to himself.

Ken resumed his pacing on the roof. Dunne and Landis did a shift change, and the afternoon came and went, the sun tracing a very slow arc through the sky.

After several long hours of watching people talk about nothing— once they'd ascertained the safety and wellbeing of their loved ones— Ken finally was next in line to use the radio. He snatched the set from Landis.

"Jorge," he said into the microphone. "I'm looking for a guy named Jorge, he's about—"

"He's here," the radio operator said. *"Been here at my shoulder, annoying the piss out of me."*

A beaming smile split Ken's face. "That would be him."

❦

Jorge elbowed Winchester through the fence. "Is that him?"

"Stop that," Winchester said. "And yes. Here you go."

Snatching the headset from the radioman, Jorge put it on and sat in a folding chair. "Ken! Holy shit, dude, I'm so happy."

"Me, too, buddy. Have you heard anything about Marie or the kids?"

Jorge blew out a breath. "Man, let me tell you. Marie is all messed up. The kids were in Mexico with her mom when everything went down. Marie hasn't heard anything from them since. Oh, and she got a new man—"

"Oh, shit. Sorry."

"No te preocupes. It didn't last. One of these *cabrones* threw him to the dead, man. You believe that shit?"

"What?"

"Yeah. One of the Dogs just *threw* him to the dead; he'd been bitten. That was the story they fed us anyway."

"I can't... and the rest of them were fine *with this?"*

Jorge shifted in his seat. "No. They've disciplined him, but no one knows what that means. None of *us,* at any rate. Hey, so you did good, huh? There's a bunch of you guys."

"We did all right. We got pretty lucky, finding a way into this place. There was some food and a bunch of first aid stations."

"Andale. Good job, holmes."

"You made it too, man. Good job too."

The conversation trailed off for a second.

Then Ken said, *"Jorge, listen—"*

"Ken, I—"

They both stopped when they realized the other had something to say.

Sitting next to Jorge, Winchester cleared his throat and shifted in his chair, clearly uncomfortable to be privy to the conversation, and to the awkward silence in between.

"*Go ahead,*" Ken said. "*Over.*"

Jorge shook his head. "No, you first, bro, um..."

"*Jorge, I just—*"

"Over."

"*What? What's over?*"

"Oop, sorry. Just saying *over.*"

"*Well, I just wanted to say that before all this happened, you know that things for me were...*"

"Yeah, I know, Ken. Over."

"*And I just, I wanted to tell you... what I mean to say is—what the hell?!*"

Jorge almost barked out a laugh. But then he realized by the tone of Ken's voice that he was serious. "Hey, I was kind of expecting an apology here, bro."

"*Shit, Jorge, no—I wasn't... Hey, can you hold for just a—Jesus, what the hell is that?*"

The headset emitted a burst of static, and Jorge winced and brushed it off his head. Immediately, he put it back on.

"Ken? Ken?!"

SEVENTEEN

JORGE'S EYES BUGGED OUT in horror as the sounds of screams and gunfire come over the radio. "Ken!" He slapped the earpiece of the headset.

Curious, Winchester flipped a switch, and the cacophony of moans and automatic fire jumped out of some speakers on his console. His eyes widened, and he grabbed for the walkie-talkie on his belt. "Q-Comms to Radio, come in."

"Go ahead."

The other survivors, who had been milling around and chatting about their talks, turned to look.

Smaller pops went off, followed again by the staccato gunfire of the Dogs' submachine guns. A voice—Jorge knew it was Ken's—yelled out *"Oh, Jesus—"*

Static poured from the speakers, and Winchester slapped the console. The needle, once floating in the green, now rested at zero. Winchester tapped the gauge with his forefinger, and the needle jumped, but then settled again at zero.

"Alert the director. There's an issue on the mainland. Over."

"Wilco."

Jorge hit the fence. "What the hell?"

Winchester shook his head. "I don't know. I'm sorry." He pulled the radio headset from Jorge's hands and reeled it in. As he wrapped the cord, he looked up at the crowd. "I'm so sorry. The connection has been lost."

"What do you mean, lost?" Jorge yelled. The other survivors began to gather behind him against the fence. "You're the go-to radio guy, right? Get it back!"

Retreating from the barrier, Winchester shook his head. "It doesn't work that way. They're not transmitting. They're—" He broke off, looking away from the crowd. "I'm going back to the comms shack. Maybe I'll get something there." He took off at a jog, leaving the distraught crowd behind him.

"Hey!" Jorge yelled. "Come back here. *Come back!*"

)

Donovan stood outside Command, knocking on the thick metal door. He eyed the retinal scanner and scowled. One more detail to remember. He felt jittery, as if his insides were vibrating like plucked harp strings. Alpha McLoughlin and the rest of the Dogs were off to the mainland, and there wouldn't be a better time.

"*Yes?*" Crispin said over the intercom.

Turning to smile at the speaker, even though there was no camera, Donovan said, "Director! I was wondering if you wouldn't mind my company during the rescue mission today. I'm still working through the Dogs' kinesthetics, and I think seeing more of them in motion in the field would—"

The door clicked and popped open an inch.

"Thank you," Donovan said, closing the door behind him. "I know the Dogs won't be on the mainland for a little while yet, but... what is that?"

The radio crackled as Donovan asked the question.

"Director, Radio, come in."

Donovan drew up next to Crispin, who was biting the first knuckle on his right fist and staring at the touchscreen in front of him. Donovan looked at the labels on the two video feeds currently featured: *Dunne* and *Landis*.

On both screens, rifle barrels pointed out from a first-person perspective, spitting fire as they swept back and forth.

Crispin picked up the radio. "I'm seeing it. Thank you. Keep this channel clear."

"Is this another training scenario?" Donovan asked.

"They're under *attack*," Crispin said. "They're under attack, and I don't understand *how*. From the initial reports, the North Regional building was fortified." He slapped the console. "How did the zombies get in?"

Onscreen, the dead staggered through the roof access and into the Dogs' line of fire. They came in all shapes, all sizes. An extremely fat woman waddled in a floral-print muumuu, holding her gargantuan arms out in front of her, dragging dark coils on the ground between her feet. Dunne sprayed her, and bullet holes stitched her from massive belly to flabby shoulder. Another line appeared from chin to forehead. She fell in slow motion, almost majestically, holes spilling out curds of fatty tissue; and then she lay still as other undead predators stepped all over her, pressing out more bloody curds.

"Where are they now?" Donovan asked. "Is that the roof?"

"Yes. They were up there to get a better radio signal."

Donovan's eyes widened. "The zombies made it to the *roof?*"

Crispin shook his head. "That should have been impossible. But there it is. Jesus Lord, most of those people aren't even armed. If the Dogs don't dam that doorway, they're all done for." He slapped the console again. "Come on, Dunne, pull it together!"

Snapping his fingers, Crispin pulled the keyboard from under the console and started typing, fingers dancing on the keys. "Yah-hah! I know what they need. Situation's a little too real, so... adjust endorphins, serotonin levels, all right. Spike *this*, dial back the adrenaline..." He looked back up at the screen. "How's that, you magnificent bastards?"

The screen showed the change through the Dogs' eyes. Dunne finished one magazine and the first-person view shifted down as he swapped it out and switched his gun to single-shot. Then the whole picture lurched and went lower. At first, Donovan thought the Dog had gone down, but the picture leveled quickly.

"Attaboy," Crispin said. "He took a knee. Controlled shots. One at a time." He picked up his microphone and set a switch to GROUP A.

"Master to Alpha. Upon arrival on the mainland, proceed *directly* to North Regional. Dunne and Landis need you there."

In Landis's peripheral vision, Donovan caught a glimpse of a large man with a correspondingly large revolver, calmly shooting at the undead.

Landis shifted his tactics to match Dunne's, and the picture stopped jumping as much. The dead were still coming, as quickly as they piled up on either side of the doorway.

"It's like the Hydra," Crispin said, chewing one of his nails.

Donovan clucked as he watched the dead amass against the small band of humans on the roof.

Survivors? Not anymore.

He watched as the big guy reloaded his revolver, and then the man stepped back, out of Landis's field of vision.

The neurotech surveyed the scene from both Dogs' perspectives. Clearly the Alpha Dog's rescue force would be too late to help anybody. Just as well. Donovan had been wondering how they would be able to accommodate the next group of survivors, and now it looked as if all that fretting was for nothing.

He patted Crispin's shoulder.

"Excuse me, Doctor. I think I... left the kettle on."

Crispin waved his hand, totally engrossed in the unfolding carnage onscreen. He reached for his keyboard and began typing again.

Donovan walked to the secure entrance and looked around the room. He stared for a moment back at Crispin, banging away at the keyboard.

Fool, he thought. *So close to being great, shackled by the chains of your own limited perceptions. Oh well. All the better for me.*

He slapped the door release, and the door opened on Theta Kaiser. Donovan stepped back and bowed, waving the shirtless Dog inside. The Theta laughed once and stepped into the room.

Dr. Crispin, hearing this, turned from the control panel. His eyes fell immediately on Kaiser. "What the hell are you doing, Donovan? The Dogs aren't allowed in here, that one in particu—"

Baring his sharp, sharp teeth, Kaiser growled deep in his chest and advanced on the project director.

EIGHTEEN

"HEY," JORGE SAID over the radio, *"I was kind of expecting an apology here, bro."*

Ken grimaced, plugging his ear so he could hear over the racket coming from the stairwell. "Shit, Jorge, no—I wasn't... Hey, can you hold for just a—" He glanced at the stairwell access and almost dropped the mic. "Jesus, what the hell is *that?!*"

Landis turned at Ken's exclamation and leapt out of his seat, bringing the bullpup P90 to bear. The rooftop access door hung open, and a walking corpse stood there. It reached out and moaned, and Landis fired a burst of full-auto, scything the zombie in half.

Dunne dropped his water bottle and leveled his submachine gun as more zombies came out onto the rooftop. Together, the Dogs rained lead into the growing horde, and before long, both guns clicked empty.

As they reloaded, Ken looked around. Hardly anyone else on the rooftop had a weapon of any sort. He frowned, looking back at the doorway full of dead men.

How?

With a snarl, he drew his large .44 Ruger and took a Weaver stance, his left hand supporting the right. Smoothly, he pulled the trigger and the five-inch barrel belched fire.

A look of satisfaction passed over his face. The time he'd spent on the range had paid off.

Ken fired the gun several more times, rewarded by a dropping corpse with every squeeze of the trigger. Dimly, he was aware of another man rushing forward, clenching a snub-nose .38 in his fist. Ken turned to look, and as he did, the man tripped, shooting himself in the hip.

The Dogs began firing again, and the man who'd shot himself writhed on the rooftop, swinging the gun around aimlessly.

"Oh, Jesus!" Ken yelled, and the injured man pulled the trigger on the Police Special. The bullet smashed into the radio. There was a burst of electricity, and then smoke.

"Shit!" Ken ran over and kicked the small pistol out of the man's hand.

A woman's screams turned him around. The dead had advanced from the doorway, even through the Dogs' withering hail of gunfire. And now the dead were stalking the survivors. The closest one was almost on top of Kelly, who was still screaming. Ken took careful aim, but the dead thing was too close to the girl.

Glancing around, he saw a pile of scaffolding pipes stacked against the air-conditioning unit. He levered one up with his foot, grabbed it, and then took off running.

With a leap, he brought the pipe back and down, impacting the zombie's head and snapping its neck. The cadaver fell, and Ken grabbed the girl's shoulders.

"Are you okay?"

Kelly nodded, fast.

"Good. Here." Handing her the pipe, Ken turned to see the rest of the survivors fighting off the zombies with whatever they could find, be it rocks or pipes or their own bare hands.

At the doorway, an extremely fat woman waddled up in a floral-print muumuu, her gargantuan arms out in front of her, dark coils dragging on the ground between her feet. Landis and Dunne cut her down.

The Dogs burned through another magazine each, and Ken covered them while they reloaded. As he fired, he stooped to pick up the fallen man's .38 Special. A quick glance at the idiot's still form was enough to tell he would no longer need it.

Zombies continued to pour through the doorway, and yet Dunne visibly calmed. He dropped to one knee and took single shots. His accuracy increased, and a grim smile formed on his lips.

Landis followed suit, and the two Dogs thinned the ranks of the dead much faster. Ken continued shooting the .44, wondering just what the hell they were going to do. An idea clicked in his head as the hammer of his revolver fell on an empty cylinder.

He ran to the ledge on the north side of the building.

Ah, there you are.

When they had taken North Regional as their refuge, Ken had noticed a window-washing basket parked at the fourth floor, right in front of a large hole in the glass.

"Dunne! Can either of you hold these things off by yourself? I need one of you to help."

Landis and Dunne looked at each other. Dunne jerked his head back, and Landis nodded and jogged over to the ledge. He looked down and back up at Ken.

"You've got to be kidding me."

"What? It's only twenty feet, max. Don't tell me you've never... weren't you military?"

Looking down over the edge, Landis gulped. "Heights."

"Whatever," Ken said, and vaulted over the low wall of the rooftop.

He hooted once on the way down, and then slammed into the basket, making it rock alarmingly and bang against the side of the building. Ken got up and turned to the window, where shards of glass still lined the frame.

He looked up. "While you're waiting, could you drop me one of those pipes?"

Landis grimaced and then ran to the AC unit and back. He leaned over the side and held out the pipe. "Hurry up. Once I make up my mind to go ahead and jump, I don't need an excuse to stop."

He let the pipe go and Ken caught it. With an explosive exhale, he swung the weapon, clearing the frame of glass, showering the concrete below with a hail of shards.

"Here I come!" Landis shouted from above, and Ken dove into the building as the Dog hurtled from the roof. He landed in the basket, and it let out a bang and a groan as one side of it dipped, making the whole thing tilt at a crazy angle.

Before Ken could move to help, the Dog was airborne again, tucking into a ball and rolling into the office with him. He came to a stop at Ken's feet and glared up.

"Never again."

"Wuss. Come on!"

They went through the fire door into the stairwell and went careening down the stairs. Landis caught up on the way down, leaping several steps at a time.

"Hah!" Ken laughed. "*Now* he wants to jump!"

"You going to tell me what the hell we're doing, Boy Scout?"

"*Eagle* Scout," Ken said. "And I should have never told anyone that." He gestured down the hallway. "Building's got two stairwells. First thing we're going to do is blockade the clear one, just in case."

On the second floor, they burst out of the stairwell and ran down the hallway a few feet. "This won't take both of us," Ken said, slightly short of breath. "I set it up so any single person could trigger it."

Landis assumed he was talking about some sort of trap. "So why am I with you? If you made me jump off the roof just so you could show off..."

Ken stopped running and leaned over, hands on his knees. "No," he said, panting. "Yank that cord."

Shrugging, the Dog walked over and pulled the cable. A terrific crash came from within the stairwell. He nodded. "Very nice. What did you do for a living, Boy Scout?"

"Construction. Now come on, we've got to get to the bottom floor, get the rest of these things out of the building. It looks like there aren't too many more outside." He cocked a thumb over his shoulder. "That way is easier down the stairs, but a pain in the ass to get through the blockade. This way is hard going down, since that's where all the dead folks are. Which one you want?"

Landis popped his neck. "I'll take the hard way."

Ken smiled. "Good. See you in the lobby, yeah?" He put out his fist and the Theta Dog bumped it.

Taking a series of quick breaths, Landis rolled his shoulders and gripped his gun tighter. "Here we go."

He slammed the door open and knocked one of the zombies back. Raising the gun, he popped off several rounds, dropping the dead men in the stairwell above him. The moaning and gunshots in the stairwell echoed and mingled to create a new sound altogether, and Landis wondered for a moment whether he had chosen the wrong door.

❧

Ken raced down the other stairwell, hoping his installation in the lobby would work out like he had envisioned.

He got to the bottom of the stairs and opened the door. Holstering his gun, he kicked at the shims holding the barricade together, freeing a pair of mop handles. He threw these aside and then pressed his back against the wall, putting one foot on the couch, which sat to the right. With everything he had, he *pushed.*

The barricade wobbled, and he hooted, dropping to both feet and throwing his shoulder against the couch. With a grinding sound, the barricade of furniture and office gear came down with a crash. Ken leapt over it and ran to the bend in the hallway. Closing his eyes and offering a quick prayer, he grabbed both the big .44 and the .38, then peeked around the corner.

Zombies milled in the lobby. Now that they had nowhere to go, they stood there, and Ken knew they would continue to stand there until either something outside drew their attention, or they were killed.

"Come on, Landis," he whispered. "Please make it. Please, please, please."

The sound of gunfire came from the other side of the building. Single shots, and then someone was yelling, nonstop and loudly. There was a loud bang as the stairwell door was flung open; the gunshots and yelling got louder.

Ken came around the corner, guns up and firing.

The zombies in the lobby turned back and forth between Dog and man, confused as to which one they should go after first. They were mowed down like wheat before the guns of the defenders.

Landis and Ken stood in the room, looking down at the bodies.

"It worked," Ken said.

The Dog shot him a look, then burst out laughing.

)

"Does it hurt?" Landis asked, spraying a bite mark on Dunne's shoulder with antiseptic.

"Yeah. Burns. Even more with that shit, thanks."

Ken turned from supervising the rebuilding of the barricade and walked over to the Dogs. "What happened?"

Dunne grimaced. "I was doing fine on the roof. The dead shits in the stairwell were starting to wear thin, so I got up and walked the last of them down. Then the idiot who shot the radio got up and followed me, I guess."

Cursing, Ken turned away. "I should have put one in his head."

"Yes, you should have," Landis said. "Fucking Eagle Scout, indeed."

"I'm sorry. I didn't think he would... do you hear that?"

Everyone quieted; the working party and the Dogs all hushed, and when they did, they heard it too.

Moaning.

"Shit," Ken said. "All the shooting must have drawn their attention. Do you think you guys could hold them off? Hey, are you listening to me?"

The Dogs sat with vacant expressions on their faces. Unmoving, unresponsive.

"Dunne? Hey. Landis? Hey, Earth to Landis!" Ken turned back to the work party. "What are you waiting for? Get moving!"

The workers scurried back to the barricade, setting it up with a new sense of urgency. Ken jogged to the door and looked down the street. More of them were coming. A lot more. He looked back at the Dogs, who had finally stood up.

"Thank you," he said. "If there's anything I can do... hey, where are you two going?"

As one, Dunne and Landis had turned and started marching quickstep away from Ken. They reached the door and turned away from the approaching zombie horde, breaking into matching clumsy jogs as soon as they were outside.

"Hey!" Ken shouted. "What the hell?!"

NINETEEN

CRISPIN HIT THE ENTER KEY and let out a long, slow breath. "It's done," he said. "Alpha McLoughlin's team has gotten the order to stop. They're now waiting for Dunne and Landis, who are on their way. Then the entire party will return to the marina. What the hell is wrong with you? Both of you. All those people."

Donovan chewed the end of his thumb. He'd been watching Crispin work, trying to follow the code and syntax of the Command language, but it was like trying to learn French by watching somebody sign it. After it was up once, it was gone. The strings of code disappeared every time Crispin hit ENTER.

The neurotech finally let go of his thumb and pointed it at the director. "One of those Dogs was bitten."

Crispin grimaced. "Theta Dunne, yes. First time. We don't even know how the virus will interact with the Dog's biology, and—"

"Dispatch him."

"What?! Do you realize what we're up against here? If anything, we need Dunne back here as soon as possible. No, sir. I am *not* going to sacrifice—"

Theta Kaiser was there before the director could finish, snapping his sharp teeth in the man's face. Crispin got a close-up of Kaiser's canines, and some of the rebellion went out of him. A small part of him wondered at Kaiser's savagery. He had always been the hardest Dog to control.

Donovan stood at the panel, stroking its brushed aluminum surface. "I assume this system has some sort of termination sequence? I bet it does. How would you do it, Doctor? What kind of man are you, really? Would you constrict a blood vessel in the brain? Or would you use something more exothermic? You can tell me." He leaned in and lowered his voice. "Just between you and me. You seem like the kind of man who always has insurance policies."

Crispin didn't answer, but his skin flushed even more, and his pupils retracted to pinpoints; Donovan had his answer. He could, if the need arose, dispatch a single Dog. He nodded, happy again and smiling.

"What a very well-engineered system. I congratulate you. If this weren't a super-secret installation and, you know, if the dead hadn't eaten the academy, you might well have won the Nobel Prize." He waved his hands at the world around them. "Instead we have this. How unfortunate. And now, as to our equally *unfortunate* Theta Dunne: dispatch him."

Eyes taking on a sheen, Crispin began typing again, wishing he had listened to his intuition. He hadn't liked Donovan from the start. He'd been right not to.

Perched over his shoulder like a vulture, Donovan tried to follow the string of commands, but the algorithms were beyond him. Accepting that as a fact for now, he moved to the right and watched the touch-screen. It was split, Dunne on one side, Landis on the other. They walked together through the ruins of downtown.

Dr. Crispin's eyes darted from the keyboard to Donovan's reflection on the big screen. He began to type faster, adding a parallel command in the syntax string. It was a short command, and this would be the fourth time he'd sent it. Any Dog receiving this directive would have to obey promptly and decisively.

Except Kaiser.

Damn his eyes!

Crispin hit ENTER and waited. Sliding his gaze sideways, he caught a glimpse of Kaiser grimacing. The Dog fidgeted for a moment, flexing and rolling his shoulders. But then the moment passed.

Looking up at Donovan and seeing his attention riveted to the LCD, Crispin began to type again.

Onscreen, the Theta Dogs walked side-by-side down the street, headed back to the marina. Dunne licked at his shoulder wound, which wasn't healing as it should. The edges of the bite were ragged and dark red. Faint lines radiated outward on the surface of his skin.

Infection.

Landis reached out, maybe to help, and Dunne snarled and snapped his teeth at him. The other Dog pulled his hand back, eyes wide but worried. Licking his wound again, Dunne kept his eyes on Landis.

Donovan blinked a few times. Watching the same thing from two different angles, as fascinating as it was unique, was giving him a headache. He put out a hand, wishing there was a way to jack directly into the Dogs' sensory input. To live what they were living. To fit them on like a glove.

He noted that Crispin was still typing.

"What are you doing?"

Fingers clattering on the keyboard, Crispin looked up. "What? I'm doing what you told me."

"Why don't you just show me how to do it then? You're taking too long."

Crispin's teeth showed for a moment. "Look, you must realize that something like this, terminating one of my creations remotely... I didn't make it *easy* to do. This is not a command I had planned to use willy-nilly." He typed faster, re-keying the directive to Theta Kaiser, along with Dunne's final command. "As a matter of fact, if you've been paying attention at all, you would know that quite a number of things need to happen before the final command. If every protective function in the Pavlovian Chip isn't shut down, the command could trigger an—"

"Director," Donovan said.

"Yes, yes—there!"

Crispin hit the ENTER key, and the three of them turned to the monitor. Dunne's half of the screen flashed bright white and then went dark. Through Landis's point of view, Donovan watched as Dunne took a stutter step. His eyes rolled back and his head shook once, violently. Blood poured from the Dog's ears and nose, and he fell over, stone dead. He didn't even twitch.

Crispin had not stopped typing. He had reworded the command to Kaiser, putting it in terms so strong, if the Dog did not comply, surely he would sustain some sort of damage. Had to. Crispin also added a rider, activating the loyalty protocol. For the other Dogs, this step was unnecessary, but for Kaiser, Crispin could only hope.

Again, he hit ENTER.

Donovan hooted. "Good job, Doctor! I know this seems an odd time to say it, but I really admire the system you've pioneered here. It's not often that I come across something so revolutionary. Now, if you would be so kind—"

He stopped, feeling hot breath on the back of his neck. Donovan turned, finding himself face to snarling face with Theta Kaiser. The Dog loomed over him, fangs bared, growling deep in his chest as drool oozed from the sides of his mouth. Kaiser sucked huge breaths of air, his chest and diaphragm working like a bellows.

"Kaiser?" Donovan asked in a small voice. "I thought we were together on this." He took a step back and cried out as the Dog tensed.

Kaiser lunged.

But to the *left*.

Crispin's eyes widened in the split-second he realized that Kaiser had defeated the command. Then the Dog was on him, his sharp, sharp teeth buried in Crispin's throat.

Kaiser shook his head, worrying at the director, and when he stepped back, he pulled out two inches of red and black gristle in his mouth. His eyes danced with bizarre mirth.

Doctor Crispin's throat made a sucking sound as he watched his own blood jetting away from him, and the thought went out of his eyes. He fell over the console, fingers scrabbling at the ragged, gory hole in his neck as he coughed and sneezed out gouts of blood.

Crispin's chair tipped over, and he hit the floor. His legs kicked and he rolled onto his belly, pushing himself up. The jet from his throat pumped one last time, and then the strength went out of his arms. He fell down, smacking his face into the cold concrete. Finally, still.

Kaiser turned to Donovan, who had backed up all the way to the large screen. The Dog grinned as he chewed on the chunk of muscle and windpipe he had torn from the project director's throat.

"Good... good boy," Donovan said.

He fell to his knees and gripped his stomach and mouth. He couldn't stop it; the vomit came up and sprayed through his fingers and out his nostrils, his breakfast and bile hitting the floor, mixing with Crispin's swiftly-cooling blood.

TWENTY

KEN AND HIS SMALL GROUP were frantically clearing bodies out of the short hallway to the stairwell. The gunfire had attracted even more undead attention, and he wanted the bodies out of sight before the rest of the zombies arrived. And there were plenty of cadavers to go around.

He had already decided that the ones in the stairwell would have to stay put. He and his team certainly had the manpower to move them all; they could have easily dumped them out a window at the back of the building. But right then, Ken knew that nobody had the heart for it.

And while he didn't know the inner workings of the zombie mind, he knew they always investigated fresh corpses. Always. So the lobby had to be cleared if they wanted any kind of lasting peace. While everyone else was happy to wait for the Dogs to return, Ken had a bad feeling about them.

A piercing whistle stopped work; the roof sentry had seen something. Ken left the work detail and ran to the front of the building and looked out. Zombies on the lawn, what else? He looked up at the sentry and put his arms out. *What?*

"Dogs!" Kelly yelled. "A whole group of them!"

Ken hooded his eyes with his hand. He spotted them, far away on the rise. He saw their bus and their tow truck.

"They're coming *back!*" Kelly cried.

Ken grimaced. The work detail started hooting and clapping, and it just made him feel worse. His next move wouldn't be popular, but he was the leader and it had to be done.

"Okay, everyone, let's get back to work! We get this place back to how it was before more zombies get through. If the Dogs are really coming, we'll let 'em in. But until they're here knocking on our door, let's keep working."

The assorted men and women of the work group shrank a little, as if Ken's words had let all their air out. And he supposed it had. But he would be damned if he let their hopes get up only to be dashed *again* by the Dogs.

He led by example, attacking the job in front of them with renewed vigor. Maybe the Dogs were coming to take them back to the island. Maybe they weren't. He still couldn't believe the way Dunne and Landis had just walked off. He slammed a corpse off to one side.

And before we go anywhere, I'm going to figure out how the zombies made it up to the roof. That was no accident. Someone had to have let 'em up. And when I find out who...

Rifle fire started behind him. Single pops from multiple gunmen.

Ken knew time was getting short. If his people weren't behind the barricades before the front of the building was overrun, that would be it for them. And all their hardship, all their heartache, would be for nothing.

❧

At the crest of the hill, the Dog convoy had stopped. McLoughlin could see through his binoculars that the survivor cell almost had their barricades back into place.

"They're set up pretty well."

"They are," Samson said from the wrecker. "The pair of shooters on the front steps are doing a good job."

McLoughlin nodded. The men with rifles were taking single shots, not rushing, showing remarkable poise for civilians.

To have survived all this so far, they'd have to.

They were slowing the tide of oncoming dead, but that's all they were doing. Still, North Regional was a defensible position. Especially after reinforcements.

So, the sixty-four thousand dollar question was: Why had Crispin ordered the Dogs back to base?

"Incoming," Rose said at McLoughlin's side. "Thetas Dunne and Landis."

Absently, the Alpha nodded, still peering through the binoculars and counting heads at the building. There were more than just a few survivors. They had done well, even after the Dogs left. The work crew was moving quickly, the gunmen were doing their jobs admirably, and the lookout on the roof had spotted the Dogs.

So, why?

He dropped the binocs and waved Dunne and Landis on. Maybe they would have some kind of intel on the order to pull out. It looked to McLoughlin that Dunne was acting strangely. He was also wounded. Their orders had been to hold off on the Change unless absolutely necessary, because once they had done it, that would be it until they could hit the recovery ward. But now that reinforcements had arrived, Dunne should have changed to accelerate the healing process. So why hadn't he?

As if prompted by the Alpha's frustration, Dunne stopped walking. His head shook once, and he fell over, leaking blood from his face. It ran in thick rivers back down the hill. Landis dropped to his knees in front of Dunne and yelled for help. His own head came back as he roared, and the Change was on him.

Alpha McLoughlin jumped off the bus and sprinted over to the Theta Dog. Hayte, Kristos, and Rose were right behind him. The drivers, too scared to be anywhere the Dogs weren't, fired up the vehicles and drove after them.

"What happened?" McLoughlin roared, grabbing Landis's shoulder. "That was... that was the terminate order."

Landis pointed his clawed hand at Dunne's wound. He growled something, and McLoughlin barely understood him: "Bitten," he'd said.

"Was this why we were called back?"

Landis pointed at the North Regional building. "Dead."

More gunshots rang out from the building, and the faint sounds of screams floated uphill. McLoughlin grimaced. Whatever commands Dunne and Landis had received, the director must have also shut out their auditory centers and had told them the survivor cell was dead and gone, a lost cause.

But why, goddamnit?

Samson whistled from the back of the wrecker. "Boss, I know we've got our orders, but if Command issued them under the pretense that those people are dead..."

119

His words hung in the air for a moment. The rest of the Dogs shuffled their feet and looked at their Alpha.

He looked down at Dunne's body.

Samson was right. None of this made any sense, not one bit of it. From rescue to retreat in less time than it had taken to plan it.

On the other hand, when has the Master ever done anything for no reason? There has to be a reason. Always has been, always will be. It's the paradigm we live by.

"Load up the body," he said. As Hayte and Rose moved to do this, McLoughlin climbed back atop the bus. He looked through the binoculars.

No surprise, the survivors were doing well. Better than that. Armed members of the barricade crew had joined the gunmen on the steps, and instead of just slowing the horde, they had thinned the zombies to a point where they were no longer an immediate threat. Retreat into the building would be a leisurely thing, and an evacuation would be safe, as safe as the last one. Maybe more so, considering that the survivors who had stayed behind were mostly armed men, ready to be reunited with their families on the island.

We should go get them. We should take the rest of those zombies out, pick up the survivors, and all head back to base.

He hung his head and lowered the binocs.

This is who we are, he thought. *My words.*

Alpha McLoughlin slapped the binoculars in his hand. He could feel his pack staring at him, waiting for him to make a decision. And whatever he decided, they would follow. If he said then that they were to storm the gates of Hell, they would go howling.

They were loyal. And he would be loyal, too.

"We are not a group of individuals," he said. The Theta Dogs all looked up at him as he stood on the bus, their quiet conversations done and forgotten.

"We are not freelance contractors. We are not civilians. We are a pack. We are the Dogs of War. And we do as we are told. Back to the marina."

❧

Ken, on the roof with Kelly, put down his own binoculars and spit over the side into the street. Everyone watched as the Dogs' small convoy pulled away. The fact that Ken had been *right* not to wait for the Dogs gave him no comfort. But at least he had kept his people's hopes from getting too high. Maybe. There was little enough solace in that.

Ken spit again.

He hated this new world they lived in.

TWENTY-ONE

ALPHA MCLOUGHLIN'S TEAM had been off the yacht for less than a minute before they heard the news: Project Director Crispin was dead. A sweating and frazzled Dr. Donovan was on the pier waiting for them, being the most sincere since he'd stepped foot on the island.

"I don't know, I don't know," he said, repeating it every few sentences. "Kaiser, he just *snapped*. After your Theta got bitten—"

"Dunne," McLoughlin said.

"—Kaiser went ballistic. But I think it was the termination command that put him over the edge."

McLoughlin's eyes narrowed. Even in human form, he could smell the tang of Dr. Donovan's vomit. And in the vomit he could detect the very smell of Donovan's fear. Some adrenaline byproduct or another.

"So Kaiser was inside Command?" McLoughlin asked, directing the question at Luke Jaden, who stood nearby, hands folded behind his back.

"Yes—" Jaden began, but Donovan talked right over him.

"Dr. Crispin and I were running an experiment. I had some theories about Kaiser's disobedience, and we needed the, uh, we needed the controls to test it."

"Sounds like it backfired," Jaden said, meeting the Alpha Dog's eyes as if to stress some sort of unspoken significance.

He thinks it's weird, too, McLoughlin thought. *Kaiser in Command.*

"Where is Kaiser now?" the Alpha Dog asked.

Donovan shook his head. "Did Crispin... did he have any contingency plans set up in the event of his death? A will, or...?"

The question took both McLoughlin and Jaden by surprise. As well thought-out as this entire operation was, neither of them could fathom how such an important detail could have been overlooked.

"I don't think he thought he would ever die," Jaden said.

Donovan sighed for some reason, and McLoughlin couldn't determine whether it was out of relief.

"Well, I guess it makes sense for the second-in-command to take the helm," he said, frowning at the ground. "At least until we can elect someone else. So that's just what we'll do. And I promise you, I will not let this stand. Kaiser will be prosecuted, or court-martialed—or whatever it is we do—to the fullest extent."

After a while, the Dogs left the neurotech wringing his hands on the pier, and Jaden accompanied them toward the barracks. He spoke privately with McLoughlin on the way.

"Did you check the security cameras?" the Dog asked.

"Yes, and it seems Donovan did, indeed, escort Kaiser to Command, just like he described when I interrogated him. But Kaiser won't say shit, and there's no footage from inside the building."

McLoughlin thought about that for a second. "You mean there aren't any cameras in Command."

"You say that like it doesn't surprise you."

It didn't. Crispin was typically the only person who ever entered Command, so the level of privacy didn't surprise him at all. But the level of oversight certainly did.

"I'm going to check into a few more things," Jaden said, "perhaps canvass." He and McLoughlin nodded to each other, and then the head of security broke off and started walking the other way.

McLoughlin's pack proceeded to the barracks. They needed rest. And therapy.

As they passed the Q section, Samson couldn't help but notice the despair in the survivors' faces. Some of it was for their savior, Dr. Crispin, but more than that, the Dogs had come back empty-handed; no more survivors. Samson took a longer look into the fenced-off area and saw that someone had torn a black dress into strips; a pair of girls was passing them out for the survivors to tie around their upper arms.

Hayte, for his part, was chanting in a low voice, then shaking his head and doing it again.

"What's that?" Samson asked.

"I'm preparing a Song for Crispin. I'm not a true Singer of my people, but I know the way. And, you know, I might be the last of my people, so perhaps I can Sing him to the afterlife without offending the Faraway Gods."

Kristos clapped the Amerindian Dog on the shoulder. "That's beautiful, Hayte. Really. I don't... I know I rag on you, but that's a really nice thing."

Beside them and nodding mutely, Rose agreed.

Jorge watched the Dogs walking past the quarantine. He wanted to call out to them, to get news of Ken and the other survivors, but he had a feeling that he would simply be ignored. He looked over at Marie and lifted his chin.

"Hey. Now they know how we feel. Maybe now we'll get some real action from them."

Marie pursed her lips. She was clearly humoring him. Taking a deep breath, Jorge pushed that thought away. She was hurting; losing Paulo and having no clue whether their kids were safe... he was prepared to give her more leeway than before. Quietly, Jorge went over and sat down next to her. He patted her knee.

She looked over at him, eyes brimming with tears. Jorge saw them and his heart cracked, just a little. This wasn't his Marie. His Marie had been full of fire, and piss and vinegar, and guts and steel. *This* wasn't her.

This new person, this stranger, leaned her head on his shoulder, and he let it rest there.

"Marie," he said. "Baby, I have a question for you."

"Hmm?"

"When did your feet get so big?"

He felt her stiffen next to him. Her head came up; not a lot, but enough to take the pressure off his shoulder.

"*¿Que dijiste?* What about my feet?"

Jorge stifled a laugh. "I said, when did they get so *big?*" He shook his head. "I don't remember them being so fat. You been hogging the chocolate?"

Marie sat up straight. "*Chingate, cabron.* You know what? I wish they'd thrown *your* ass off the boat."

"Hey, now. I'm just asking."

Marie got up and stomped away.

"Marie!"

Her only response was to spit and hold up a middle finger while she walked off. Jorge smiled and slapped his thigh.

"That's my girl."

)

Holly Randall sat with her engineering group in the galley, watching her coffee cool. Intellectually, she knew that the molecules of coffee were losing their vibrational energy to the molecules of oxygen and nitrogen in the air around the cup, but emotionally it was a metaphor for life. You start off all hot and ready to scald something, and then you cool to room temperature. Or something.

She shook her head.

I need to get some sleep.

Holly looked around the galley, surprised to see how many people were actually in there. The place was quiet. Eerily quiet. Everyone absorbed in their own recollections of Dr. Crispin. Even the IT Lucies were subdued.

"Is this seat taken?" Jaden asked.

Holly shook her head, and the security man sat.

"Are you holding up all right?" he said.

The engineer blinked. "I, uh... yeah. I think so. It's just so weird, you know? The whole world out there is dying or dead, and none of us really tuned into it, I guess."

Jaden smiled. "It takes something close to home."

Gary and Scott, the neurotech interns, began punching each other in the arm. Nurse Joshua clapped his hands to the sounds of fist striking arm, keeping a cadence with it.

Holly raised her eyebrows. "Exactly like that. Here we are, fraying at the edges. And you know, it's not like..." She looked up. "What is *this*?"

Jaden turned to see a pair of techs dragging in the podium. Dr. Donovan stood waiting, looking as if he had just gotten out of the shower. When the podium was set, Donovan stepped forward and turned on the microphone.

"Good afternoon. I'm glad so many of you are here." He had some three-by-five cards that he looked at, then stuffed into his pocket. "Sorry. I had a speech written out, but now that I'm here, and you're here, I don't know.

"What I want to say is this: once Dr. Crispin's remains have been... *processed* by the medical team, we'll hold a service for the Project Director. If anyone has any suggestions for a fitting location for the memorial, I'm ready to listen. You all knew Dr. Crispin better than I did, but in the few short months that I had his acquaintance, I can say he was a true visionary."

Weepy Lucy broke into sobs, and Doctor Ron put his arm on her shoulders. He nodded to the other nurse, Alison, who put a hand over her shirt pocket. Jaden saw several hypodermic needles there. Evidence. But at this point, he had bigger concerns than pill poppers and junkies.

"I wish I could say more to make things easier for everybody," Donovan said. "All I can do is offer this, from Summer Chan. Ah, she's one of my interns. She wrote this, and I had wanted to save it for the service, but, well, here we are..."

I thank you for everything you've done,
For shining light when there was no sun,
You lit the way to a better day,
You gave us hope when there was none.
We'll terribly miss your guiding light,
We'll miss your gifted, brilliant sight,
And though you're gone, you gave us dawn,
An end to this endless night.

He put the paper with the poem down, and some light applause broke out. There were quite a few wet faces, and Weepy Lucy had put her head down on the table.

Jaden watched Donovan over the rim of his cup, his eyes cold.

❯

Samson and McLoughlin were in the Alpha's office. The door was shut, blocking out the sounds of the big barracks room. McLoughlin sat with his feet on the desk, fingers laced behind his head, staring at the ceiling. Samson stood against the door, arms crossed.

"If you're asking me," Samson said, "I'm going to be honest. I don't know. I mean, he says he's in charge, but..."

"Who put him there?" McLoughlin finished his friend's sentence. "Right. Well. He was second-in-command, Dr. Crispin said so himself. I think it might be our duty to continue to serve the leader of the project. Until proven guilty, right?"

Samson shrugged. "Things were so much easier before all this shit. This morning, we had structure. We had a rigid chain of command." He threw his hands in the air. "Now? The only one I know to follow is you, man."

"Don't do that," McLoughlin said. His feet came off the desk and he swiveled his chair to look at Samson. "Don't just put it on me. We've known each other too long for that. You know I need your input, so yes. I am asking you."

Looking up at the ceiling, Samson made clicking noises with his tongue. "All right. In the absence of having a copy of *Robinson Crusoe* to draw wisdom from, you'll have to make due with whatever's in my noggin. This is what I think. Are you paying attention?"

"Will you go, already?"

"I think you should follow if, and only if, your leader is taking you someplace good. Someplace safe. And then only if the way is honorable. That's what matters. If not..." He looked at Mac. "If your leader isn't fulfilling his role, then perhaps you should be the one who leads."

)

"That was low, Doc. I mean, I knew you had it in you, but I didn't expect it to come so fast." Kaiser gripped the bars of his darkened cell and stared out of the shadows at Donovan. "I have to say. I did not see that one coming."

Donovan gave the Dog a tight smile. "Safety first."

Kaiser laughed. "You know, I was a little shocked when I found myself changing back, but then when you made me go to sleep." He applauded. "And I wake up here."

"That's right," Donovan said. "And without the benefit of hormone therapy, that's the last time you'll go through the Change for the next four weeks." He waved his hand. "But this is just for show. Come on, you know this. I just need you in here until I can tell which way the wind is blowing with security. And the Alpha Dog."

With a snort, Kaiser let go of the bars and backed to his cot. "Big Mac ain't gonna take it. Maybe at first, but when he gets a whiff of the real you, and he *will*—" He spit at the sink in the corner of the cell. "Your position won't mean anything. Alpha McLoughlin is a big, furry Boy Scout, and he'll break his own back doing the right thing."

Donovan tapped his chin. "Well, then. I'll just have to be extra careful with my stated intentions, won't I? At least for long enough to win him over. I'll be a man of the people."

"It won't be enough. He'll know. He's the Alpha Dog."

"Don't tell me he can smell lies. You're being ridiculous."

Kaiser leaned forward on his cot, letting his canines show in the low light. "Let me take care of him. I'm stronger than he knows. I can get rid of—"

"Sit," Donovan said.

In this instance, he did not intend to share his schemes with the Theta. But if there was one thing he absolutely would not do in this new world, it would be to throw away any asset. McLoughlin still had a chance to come around. And until he did, Kaiser would have to get comfortable in his six-by-six cell.

"Good day," Donovan said, and then turned to leave.

Kaiser exploded off his cot, roaring and tearing the sink from its foundation, throwing it against the bars. Shattered porcelain followed Donovan to the door.

TWENTY-TWO

"THAT'S IT? That's all the ammunition we have left?" Ken Bishop stared at the small collection of piles, bullets separated by caliber. For his big .44 there were only four rounds, not even enough to fill the cylinder. The other gun he'd picked up was now a .38-caliber paperweight. The rifle ammunition was almost all gone after repelling the horde of walking dead. There were exactly two shotgun shells. "We've almost returned to the stone age."

Kelly wrinkled her nose. "It looks bad."

"It *is* bad. Once these are gone, we're back to using clubs and rocks."

He bit his lip, staring at the tabletop where the ammo rested. They had more nine millimeter rounds than anything else, but even those were in short supply. Enough to cover one food run, maybe. He already knew there was no ammunition to be found in a five-block radius. Not in this part of town. He almost wished they had holed up in a seedier district, someplace with pawn shops full of guns.

Ken looked at the bullets, hoping no one would ask why he was counting them. "*Just to know how many there* are" seemed like a pat answer, but he had never really been that skilled at lying. Even little white lies. He really hoped no one would ask The Question.

What about the people who got bit?

"Pack this up. Pick out the three best shots and distribute the nine mil stuff to them. I'm going to check on the radio."

Kelly started counting the bullets as he headed for the rooftop. Julius had said he'd be up there, where the breeze was nice and the sun was shining with no shade, nothing in the way. Why that was important, Ken didn't ask. He didn't care much, but he was curious as hell.

Earlier, Julius had made him and three other guys muscle up an old rear-projection TV they'd found in one of the storerooms, plus a big overhead projector, a folding chair, and a set of shelves. He'd also raided desks for all kinds of stuff, filling the pockets of his overalls with large paperclips and rubber bands. Afterwards, Julius had grabbed the lookout's binoculars and had herded everyone else away, closing the door.

That was an hour ago.

Ken opened the door to the rooftop and stopped in his tracks. "What the hell is that?"

Julius, an older man with wiry grey hair, looked up and waved. "Check it out! Solar soldering." He pointed as he spoke. "This big ass lens is out of the projector, the one under it is a desk magnifier, and of course, you recognize the binoculars."

"What?"

"Well," Julius said, bending his head down, "you asked if anyone could fix the radio. I took a look, and the only thing *wrong* with it is the damage to the high-voltage unit. So, I stole the HV card out of the TV and soldered it in."

Ken, whose only previous experience with soldering involved a pencil-like soldering iron and a 120V outlet, just blinked at the contraption cobbled together from office materials. "How?"

"Thank you. Usually people want me to shut up at this point." He pointed a grimy finger at the lenses. "Area over focal point gives you the magnification, right? Right. So, big lens takes the sunlight and concentrates it. But the overhead projector wasn't made to really focus something down. The contrary is true. So, I aimed that at the desk lamp magnifier, which really intensified the beam of light, and then pointed *that* through the binoculars. Backwards. We easily hit our target five hundred degrees." He slapped the radio. "And here we are. After I snapped the HV card out of the TV, I scraped the rest of the solder off the other cards and used that to connect it to the radio."

"You fixed the radio?"

Julius put his hands up. "What did I just say?"

Ken picked up the headset. "We're good to go, then?"

"Yes, but for how long? Who knows? The high voltage card doesn't put out exactly what we need, so the radio will work, but sooner or later the card will burn out."

Nodding, Ken put the headset on and hit the power switch. "As long as it works." Then, into the microphone, "Come in, Dog Pound. This is North Regional."

A moment later, the radio crackled. *"North Regional? This is Dog Pound. We'd heard you guys were toast."*

"Yes, but not burnt toast. So is that what happened? Is that why the Dogs left without us? They thought we were dead?"

"Ah, yes. No. There were complications. Unforeseen complications. In the plan."

Through gritted teeth, Ken said, "Well, is there another team on the way? We've run into our own complications over here. We're low on ammo and food. We have wounded."

"Another rescue attempt has been postponed."

"Until when? You know what? Never mind. I'd like to speak with Jimmy—"

"We aren't allowing any personal calls. Not at this time."

"It's not a *personal call*. He's my, uh, second-in-command. I need to talk to him, see if everybody from North Regional is doing okay."

"We aren't allowing any personal calls at this time."

"It's not... fine. That guy, Jorge—"

"We aren't allowing any personal calls, sorry."

Snapping the radio off, Ken had to restrain himself from launching the damn thing off the rooftop. He handed the headset to Julius. "Thank you for getting this rig working, Julius. For all the good it did us."

He turned from the older man's confused look and headed to the ledge. He could hear Julius's feet moving on the pebbled rooftop as the fix-it man tried to decide what to do next.

"Does that mean—?"

"Not now, Julius. I don't have any answers for you. If you see anybody else on their way up here, turn them around."

Ken looked over the large roof, estimating the footprint this building put down. He sighed. The barricades downstairs had lasted for them pretty well, but after this goddamn *invasion*, nothing had gone back together quite right. If it came down to it, the barricade wouldn't last through another mass attack. North Regional had been good for them before, when the group was large and better-equipped, but it was too much building for the handful of them, especially now, when they were practically out of ammunition. And he still didn't know how the zombies had gotten inside in the first place.

So now what?

The empty eyes of the surrounding buildings taunted him. He and his team of scavengers had been in and out of those places, stripping them bare of anything useful. And now? They needed something else, and they couldn't get it around here. And beyond all that lay the marina, the gateway to the island, where the Dogs had promised refuge.

Before they turned around, that is, leaving everyone high and dry.

Grunting, Ken turned his back on the view and looked around the rooftop. It was hardly any better. Instead of seeing the big, dead city, he saw large brown stains on the pebbled roof. Large spots where the rocks had been disturbed by shuffling feet and falling bodies. He saw the spot where everything had changed *again*, and his sense of security had been ripped out from under him.

He also saw the spot where he and his small group of able-bodied volunteers had thrown over a dozen corpses into a big pile down below. After the first couple, they had paused to stuff their ears with cotton to block out the sounds the bodies made.

Some of the bodies were from the invading zombies.

Some were not.

With that image firmly in mind, Ken went back inside, passing a fire axe on the way. He paused for a moment, catching the reflection of a tired and frustrated man in the glass. "Shut up," he said to his reflection.

On the fourth floor, Kelly met him at the stairwell entrance. "You're back. I was just coming up to see you. Did Julius fix the radio?"

Ken nodded.

"Wow! I didn't think he'd be able to. What did they say?"

"They're not coming," Ken said, slumping down the handrail. "They're not coming and I can't talk to anybody."

Kelly chewed on that. "What the hell happened over there?"

Ken shrugged, staring down at his boots. He liked Kelly, he really did, but right then he wished she would just stop asking questions. Everyone asked him questions.

"What are we going to do, boss?"

He ran his fingers through his hair. *Questions like that one.* He put his head down and closed his eyes.

"There's nothing else for it. This place is just too big for us now. It's not safe. We're going to have to move to someplace more secure. Someplace that we can hold with just a few of us."

Kelly twisted her fingers together. "Move. All right. But what about... you know." She nodded toward the downstairs. "There's a group of us that won't make it too far."

And there it was. The Question.

What about the people who got bit?

"Close the door," Ken said.

Kelly turned and eased the stairway access door closed, but didn't turn back around. She knew the question she was asking.

"We're going to have to restrain them," Ken said. "As comfortably as we can, right? I don't want it to be a *thing*. We just have to make sure they understand. It's for the greater good. For everyone."

Nodding, Kelly dropped her hands from the door.

"And what about—"

"Hey," Ken said, softening, touching her arm and gently pulling her around. He decided that maybe he felt a little better after talking about it with someone. Maybe he felt less like a monster if someone agreed with him. "We can talk about this. Turn around, all right?"

She did, facing him. Her lips were set tight, her brows furrowed. "I know why you were counting the bullets, Ken. And it wasn't just to see how many we had." She took a shuddering breath. "What are we going to do after they... turn?"

Even though he knew it was coming, even though he welcomed it, the question hit him in the gut, knocking the air out of him. He hated the answer, and went back to wishing she hadn't asked it. He wished he didn't have to raise his weary arm and point behind him. Up the stairs.

At the fire axe.

TWENTY-THREE

"I DON'T CARE, MR. JADEN," Donovan said. He slapped down the clipboard that the security chief had handed to him. "I don't care what Dr. Michaels' report has to say. I don't care about the initial screening. And I do not care about anybody's feelings." He pointed at the quarantine area. "They are getting checked again, and it is already happening."

Jaden put his clipboard to the side, the list of survivors and initial examination results ignored. "These people are scared, Doctor, and they've already been checked. This is unnecessary, and a waste of my men's time. We're stretched tight as it is, and some of the men are pulling triple shifts. You *do* realize that we have no more overtime to pay these people, right?"

Dr. Donovan reined himself in a little bit, suddenly aware of the audience that had gathered on the other side of the fence. "Mr. Jaden, do what you have to do to make this work. Figure it out. That's why they made you the chief, isn't it?" He turned away, clasping his hands behind his back. "Instead of overtime, offer increased alcohol rations. You can reduce your patrols if you have to, or at least cut a man from each patrol unit. And the endless escort details. Remove the guard from the communications shack. We're on an *island*, Mr. Jaden. I don't think we have a lot to worry about."

He turned to the quarantine area. "And you people. This is just a precaution. There is no need for you to worry. Our safety, all of our safety, is my number-one priority. I am responsible for every man, woman, and child on this island, and that means you now. I will *not* let anything slip through undetected.

"If it makes you feel any better, the Dogs are also being screened. Just like you." He turned to face Jaden. "Make it happen. *Goodbye.*"

Nodding to the security chief, he stalked off to the inspection tent where Ron and his nurses were carrying out the screening. Donovan grimaced when he saw that no one had been assigned into quarantine yet.

"What did I tell you, Michaels?" he said as he stepped inside. On seeing the patient sitting there, he covered his mouth and nose. "What is that?"

Dr. Michaels sat with an older man, who was buttoning a dark-blue work shirt. Michaels looked up at Dr. Donovan, confused. "What is what?"

"That!" Donovan pointed at the red skin on the patient's neck.

"I have something?" the patient asked, putting his hand to his own chest. The man was in his fifties, and was smaller than he had been, if the tent-like fit of his work shirt was any indication. His querulous voice rose as he asked the question.

Ron Michaels scowled. "Yes, Mr. Greene. You have a chest cold. I have something for you; it's an expectorant and a cough suppressant. Take two teaspoons every four—"

"No," Donovan said. "Absolutely not. Put him in quarantine."

"But I'm already in quarantine," Greene said.

"You shut up," Donovan snapped. To Michaels, he said, "Put him in quarantine until he gets over his chest cold. If that's what it is. Are you sure he hasn't been bitten?"

"Would you like to see the pictures?" Michaels asked. "We took pictures of everyone the first time through, and we thought, what the hell? Let's take pictures this time, too."

"I just want to make sure you've been thorough."

Michaels stood. "This man has been examined thoroughly, Doctor, as has everyone else who's been through this tent. Unless you intend to relieve me and carry out the examinations yourself, I suggest you stop questioning everything I do."

Donovan's nostrils flared. "Quarantine him. And anyone else with an illness, however slight. *Or* however serious. I don't care what you *think* it is."

Frowning, Dr. Michaels turned and nodded to the security man. To his patient, he said, "I'm sorry, Mr. Greene. You heard the project director."

"This is a travesty," Greene called out as the security man led him away.

"That it is," Michaels said under his breath. "Alison, who's next?"

The nurse waved the next patient in. A walking skeleton entered the tent, pulling a baseball cap off to reveal a smooth, bald pate, white as a cloud. His red coveralls hung on him as if he were a coat rack instead of a human being.

"Ah, Mr. Evans. I'm so sorry for this inconvenience."

Donovan made a face. "Jesus, Doctor. Why isn't this man in isolation?"

Evans turned to Donovan. "Don't worry about me, brah. What I have isn't going to spread anywhere." He shrugged. "Least ways, it won't be spreading from me." He laughed, a broken sound that terminated in a coughing jag.

Michaels pushed a clipboard at a pale-faced Donovan, who snatched it away and read the top sheet.

"Oh," he said, relaxing slightly. "Thank God."

"Whatever," Evans said, looking around the tent. "I was in chemo, but then..." he put his hands out in front of him and moaned, crossing his eyes. "I almost let them have me. Walking dead, meet walking dead."

"Well, I'm glad you didn't give up," Michaels replied.

Evans looked at him. "*I'm* not. What I really want is a smoke."

"Quarantine him," Donovan said, tossing the clipboard away. "I don't want his bad attitude or his death wish infecting the others."

The nurses' jaws dropped.

"Are you serious?" Joshua asked.

Donovan exploded. "Of course I'm serious! Attitudes are infectious. They will leap from person to person like a fire across roads and rooftops." He shook his head. "I can't believe you. Have you ever heard of *morale*? This man clearly no longer wishes to live—"

"You got that right," Evans said.

"—and I don't want that to get around. Can you imagine, a group of survivors who have given in to despair? And who's to say it would stop at the fence? No. Quarantine this man."

The guard returned from taking Greene away, and Evans walked over to him. "Looks like I'm off to quarantine. You better take me away before I break my fist on this asshole's face."

Michaels pinched the bridge of his nose as the guard escorted yet another survivor out of the tent. "This day will never end. Who's next, Alison?"

The nurse stepped outside and waved the next patient forward. Jorge limped into the tent, favoring his leg. "I think my erection has lasted for more than four hours, Doc."

"What is this, now?" Donovan asked.

"Ah, I'm just giving you a hard time. I was in a car wreck," Jorge said, smoothing down his bristly mustache. "I told these guys before, I was in this chick's lovebug and—"

"Quarantine," Donovan said.

Jorge crossed his arms. "You said what? Quarantine? We're *in* quarantine, *pendejo*."

"It looks like a bite to me," Donovan said to Michaels. "What's your professional diagnosis, *Doctor*?"

Joshua lifted his face from the laptop. "According to the pics we took on the initial screening, the shape and depth of the wound is consistent with the story he told about the car wreck."

"Nobody asked you, Nurse Joshua," Donovan said. He raised his eyebrows at Michaels.

"Let's see it," the doctor said with a sigh, gesturing for Jorge to drop his jeans.

"Oh, what*ever*. *Cabrones*. You just couldn't wait to see me naked again. This whole screening thing, it seems elaborate for little old me." He winked at Alison as he fumbled with his belt buckle. "You, blue eyes, it's okay. Understandable; I'm a sexy beast. But these guys? I know the guy-to-girl ratio is a little skewed, but come on. I don't want to make any judgments, it being the end of the world and everything—"

Donovan snapped his fingers at the security man, who had just returned.

"Just strip, already," the guard said. "Zip it."

"I got nothing to hide," Jorge said, dropping his pants. "Hey, Doc, while I got these down, you want to help me weigh my junk? I got a bet on the side."

Ignoring Jorge's banter, Michaels crouched down to get a better look at his wound. He shined a flashlight at the puckered skin. "It's not healing up very well. It's obvious your leg is stiff from your limp. We'll take your temperature and—"

"Quarantine him. Isolation," Donovan said.

"Hold up, of course it isn't healing right." Jorge took a tottering step forward, hobbled by his jeans. "You got me eating rice cakes and mushrooms, for Christ's sake. You give me a goddamn steak and a couple of beers, and this will clear right up."

"Isolation," Donovan said to the guard, who stepped forward with a hand on his sidearm. While he had been laconic about the old man and the cancer patient, a potential bite was just the thing to wake him up to his full duties.

"All right, all right," Jorge said, turning and walking out of the tent, taking short steps with his jeans still around his ankles. He glanced back over his shoulder. "You still looking, perverts? I know you are. My ass is getting hot."

Smelling trouble, Donovan followed the guard and Jorge out of the tent. "Don't let him talk to anybody."

"Ha, I knew it!" Jorge barked. "Chasing me down. But you can't *have* any if I'm in isolation."

"What're you going to do with them?" a woman asked. She was in her mid-thirties with very long, dark hair and a thick accent. She was stealing glances at Jorge as he was taken away.

"I'm going to quarantine them," Donovan replied. "For everybody's safety."

He looked at the line of people and made a quick estimate of how many survivors would end up in quarantine. A good half, at least once he got Dr. Michaels to fall in line. And then, if he wanted to, he could just... forget about them. If they were in quarantine, isolated from the rest of the survivors, all he had to do was not feed them or give them water, and they would die out on their own. He didn't even have to waste bullets.

But not yet, he thought. *Not until the Dogs are done with their screening. And on my side. Who knows? Maybe that's how I'll test their loyalty, by setting them on this rabble.*

He frowned. The thought of letting these people die sat all right with him, but actively participating in their deaths gave him pause. He made a fist, trying to feel like somebody who could order violent, messy death.

It's a new world. I have to become something other than myself if I want to survive. No, if I want to thrive. I have to inure myself to the less-pleasant aspects of the job. Right now I have Kaiser, and he would gladly do it for me, but I won't always have Kaiser.

And I won't always need him.

His thoughts were interrupted by Summer Chan. She yelled to him as she ran up, her long, straight blond hair flying behind her. "Dr. Donovan! Sir!"

He looked up at her. "Are you done screening the Dogs, Miss Chan?"

She shook her head. "Sir, you need to come see this."

TWENTY-FOUR

KEN SAT IN THE STAIRWELL of the North Regional building, completely cloaked in plastic wrap. Underneath, his shirt stuck to the sweat on his chest and back.

The plastic had come from the break room, and Kelly had used it to dress him in a makeshift biohazard suit. He felt as if he were being smothered to death by a giant, hot plastic hand; the distraction was welcomed.

Ken flinched when the head of the axe suddenly chinked into the stairwell floor. It had slowly slipped from his grip. Almost so slowly he hadn't noticed it. The sound of the head biting into concrete sparked some sort of flash across his eyes. Not a memory, per se, but a glimpse.

An axe chinking into concrete, striking sparks.

He heard footsteps.

"Ken?"

Kelly opened the door before he could decide whether he really wanted to let her in.

"Yeah," he said.

She peeked in and saw him looking up at her.

Earlier in the break room, when she'd been wrapping him up, Kelly's hand had paused briefly, tucking a length of plastic into the waist of Ken's jeans.

Their eyes had met.

She was beautiful in that moment, looking up at him. Under any other circumstances Ken would have kissed her. Instead he just watched

Kelly's tears glisten and spill, and suddenly he was hugging her while she cried about how everyone had lost so much.

It spoke volumes of her that she was now back to being mentally stable enough to come tell him the news.

"Ken, they're..."

"I know."

It was written all over her face. He didn't want her to have to *say* it too. He could hear them, *those people* in the other room. The ones who had been bitten.

They had fallen silent for the last three minutes. But now he could hear them because they had started to moan.

They had woken up.

"Kelly!" the pastor yelled from the other room. There were sounds of a minor struggle, shoes scuffling on concrete, people grunting, groans.

She glanced at Ken and then ran out of the stairwell to go help. He couldn't believe she was that strong.

He couldn't even get up.

Ever since junior high, Ken had had a tough time taking tests. It was just the anxiety.

The hardest test he'd ever had to take was for his contractor's license. He *knew* everything on it, but still, it was a big one, deciding the difference between his status as *employee* and *employer*.

Left on his own, Ken might have put it off forever. But then Jorge had told him, "How could you let a little old piece of paper get the better of you? You're Ken motherfucking Bishop!" and Ken had said *hell yeah!*

It had also been Jorge's sage advice to drink a little before taking the test. He'd said, "It'll help loosen you up for the fight."

Ken had laughed at the time, and then had proceeded to take one too many shots. But had he passed anyway? Yes. Yes, he had. So what was the *problem?*

That very day his wife had served him with the papers.

And then *the episode*, drinking too much.

He had just gotten so angry.

He couldn't believe it, that things had been allowed to go so well for him, only to be shot down right in front of him, and all at once. He just didn't understand the reason for it. Any of it.

Even the bar fight.

It was just some local idiot who had run his mouth off playing darts. Something like *he'd* fuck Ken's wife.

He and Ken had both ended up in the hospital. But only Ken had ended up in anger management.

Now he flinched when he heard the pastor shout, "Where the hell is Ken?!" and then *those people* in the other room continued to moan.

It was so hot in the stairwell. Ken felt like he was about to pass out. He was *panting*. Both sweat and saliva dripped from his chin.

He wished Kelly had wrapped the plastic tighter. He didn't want to feel his hands. Wanted to pretend it was someone else doing this. Didn't want to think about how these people had names.

Sparks on concrete—and then suddenly he was jumping up and bursting from the stairwell, crinkling and carrying the axe.

)

Ken burst into the public restroom, and started stripping off the bloodied plastic. He tried not to touch it. Tried not to get any of it on his hands. But he moved fast. He had to get it *off*.

In the sunlight filtering in, he could see that he was completely coated in strings and dollops of it. The blood had run a little and had streaked, but on some folds of the plastic it was still richly beaded red. Little tributaries of the stuff.

Keeping his plastic-wrap gloves on for last, Ken managed to pull everything off and wad it all into the trashcan, all without making contact with the blood. He had taken a class once on decontamination techniques. It had worked wonders for the asbestos job, but he had never thought it would be useful in real life.

Ken went to the mirror and immediately paled. He felt it happen, the heat in his face draining away as if blood flow had just switched off. The pallor of his cheek made the bright-red drop stand out even brighter.

Ken rushed into one of the stalls and dropped to his knees, splashing his face in a bowl. The toilets were one of the group's only sources of drinkable water, aside from the hope of falling rain. He hated to ruin any of it, but...

He fished under the stall door and grabbed a sock, which he used to scrub his cheek.

Not too hard, he thought. *Can't rub it raw.*

The thought piqued a sudden gag reflex, and Ken hunched over the ceramic pot. His whole torso clenched as he tried not to puke. The reflex was so intense it wrung a squeak from the back of his throat.

Then he was breathing hard and spitting—he hadn't puked.

He wished he had.

In the silence, it became painfully aware to him that the moans from the other room had been silenced.

After a few seconds, Kelly poked her head in. "Ken?"

His eyelids trembled as he hovered over the water, which he knew was trembling too—he could feel it, everything trembling. Was it coming from him? Was it coming *for* him? Was a drop on the skin enough? His stomach gave a wrench again as he thought about it.

"Ken, we really need to get going."

In the echoing acoustics of the bathroom tile, he could hear his people shouting from down by the barricade, and then he could hear the things outside again, pounding to be let in. The commotion earlier, and the sound of the axe striking concrete, must have roused them.

The axe had struck concrete over and over.

Wouldn't be much longer now.

"Kelly," Ken said, "did you... cover them up?"

"Ken, please—"

"Did you cover them up?!"

"Yes, of course. We were very respectful. The pastor even said a few words."

Ken nodded, even though Kelly couldn't see him. He swallowed one last mouthful of thick, viscous saliva and said, "I'll be right out."

He knew he was alone again when the pounding and constant moans quieted back down—the door had swung shut.

Finally Ken opened his eyes.

He could see his own silhouette reflecting in the toilet, staring right back at him.

In the water, he also saw a little diffused ribbon of pink.

The blood spot from his cheek.

Ken met his own eyes in the water, but his reflection's eyes were different, alien, just gleaming slivers where the incoming sun highlighted the whites. It stared back at him without intelligence, a mocking glimpse of a possible future.

One last time, Ken's body seized up. The sob was dull yet sharp, and it speared him from neck to gut. But it barely made it out of his mouth.

Ken pushed himself up from the toilet, took one last deep breath, and left the restroom to go help. It was his job, after all. Just another employee.

TWENTY-FIVE

THREE THETA DOGS paced around the barracks in Alpha McLoughlin's wake, talking amongst themselves in low voices. McLoughlin had heard news from quarantine. Something had been found during the screening of the Dogs, but he hadn't heard what it was, or whether it was Kristos or Samson. The six Sigmas milled aimlessly in the middle area. Alpha Mac turned suddenly, and all the Dogs stopped to look at him.

"What? *What?* I don't know what's happening now. Nobody does." He gritted his teeth. "Why are you still following me?"

The Thetas looked at each other. Hayte and Rose looked to Landis, who sighed. He hated being the spokesperson, especially when Mac was in such a foul mood.

"We heard about the memorial for Dr. Crispin. And we were kind of wondering, you know, if we could do something of our own. For Dunne."

McLoughlin's face lost some of its harsh lines.

"Yeah," he said. "Yeah, of course. When the rest of the pack gets back from the screening, we'll talk about it."

His face reddened a bit. Kristos and Samson had yet to return from the screening, and word had gotten back there was something wrong. But they were always finding something wrong. Without fail. The neurotech interns meant well, but they were using prototype equipment on next-generation biosystems. There was no real training program for it.

The techs always found something in their scans, and it was never anything. McLoughlin shook his head.

Open jaw, insert paw.

One of the Sigmas straightened and walked over. The man had tattooed the number 37 between his eyebrows. All Sigmas had a number, stenciled on their uniforms in place of their names.

They understood that their value in operations was low. Instead of letting it crush their spirits, they took it as a badge of honor; every war needs its foot soldiers. So one day they had snuck off the island, and the next day they returned with the tattoos: the numbers on their foreheads; and on their backs, MORITURI TE SALUTAMOS.

McLoughlin hadn't found it in his heart to punish them for it. Dr. Crispin had felt otherwise.

Sigma 37 stopped in front of Alpha McLoughlin and came to attention, standing ramrod straight, thumbs down along the seams of his BDUs, his shoulders thrown back and his feet together. "Respectfully request permission to speak freely, sir."

Out of the corner of his eyes, McLoughlin noted the Thetas had turned to listen.

"Go ahead, 37."

"Thank you, sir. We, meaning the Sigmas, have waited for a long time for an opportunity to pull our own weight, sir. We were in training with Theta Dunne. He had ideas on how we should work together, since we're not as strong or fast as the Thetas. A modified pack attack."

The Alpha looked over at the Thetas, who were smiling.

"If there is another rescue op, sir, we would like to ride along. We were waiting for Dunne to make the suggestion for us, so we could stage a demonstration, but..."

"I understand," McLoughlin said.

"Thank you, sir. With Theta Kaiser in the brig and Dunne KIA, we are ready to do our part."

"When the rest of the Dogs are back, we'll talk about that too. Dismissed."

Sigma 37 threw up a crisp salute, which McLoughlin returned. Smiling.

❧

"Which one is it?" Donovan asked, walking quickly to keep up with the younger, taller intern. Summer Chan opened the door for him and he breezed through, ignoring her answer. They were already there, he would see for himself.

He stopped short of the doorway into the Dogs' examination room. There was dark blood everywhere, and he wasn't sure whose it was. Kristos stood behind Samson with his arm snaked around the Beta's neck, struggling to lock in a rear naked choke. Samson, streaked with blood, was snarling at Scott and Gary as they cowered behind an instrument cart. Both Dogs were still in human form, straining against each other. Donovan took all this in, then crouched down to get a better look at the red marks on Samson's leg.

"Is that a bite?"

"We think so," said Summer Chan, brushing her blond hair out of her face, smearing a bit of the blood across her forehead. "We haven't been able to get close enough to tell. As soon as we tried to check it—"

"It's a bite," Kristos snarled out. "I can smell it."

"Well," Donovan said, rubbing his temples with his forefingers, "he'll have to be quarantined, obviously."

"Great!" Kristos shouted. "That's just great. Now how about some tranquilizer over here?"

Gary and Scott both turned and dove for the red plastic cube on the wall, tangling limbs as they reached for the handle. "Let go!" Scott yelled as they both stumbled to the side.

"Boys," Summer muttered. She skipped over and knocked them both out of the way, then ripped the box open. Inside lay a matte-black pistol. She turned with it, leveling the barrel at the struggling Dogs. With a slight trembling in her hands, she put her thumb on the firing stud on the top of the gun.

"This has to go in the neck," she said. "Your systems are so good at keeping out—"

"I don't care!" Kristos yelled.

"Fine. But you'll have to move your arm."

"Bullshit," Kristos said through gritted teeth. "I move my arm and you're a dead woman."

"Well, there's no other way!"

Kristos heaved back on Samson, who was still reaching out, looking to grab anyone foolish enough to come close. Reason was gone from his eyes.

"We better do it before the Change hits him," Kristos said.

"That is a good idea," Donovan added.

Summer yelled, "Then move your arm—move it!"

147

Pulling back on the Beta Dog with all his might, Kristos arched himself backwards, and when he couldn't go any farther, he counted down.

"Three. Two."

Samson roared.

"One!"

Kristos let go of the Beta, who lunged forward. The muscles in his arms started to ripple as he began the Change, and Summer Chan dropped to one knee, aiming the gun.

Pock!

A little dart buried itself in Samson's neck as he plowed forward. Summer curled into a ball, and the Beta Dog's knees hit her. He fell, smacking his face on the bloody cement. His breath came in rasps, and the Change reversed, hair and extra cells shedding all over the floor. The bite on his leg festered and bled.

"Now what?" Kristos said.

Donovan snapped his fingers. "Pick him up. I know where we have to go. And someone sterilize this mess!" He turned. "You, Chan."

"Yes, sir?" the intern said from the floor.

He smiled with warmth. "Good work. Clean yourself up and go get Alpha McLoughlin. Tell him to gather the Dogs and meet me by the sparring cage."

)

As he waited for the Dogs to show, Donovan paced outside the fenced-in area, tapping his chin and cursing Crispin's memory. *You contrary bastard. If you'd left me the termination codes, I could do this myself.*

He stared down at Samson's form, watching the midsection rise and fall with the Dog's heavy breathing. The tranquilizer had worked immediately, but no one knew for sure how long it would last, because it had only been used on a Sigma before. Metabolic rates varied with each Dog's strength level, and sooner or later, the sedative would be out of the Beta's system.

Plus, there's the virus.

The sound of running feet turned Donovan around, and he smothered the smile that wanted to sprout on his face. His tools couldn't know the spirit in which they were being used.

Putting a dour look on his face, he stepped forward to greet Alpha McLoughlin.

"I'm sorry for you to have to find out this way," he said, extending a hand to the big man. McLoughlin brushed past the new project director and locked his fingers in the fence of the sparring cage.

"How long has he had it?"

Donovan stepped up next to McLoughlin. "I was hoping you'd be able to tell me that. On your last operation, the Dog Pack pulled back before any engagement with the zombies at North Regional, isn't that right?"

McLoughlin scowled. "That's right. But when we got to the marina, Samson cleared the pier. God *damn* it!" He hit the fence. "Why didn't you say anything?"

"He can't hear you," Donovan said.

"Tranqs?"

Donovan nodded. "He became irrational in the exam room, and if Theta Kristos hadn't been there to hold him back, who knows?" He sidled in closer to the Alpha. "I know this is all very sudden, but a decision has to be made. Now."

Alpha McLoughlin looked down at Donovan. "What are you planning, Doctor? He's isolated. That much is certain. Dr. Crispin factored in our abilities when he built the sparring cage." He bunched his hand into a fist and hit one of the beams that supported the fence. "Even me. In full Change, on amphetamines and adrenaline, there's no way I could get out of this cage."

Rubbing his temples again, Donovan closed his eyes. "I understand that. I do. The thing is, Alpha, we have a population of survivors who have also just been screened, and they've been split yet again. A great many of them have gone into extra quarantine, and we can't be seen *favoring* the Dogs.

"Samson is a special case. This may sound callous to you, but as a scientist, I would like to study him as the bite takes effect."

McLoughlin's face clouded over.

"But I'm not going to favor him. I can't." Donovan looked back over his shoulder at the large quarantine area, just within sight of the sparring cage. "These people are us now. They are us. And we have to apply everything equally. Samson is effectively quarantined, yes, but we sent all the others into the kennels underground. Samson will have to be in isolation there, too."

"Yes, sir," McLoughlin said. "I'll move him. He's part of my pack, and I'm responsible for this."

Donovan stood back while the Alpha opened the cage. As the larger man stepped inside, Donovan scurried forward and closed the door behind him, locking it.

"Just a precaution," he said. "We don't know how long the tranquilizers will last, remember? When you're ready to carry him out, I'll open the gate."

Mac looked down at Samson, whose eyes were open.

Barely suppressing the glee in his voice, Donovan said, "The other option is to kill him."

McLoughlin turned to face the neurotechnician.

"I won't do that."

Donovan laced his fingers into the fence. "Do I have to make it an order, Alpha McLoughlin? Do I have to remind you that I am now in charge?"

The Alpha simply crossed his arms and glared at him.

"Fine," the new project director said. "Alpha McLoughlin, I order you to kill Beta Samson."

"I won't."

Samson rose up behind him.

TWENTY-SIX

KEN SAT WITH HIS BACK against a brick wall, holding the big .44 to the side of his face, wishing he had more ammunition. He already regretted telling Kelly he would get a bus "or die trying." If he was being honest with himself, he'd felt a little like dying when he left. Taking care of the people who'd been bitten...

He shook his head.

Already, he was seven blocks from North Regional with nothing to pay off. No bus, no guns, no ammo. Just lots and lots of dead people, up and walking around. Waiting for him to screw up so they could *eat*.

He risked a quick glance around the corner. The parking lot of the gas station was almost empty. Only one or two zombies wandered around there. Ken laughed out of his nose.

I guess the rest of them got bored.

What he really wanted right then was to get into the gas station and find a city map. Maybe then he could find a school. He knew from driving through morning traffic that there was a bus depot in the area somewhere. He just had to find it.

There was also a Greyhound station, but that was farther into town than he wanted to go. Ken suspected that the closer he got to downtown, the denser the bodies would be. And the gridlock. He had a brief vision of himself as Clint Eastwood in *The Gauntlet*. Smiling, he dismissed that. Julius may have been a wiz, but Ken thought TIG welding might be outside of the old man's area of expertise.

He looked around the corner again and saw that the zombies were both facing opposite directions. He took a series of quick breaths and hoped he wouldn't have to pull the trigger on either of them. It wasn't them he cared about; it was the noise.

Like a bear, Ken lumbered around the corner and started running. His arms and legs pumped, propelling him across the parking lot in relative silence, only the *slap, slap, slap* of his shoes giving him away.

It was enough. The dead, both of them, turned to look. By the time they got turned around, though, he was already past them and around the corner of the convenience store.

Ken smiled grimly and holstered his revolver. There on the ground was a baseball bat, blood and hair all over the business end. Whoever had dropped it might not have made it, but Ken decided the bat would be much better than the .44, as far as stealth went.

He jumped back around the corner of the convenience store and swung the bat. The heavy end struck one zombie's skull with a loud crack, and the dead man in the nurse's uniform went down. Ken turned and saw the other zombie, wearing the bottom half of a firefighter's outfit. The corpse's jaws opened as it bore down on him, and he jumped at it, swinging the bat in an overhand smash that shut it up forever.

This again.

He stood over the corpse, wondering whether he was looking at an ex-male stripper. Wiping the bat on the rough fabric of the dead man's pants, he decided he didn't care. He couldn't afford to care.

Ken turned to the convenience store and hoped the door wasn't locked. Glancing around, he walked over and put out a hand, then sighed when the door opened to his slight pull.

As the door closed behind him, he surveyed the inside of the store, all senses on alert. Even though he was certain the store was vacant, he was past taking chances. No matter how he'd felt about himself at the beginning of the day—

The axe head came down, over and over.

—now he was on a mission for everybody else. The people at North Regional were counting on him. And he would not let himself get killed, because any oversight or stupidity would essentially get them killed too.

The aisles of the store were clear, and the door leading to the storage area was closed. He jogged back there and twisted the knob: locked.

"Good," he said.

Back at the front of the store, he rifled through the area maps, looking for one that was less generic. He found one geared towards tourists and smiled, thankful again that his group had chosen to hole up on the outskirts of town.

Unfolding the map, he smoothed it out on the counter and found the gas station.

"Marker," he said, and turned to look for one. He found one, and also snagged some high-protein bars and two tiny energy drinks.

At the counter again, he marked the intersection next to the convenience store, circled the North Regional building, and started looking for someplace he could snatch a bus from. Chewing on a runner's snack, he kept an eye open for places to migrate to as well. Julius had been helpful there, informing the group of a machine shop that wasn't too far. Someplace like that, the doors would be heavy and the locks would be stout. Plus, there would be plenty of tools they could use as bludgeons, if they had to.

Ken stabbed a blunt finger down on the map. "There you are."

He noted the cross streets and then folded the map, jamming it into the back pocket of his jeans. Turning to leave the store, he had a thought.

Behind the counter, someone had left quite a mess, stuff thrown off one of the shelves. On the clear spot of the lowest shelf, Ken spotted a small black box.

Smiling, he opened it and found a short Walther PPK .32 automatic, fully loaded, along with an extra magazine full of bullets.

Two magazines. Beautiful.

He moved the stuff on the shelf some more, hoping to find a box of bullets, but his good fortune had come to an end.

He went to the front doors and closed his eyes. Eight blocks to go. Could he do it at a dead run? Already, just from the single snack bar, he felt better. Quickly, he downed one of the energy drinks and stretched.

Probably look ridiculous, like a lumberjack doing yoga.

Ken pushed the door open and started off with a light jog. Twelve steps from the store, he heard a moan behind him. Still jogging, he turned to look, and there was the rest of the party that had left the parking lot earlier.

The zombies had returned.

Ken ran a little faster, but then stopped. As long as it was just that group, he only had to stay ahead of the pack. No need to burn himself out right away.

As he crossed the first intersection, another moan started on his left. He grimaced, but didn't bother to look. He wasn't going that way, so it didn't matter.

In front of him, a pair of zombies in his-and-hers clown suits staggered into the intersection and turned to face him. The man's wig had slipped off, revealing matted brown hair, and old streaks of blood that ran down and ruined his makeup. The woman still wore her wig, but instead of a red clown nose, she had just a hole in her face.

They, too, began to moan.

"I hate clowns!" Ken roared, raising the bat and scything it through the air. It caught the man and forced him sideways into his sidekick, knocking both of the clowns off-balance. Ken kept on running, reining in his desire to stop and pummel them until they shut up.

He really did hate clowns.

He reached the third intersection and turned left, only to pull up short. From curb to curb, dead folk of all shapes and sizes turned, alerted to food by the moans that haunted Ken. He looked around, wondering just what he was going to do *now*.

The street sloped down away from him, and he knew if he got past this knot of zombies, he'd be all right for a while; past this residential neighborhood there was a park.

A big white Ford truck sat at the top of the hill. Ken smiled. The driver, whoever he or she was, knew a good truck, but didn't know shit about parking on an incline. The wheels were turned out instead of in. Running to the truck, he peered in through the glass, confirming it was a stick shift. He raised the bat and smashed open the window.

Zombies were closing in, from behind and in front. Ken got into the truck and scooted over, leaning down and away from the window. He poked his head up over the dash, waiting for the dead to get a little closer up the hill, but not too close. Too close, and the truck wouldn't build any momentum.

Now.

He released the emergency brake, and immediately the truck began to roll away from the curb. Ken hooted as it made its first impact, then it was all rumbling and moaning and arms reaching in through the busted window as the truck plowed through the rows of zombies. The shuddering stopped, and Ken looked up—his face bounced off the dashboard as the truck rammed into a four-door Lincoln across the street.

Popping the door open, Ken leapt free of the truck and started swinging the bat. He'd cut a diagonal path through the thickest part of the zombies, but he was still surrounded. The bat cracked from skull to skull, smashing down on arms and shoulders.

Grinning, he decided that breaking collarbones was just as good as anything else. It kept them from reaching out and grabbing at least.

He hopped up on the roof of the Lincoln, then ran over the top of the car and leapt onto the top of the van parked behind it. He kept running, jumping off the back end of the van and landing awkwardly against a blue U.S. mailbox. Something in his knee protested, and he hobbled away, still four blocks from the bus depot.

The zombie mass staggered after him, their unending moan setting his teeth on edge. He limped as fast as he could, each step a bit of agony in his leg.

"Aspirin. Ibuprofin. No, I got *energy drinks*, bah!"

Hobbled the way he was, Ken wasn't gaining any ground ahead of the horde. It was a case of the tortoise and the hare anymore. He had to keep moving.

Ken cracked open another energy drink and sucked the bitter liquid down.

At the next intersection, he veered right, glimpsing the park. He breathed a sigh of thanks; the place was empty and green, and if he hadn't had a bad wheel, he might have stopped to enjoy a moment of peace and sun.

He noticed, idly, that he was breathing pretty hard through his mouth. He closed it to swallow, and found his mouth full of blood. He spit and put a hand to his nose; it was mashed down and to the side.

Looking behind him, he saw the zombies just a touch farther away. Maybe.

He stopped and dug the marker out of his pocket, then jammed the end of it into his nose. He took a couple of deep breaths and yanked it sideways, setting the cartilage with a crispy, crunchy noise. A groan forced its way out through his gritted teeth, and he kept moving.

He spit blood again.

I got to stop this nosebleed.

But he kept moving instead, now only two blocks from the school he'd marked on the map. As he cleared the end of the park, the entrance came into view, and Ken's face broke into a wide smile as he saw three school busses sitting there.

A thumping sound from the school killed the smile.

He looked, and in each window along the side of the long building, there were children, looking dead and a little chewed-on, smacking at the glass of the windows with the flats of their little hands. Ken turned away, gulping another mouthful of blood.

The thick metallic taste was starting to make him nauseous.

He came to the first bus and pushed open the door. A stench wafted out at him, weeks of decay and dry rot, and the driver hauled himself up in the rear seat of the bus. Ken went up the stairs and took a second to close the door behind him, then turned down the aisle with the automatic .32 in his hand. He pulled the trigger once, and the sound and the recoil and the new smell of cordite released a flood of anger in him. He kept pulling the trigger, making the corpse of the driver dance before the slide locked back.

Dragging the thing to the emergency exit, he tore the key ring from the driver's belt before popping the back door open and dumping the body outside. The horde was right behind the bus, and he shouted, spraying blood off his lips.

"Go away! Just get the fuck away from me!"

Hobbling to the front of the bus, he found himself crying.

The kids.

He plopped down in the driver's seat and started the engine, then put the bus into drive and pulled away, leaving the mass of undead behind him. The bus lumbered into the street, and he headed back to North Regional. Fifteen short blocks.

As he turned onto the avenue where the big building squatted, his heart sank.

Even more dead had gathered out front. They were spilling out of the lobby.

Ken stopped the bus and stared. The top of his building was belching smoke.

He checked the rearview mirror, seeing the pair of clowns round the corner, followed by a different mass of zombies.

Clowns.

Kids.

Ken sneezed blood and wiped at his eyes.

Up on the second floor of the North Regional building, he could see Kelly behind the window, pointing down at the bus and yelling something. A desk came sailing through the glass, and its drawers opened, scattering papers and pens and a family photo. The desk landed on a bug-eyed zombie down below.

Ken leaned out the window. "Well, come *on*, then!" he shouted up at his people.

He reloaded the .32, picked up his .44, and opened the bus door.

TWENTY-SEVEN

ALPHA MCLOUGHLIN CAUGHT Samson's wrists as the Beta's hands shot for his throat. McLoughlin twisted, turning the Dog's momentum away before jamming an elbow into Samson's armpit to push him off.

"Stand down!" he shouted.

Samson staggered away but stopped himself from slamming into the cage. He craned his head around to stare at Mac. The Beta's upper lip twitched, but he said nothing. Instead, he turned, keeping in contact with the fence. His stare emptied of emotion.

McLoughlin took a step back. "Look, whatever it is, we should just hold tight, ride it out. If you got bit... Sam, if you got bit, why didn't you say anything?"

Samson didn't respond. He just leaned forward, drooling, sneering, showing bloodstained teeth.

"*Did* you?" Mac said. "When you went to clear the pier, did one of them get you?"

"Stop stalling," Donovan said. "I gave you an order, Alpha."

McLoughlin turned to shut the director up, but then saw the rest of the Dogs arrayed behind Donovan, their faces blank. All of them were watching, totally invested in whatever happened next.

McLoughlin knew what they were thinking.

What if it were me in there?

"If you got bit, Sam, I don't know what will happen. Maybe our systems can fight it off. But this? This won't fix anything."

Samson burst away from the fence, flinging himself headlong at McLoughlin, who caught the charge and threw him over his hip. The Beta landed hard on the concrete floor of the sparring cage, not even rolling to absorb the impact. Instead, he landed face-first, bouncing off his chest. Only then did he roll over. The wind had been knocked out of him, but he got up anyway.

Backing to the center of the cage, McLoughlin held his hands in front of him, keeping an eye on Samson. "Stay *back*." Mac stopped in the middle of the sparring area. "I'm not going to hurt you, Sam, but you have to stay back." He tried to laugh but couldn't, finding his throat too dry. "Come on. We both know how this goes. You're going to sleep."

One side of Samson's mouth twitched in a short-lived smile, and he crouched down, advancing and circling to the right. He rushed in, swiping a hand at McLoughlin's legs, then backing out. The Alpha fell for the feint and dropped his hands—Samson lunged. Together, they fell to the ground.

McLoughlin kicked his legs up, holding Samson's hips in a guard. He kept having to move his head as Samson's jaws came down, biting.

Working his arms free, McLoughlin grabbed Samson's left wrist and shifted his hips, moving his legs up until he was high enough to slip sideways and wrap his right leg over Samson's face, pulling the Beta Dog down into an arm bar. He pulled; their jiu-jitsu sessions always ended this way, with Samson in a submission hold and tapping out.

Instead, the Beta bit down at McLoughlin's calf.

The Alpha Dog moved, releasing the hold and rolling away. He made it to one knee before Samson came barreling into him again. This time McLoughlin landed on top, straddling Samson's hips.

The Beta Dog reached up, and McLoughlin dove to the outside, wrapping an arm around Samson's head and stuffing his shoulder into Samson's armpit. The choke was complete when McLoughlin kicked off to the side, applying pressure from his forearm and shoulder to cut off the blood supply to Samson's brain.

Squeezing with everything he had, McLoughlin felt his friend finally slowing down. Closing his eyes, the Alpha whispered a soft prayer that his brother-in-arms would let it go and pass out. Samson's legs kicked more slowly, and his arm, held up in the Alpha's hold, started to droop. McLoughlin gave his thanks into the dirty concrete and got ready to let go. He didn't want to hold the blood-choke for too long.

A deep growl started in Samson's chest.

Ah, no.

McLoughlin squeezed harder, crushing down with enough force to put a python to shame, but he felt it anyway; bones and cartilage under Samson's skin started to shift and change. The heat from his body doubled as all his systems went into overdrive.

"Fuck!" he yelled, pushing off and rolling away. He dimly heard Samson's howl over the rushing in his own ears as he, too, began the Change.

Donovan stepped closer to the fence, watching as both Dogs' bodies began to shift and reconfigure. A smile crept onto his face. He knew he was going to get his death match. Once the Dogs were in their bestial forms, with no one in Command to override any of their animalistic impulses, the blood would fly.

He felt the other Dogs clustering behind him and listened to their breathing change. They began to hyperventilate, the action in the cage appealing to the beast inside each of them.

Idly, the director wondered if the security cameras were recording this. He would want to watch it again later. Over and over.

The Alpha and Beta Dogs faced each other inside the fence; Mac's golden fur shone in the sun, and Samson looked every bit his antithesis, shaggy black fur absorbing the light. Where Mac's scleras were slightly yellow, Samson's were blood red, the veins in his eyeballs distended.

The Dogs snarled and snapped their jaws, circling each other, sniffing the air. Their taloned feet scraped and clicked on the concrete as they moved. Their shoulders heaved with each breath, their diaphragms pumping air in and out in great gulps.

Samson charged, leaping with his claws out. Mac dove under the attack, rolling and kicking, hitting Samson's knees and lifting his legs too high. The Beta tilted and landed awkwardly, coming down on his hands and chest.

He was quick to his feet, running at the Alpha on all fours and lunging at his midsection, jaws wide. Mac's fist rocketed up, catching Samson under the elongated jaw and sending him to the side. Samson's claws raked across Mac's hip as he passed, leaving four bloody furrows that soaked the Alpha's golden fur.

The Beta Dog turned to look at Mac, licking the blood off his talons. His bestial chuckle turned into a growl, and he began to bite his own fingers.

The Alpha, wounds already healing, jumped at Samson, gathering himself in the air. Both feet shot out like pistons, smashing Samson in the face, and the Alpha and Beta fell backwards, away from each other.

Donovan clapped, genuinely pleased by this display of skill and power. He felt the other Dogs staring at his back, but he didn't give a shit. *This* was what it was all about.

Science be damned.

Samson charged again, but Mac ducked under it. He swept his left arm around, clocking Samson behind the ear and sending the Dog sprawling. Then Mac leapt after him, still eerily silent.

Turning at the last second, Samson snapped at the Alpha's neck. Mac locked one hand under Samson's jaw, holding it away from his face but leaving his side exposed. The Beta Dog slashed and tore at Mac's unprotected ribcage, stopped only by the bigger Dog's stout bones. Samson's foot came up on that side, ripping Mac from stomach to knee.

McLoughlin stuck his thumb into Samson's eye. Using the orbital bone as a handle, he yanked to the side. Samson yipped and pulled away, and Mac's thumb came out with a sucking, squelching sound.

And finally, the Alpha Dog began to growl.

Samson shook his head, trying to clear his vision, flinging blood everywhere. He blinked his empty socket several times as he and Mac circled each other. The growl building in McLoughlin's chest got louder and louder until Donovan could feel it vibrating the steel of the cage.

The Dogs charged each other, hundreds of pounds of meat and bone smacking together in fury. They spun and slashed, clawing each other and roaring. Locked in combat, they fell to the side and rolled. One talon flew out of the melee, smacking against the steel fence.

The Dogs and Donovan watched, wondering what the hell was happening. The new project director got even closer to the fence, taking in the combat, eyes wide open.

An awful tearing sound made everyone flinch, and the fight came to an absolute standstill. Samson stood with his back to the spectators, towering over Mac, who was kneeling on the ground in front of the Beta Dog. Blood poured out onto the concrete, a red fount that seemingly had no end. The Dogs held their breath, leaning forward.

Then Samson keeled over.

The hole in his throat wasn't healing.

Alpha McLoughlin stood, a red piece of meat in his teeth, blood dripping from his snout. He spat the meat out and raised his furry arms, clawing at the sky and howling in triumph and pain.

161

TWENTY-EIGHT

THE FLAT WALTHER PPK/E in Ken's fist barked three times, knocking down the zombies directly under the window. "There's too many!" he yelled up at Kelly on the second floor. "You're not coming down through the lobby."

A pair of zombies got too close, and his .32 spit fire twice.

That's five, already. Only three more before this slide locks back.

The zombies in the lobby turned toward the gunfire, moaning louder. Ken waved at them and smiled. He looked at the foliage on either side of the walk up to the building, trying to decide whether the bus would make it all the way to the wall. Backwards, so he could use the emergency exit.

He shook his head. To make it to one of the side offices, the group would have to pass through the hallway downstairs, which was undoubtedly full of the dead.

He walked backwards to the bus. "Kelly!"

The slight girl poked her head out.

"Look around. See if you can find a rope ladder or something. Maybe some electrical wire?"

He turned and shot another zombie through the face; the dead man was close enough that Ken felt the mist of a disintegrating eyeball.

"Tell Julius we need to get you guys down."

"Outside? *Here?*"

"You'll see!"

He turned and hobbled for the bus, then hopped up the stairs on his good leg. He closed the door and wedged the baseball bat between it and the little stairwell.

Dropping heavily into the seat, Ken cranked the bus and put it in reverse. He used the mirrors to back up until he was close to the oncoming horde.

Ken slapped the lever into park and got up, limping to the back of the bus. He opened the emergency exit and pointed the .32 semiautomatic at the two clowns in the lead. Turning the gun sideways, he looked at it and shook his head. He swapped it out for the .44 in his holster and took aim.

"Fuck you, clowns."

The big gun boomed once, and the male clown stopped moving forward, instead walking in a tight circle, his left leg acting as a pivot. The clown made a full revolution before falling over. The gun boomed again and the female clown bent over backwards in an almost perfect arch.

Smiling, Ken closed the emergency door and limped back to the driver's seat.

"Much better."

He looked out the windshield. He had the attention of every single dead thing still on its feet. For a second, he thought about what Jorge might say.

I bet you're all wondering why I've called you here.

Setting his lips in a tight line, Ken put the bus into gear and pulled away slowly. As he passed North Regional, he glimpsed Julius moving back and forth inside, yanking wiring out of the wall.

Ken leaned his head out the window and yelled at the zombies. "Come on, you dead shitters! Rolling buffet of Bishop in here! All you have to do is keep up. What are you waiting for? You know you want some of this!"

He turned the wheel, slaloming the bus back and forth and knocking over the zombies that got too close. Even at his slow speed, he had to keep stepping on the brake to make sure he didn't get too far ahead of the shambling mass.

Don't want them losing interest and turning back.

Banging against the side of the bus with the flat of his hand, Ken started to sing at the top of his lungs.

Looking inside, not much to see
Reflecting no identity
Wearing the face that was given to me
Buy my anonymity
Molded thoughts a moldy brain
Filled by latest ad campaign
Passengers on the same train
Time to derail! Embrace insane
HA! HA! HA!

He turned the corner and looked back, coughing. His nose had started bleeding again. The zombies were still back there, but he wasn't singing another verse.

It didn't matter. They were coming on now, moaning together. They wouldn't be able to hear him anyway. He alternated between the gas and the brake all the way up the block, then stopped at the next intersection. The dead caught up, surrounding the bus, hands scrabbling at the bottoms of the windows.

"This is as far as the tour goes, folks," Ken yelled out the window. "You'll have to find your own way back."

He let off the brake and sped away. Two left turns and two minutes later, he was stopped in front of North Regional again, backing carefully up to the building. The rear of the bus tore away part of the overhang.

Ken put the bus in park. "Close enough."

Hobbling to the rear, he clambered up onto a seat and muscled open the emergency roof hatch. He found himself looking up at Kelly's smiling face.

"We were wondering if you'd gone off for a bite to eat or something."

He returned the smile. "Something like that. Come on down."

Julius leaned out and threw down a rope ladder made of electrical wire. The rungs of the ladder were made of sawn-off pieces of PVC pipe. Ken looked up and signaled his approval.

"Very nice."

Ten people had climbed down by the time the zombies made it back around to North Regional. The moaning made the others on the ladder nervous, and trash bags full of water from the toilets fell from their hands.

The bags burst and splashed everywhere, and water poured down inside the bus, soaking Ken's head and shoulders.

"It's all right," he said, drying his eyes. "We'll get more later. Just come on down."

Kelly ushered more people out the window and down the ladder, and still the zombies got closer.

"Don't worry about them," she said, helping a man who had a prosthetic hook for a hand descend the ladder. "The bus is too tall for them to get to us."

The truth of her words was immediately evident, but the moaning was getting louder and louder, a choral dirge that didn't abate, didn't stop. Several survivors huddled in their seats, facing inboard and looking at the floor, or at their shoes. They held their hands over their ears.

Zombies piled up against the bus, and as they moved back and forth, a tidal motion began to rock the big yellow vehicle. Ken looked out, seeing the dead folk backed all the way up to the horrid sculpture in front of the building. As he watched, one of the guy wires that held the art in place snapped with a loud, metallic *twang!*

"You have got to be shitting me."

The sculpture swayed with the movement of the horde, moving in sympathy with the bus, and before too long, the motion was too much. Very slowly, the statue started to tilt.

Absently, Ken helped another person through the roof hatch as he watched the sculpture pass the point of no return. It tottered and fell, smashing six zombies beneath it. The end of the sculpture was no more than three feet from the bus. An easy distance to step across.

"Rifle!" Ken yelled up to Kelly.

She disappeared inside the building and came back with an M1 Carbine, the last of the rifles that still had any ammunition.

"What am I shooting at?"

Ken pointed at the end of the sculpture, where the mass of zombies had regrouped. Two of them had fallen against the colossal work of art, and the motion of the crowd had pushed them up onto it. One of them, a mechanic in his former life, stood atop the sculpture and took one wobbly step toward the bus.

Kelly fired, the shot pinging off the side of the sculpture and blasting through the nose of one of the zombies. The mechanic took another wobbly step.

Kelly took aim and fired again, this time taking the zombie through the hip. When it lifted its leg to step again, the damaged joint wouldn't hold it, and the mechanic fell onto the horde like a crowd surfer at a wake.

"Is that everybody?"

Nodding, Kelly dropped the rifle into Ken's waiting hands. "Just me and Julius."

"Come on, then."

Ken opened one of the bus windows and fired with the Walther at the other sculpture-riding zombie. It did a short dance and fell off.

One bullet left in this one. One more .44.

He checked the magazine in the rifle, found three more .30-caliber bullets in there.

"You want me to drive, boss?" Julius asked before lowering himself through the hatch into the bus.

Handing him the rifle, Ken shook his head. "I got it. You just take a seat. Who has the nines?"

Julius pointed up. "Kelly has one."

"What about the other two?"

Grimacing, Julius said, "We'll have to talk about that in a little bit. After we're out of here."

Ken pursed his lips and considered pressing the issue, but Julius was a stubborn old man; if he didn't want to talk, he wouldn't. Neither would Kelly. Small as she was, she was tough.

"Fine," Ken said, shuffling to the front of the bus. He sat down and checked the mirror. "Let me know when she's in. Is this everybody?"

"Twenty souls," Julius said.

"Twenty?"

"We'll talk."

Kelly dropped into the bus and Julius whistled. Ken put the bus in gear and pulled away from the building.

"Not bad," Kelly said, slumping into the seat behind him. "Glad you came back when you did. Things got weird."

He looked up at her in the rearview. "How do you mean?"

"Just, watch where you're going. We'll have the chance to talk soon enough. You know where Julius's machine shop is?"

Ken sat up and dug the map out of his back pocket. He handed it to her and then fished the marker out of his shirt pocket.

"What the hell?" Kelly said, seeing all the blood on the marker.

"Ah, shit." Ken wiped the marker off on his shirt. "Sorry. I had some problems."

Kelly made a face and took the marker, passing it and the map to Julius, who marked an X on it and passed it back. He sat down and crossed his arms on the seatback in front of him, putting his head down.

"Wow," Ken said. "Not a word about it. Must have been bad."

Only raising her eyebrows in response, Kelly passed the map up. Ken smoothed it on the steering wheel. "Good," he said. "This isn't too far at all. We should be there in no time."

He took the bus through a turn and saw the Ford truck he'd crashed. A wriggling zombie was pinned under its front driver-side wheel. Ken tossed a salute at it as the bus rolled by. He turned again, pulling onto a smaller, narrower street.

"Oh, come *on*," he said, slowing the bus. A car wreck had closed the street about halfway up the block. An overturned Saturn was wedged between a Jeep and a Land Rover, each facing opposite directions.

"Can we push through?" Kelly asked, looking over his shoulder.

"Let's find out."

Ken dropped the bus into low gear and moved forward, slowing as he got near the wreck. He turned the wheel so that the flat of the bumper was against the corner of the Land Rover's. He goosed the pedal, and the entire wreck gave off a shuddering groan. The Saturn settled farther on its roof and slid with the Land Rover.

"Shit. I don't think I can shake it loose."

He gave the bus more gas, engine roaring in low gear. The combined mass of the wreck slid another two feet before the Jeep wedged against a parked van.

"Let's just find another way, then," Kelly said, patting Ken's shoulder.

He shrugged and put the bus in reverse. The Land Rover came with him for a second, then let go with a crash. The bus began to shudder. Ken gave it more gas, and the shudder became worse, until the steering wheel felt like a jackhammer in his hands.

Julius got up. "I'll take a look."

Ken leaned down and picked up the wedged-in bat before pulling on the door lever. As Julius passed into the stairwell, Ken reached to his left and put out the STOP sign.

"Cute," the old man said. He was out of the bus and back within seconds. "I don't know what you ran over, hoss, but that tire is shredded. We aren't going anywhere."

Ken ran his hands over his head and looked up at the ceiling. "That's..."

He drifted off as he caught movement in the rearview mirror.

"That's truer than you know," he said quietly.

The moaning began a moment later.

TWENTY-NINE

THE ALPHA DOG stood panting in the middle of the sparring cage, looking down on the body of his best friend. McLoughlin's feral yellow eyes never blinked, waiting for the Beta Dog to change back, so he could at least see Samson's face one more time. The body remained stubbornly lupine.

"Bravo, McLoughlin!" Dr. Donovan yelled. He had dropped his papers and was applauding. "That was—"

Faster than the neurotech's eyes could follow, Mac streaked across the sparring cage and locked his teeth on the fence directly in front of Donovan's face.

"That's no way to be," Donovan said, wiping spittle from his forehead. "You should be grateful you're not being punished for disobeying my direct orders." He turned to the Dogs gathered behind him. The Thetas and Sigmas all looked from him to Mac as if they were watching a tennis match.

"I am the Master," Donovan said to them. "Is that not so? Heel!"

The Theta Dogs looked at each other, unsure of what to do, but the six Sigma Dogs moved forward at once, falling into rough formation before Donovan. Inferior minds, easier to control, and resigned to their status at the bottom of the totem pole. The neurotech raised his eyebrows and turned to look at the Alpha.

"You should have just listened to me. Did you think you were indispensable? There are graveyards full of men who were indispensable.

Look there. I'm sure you never thought you would get along without your Beta."

Alpha McLoughlin slashed at the fence, ripping his still-healing forearm back open. His roar bounced off the walls and his feet scraped for traction as he tried to force his way out. But it was as he had said earlier—the cage held.

Donovan began pacing to the left, following the curve of the fence. "Here's the problem in a nutshell, McLoughlin. I can't control you just by talking to you. For whatever reason, you refuse to acknowledge me as Master. I imagine that the pile of meat on the ground over there has something to do with it—"

The Alpha Dog, following Donovan around the cage, snapped his jaws at the fence.

"—but the fact remains. If I were sitting in Command right now, with the mere press of a button I could have you standing on your head reciting Chaucer, assuming you know any. But that is an untenable situation, and we both know it."

He continued to walk, occasionally placing his hands on the fence, then pulling them away as the Alpha stalked him. They played this peculiar game of Dog and Doctor all the way around to the opposite side of the enclosure.

"Don't worry about me, though. I have a contingency plan. To tell you the truth, I never really liked you. I thought you were too good to be true. And now look at you. You've killed your second-in-command. He was high on my list as your replacement."

Alpha McLoughlin hurled himself at the cage again, impacting it hard enough to make the entire thing shudder.

Donovan crouched down, and the Alpha pressed his face up against the fence so that he and the director were almost nose-to-nose. Donovan waved his hand, beckoning for some reason.

In a low voice, he said, "But now that you've put Samson out of the running, I guess that just leaves Kaiser. You remember Kaiser. On my first day here, he put the Beta in his place, and—"

Mac snapped his jaws at the fence again. The sound of his enamel striking the steel was loud, and Donovan turned his head away for a moment. When he turned back, he was smiling.

"And finally, you insubordinate mutt, your honor guard has arrived, ready to escort you from this life, and out of my hair."

The Alpha turned to find the six Sigmas arrayed behind him in the cage, and he suddenly realized why Donovan had made the seemingly meaningless hand gesture. The Sigmas looked at each other and back to the Alpha. They were bouncing from side to side, rolling their shoulders, looking like a set of professional wrestlers psyching up for a Battle Royale. Behind them, still outside the cage, the Theta Dogs looked on with stony faces.

"By the numbers," Sigma 37 said. "Just like we trained."

Donovan shook his fist in the air. "Sic 'em!"

The Sigmas dropped to all fours, their backs bowing and their voices raised in agony as the Change swept through them. Since their bodies hadn't accepted the Dog upgrades as readily as the Alpha's had, it always hurt more as their bones grew, realigned, and changed shapes beneath the flesh.

Mac stood and threw his head back, roaring at the sky. It was a primitive, primeval sound, and the hairs shivered on the back of Donovan's neck.

Here it is, the roar said. *Come and get it if you're hard enough.*

The Sigmas broke off into pairs, two running each way as the middle pair charged ahead. The Sigmas on the left jumped at Mac. He turned with both hands out, backhanding one Sigma away, catching the other by the throat. Immediately, he swiveled back and threw the Dog at the pair advancing up the middle, and then the Dogs from the right were on him.

Even though the Alpha towered half a foot or more over the Sigma Dogs, the combined attack forced him to retreat. He slashed and clawed as he went, and one Sigma dropped out of the fight, cradling his stomach, trying to hold in his slippery guts.

The Dog who Mac had backhanded tackled him at the knees, and they both went down. The Sigma held onto Mac's legs as two others pounced, their jaws snapping for a piece of the Alpha's throat. Instead, one of them caught the Alpha's forearm between his teeth, and the Sigma backed away, dazed, pulling the Alpha's injured limb with him. McLoughlin rolled with it across the concrete, and then another Sigma darted in, sinking his teeth into Mac's shoulder.

Kicking and howling in frustration, McLoughlin shook his legs loose from Sigma 37's hold and then booted the ankle biter in the throat. The Sigma fell back, coughing and spitting up blood. The Alpha knew the injury wouldn't keep 37 out of the fight for long.

Mac rolled up, lifting his feet to wrap around the torso of the Sigma who had chomped down on his shoulder. He rolled back down and the Dog let go, flipping with the movement.

With his other hand free, Mac clawed at the face of the Dog biting his forearm. The Dog let go and Mac scrambled to all fours in time to meet the charge of the middle pair of Dogs.

The first of them came in high, and as Mac rose up to meet the attack, the other Dog slipped in low and snapped at his belly. Mac smashed the lower Sigma with his knee and grabbed the other one by the throat, yanking the little runt around and throwing him to one side.

McLoughlin leapt away then, leaving the Sigmas to regroup. All of the Dogs were panting hard now, and the Alpha scanned the six of them.

Somewhere, deep within his animal mind, the Alpha knew he couldn't win this fight.

He charged.

The Sigmas were bowled over as the hurtling Alpha Dog pushed through. Mac turned and gripped a Sigma's ears, yanking him down as he kneed, launching the little Dog backwards four feet.

Pirouetting, Mac slashed out with both hands, catching two of the Sigmas as they approached from either side. As he spun, Mac saw something that ignited hope in his chest.

The gate.

They had left it open.

Dropping to all fours, he powered to the opening in the fence. Dimly, he heard Donovan yelling for the Theta Dogs to *do something!* With a look between them, the Thetas simply stepped out of the way, letting Mac race from the cage.

The Alpha Dog glanced over his shoulder, seeing that only three of the Sigmas were giving chase. A very doggy grin bloomed on his face.

Sigmas.

Pouring on even more speed, McLoughlin blurred past the fenced-in quarantine area, where the survivors stared open-mouthed at the high-speed parade. He jumped over a small knot of security men, who scattered as the Sigmas barged their way through. One of the guards picked up his radio and began rattling off details into it.

But then Mac reached the perimeter of the island compound and hurled himself through the air, sinking four sets of claws into the wall. Slamming his hands and feet down, he climbed the inside of the wall and tore through the razor-wire at the top, which tore through him as well. He snarled at the security cameras that swiveled his way.

A dozen running steps later, Alpha McLoughlin was in the water and swimming for the distant shore.

THIRTY

"WELL, OLLIE," JULIUS SAID, "this is another fine mess you've gotten us into."

Ken snorted, then felt immediately sorry for it. "Ow," he said, holding his nose.

Kelly put her hand on his shoulder.

"Are you okay?"

Looking at the blood pooled in his palm, Ken considered the question. "I think it... only hurts when I laugh?"

"You're okay, then."

He sat with her and Julius at the front of the bus, marooned in a sea of moans.

"I wish I had some earplugs," Julius said.

"I wish I had some..."

Water was what Ken had meant to say, but he stopped himself. Looking around the bus and seeing all of the panting and puddles of sweat, he decided nobody needed to be reminded. The ones who'd dropped the garbage bags felt bad enough as it was.

The sash of every other bus window was open precisely one inch, just beyond the reach of the zombies' fingertips. The rooftop hatch was open, and most of the passengers lay either in the walkway or between the seats, the communal idea being that heat rises, so best to stay low.

Had Ken known they would get stranded out in the summer heat, he never would have suggested they travel by light of day. His rationale had been, "We want to see them coming," and everyone had agreed. They hadn't been thinking of the weather.

During those hours when the sun had burned directly overhead, Julius had rigged a tent-like shade under the roof hatch, using a couple of button-up shirts fastened together and strung up with belts. But as soon as the sunlight had started slanting, the heat had climbed in through the windows with them.

Julius, Ken thought. *What would we do without the old man?*

He looked at the lock that the repairman had rigged to secure the bus door. A piece of wire rope was tied to the door lever and threaded out and around one of the door hinges, where it was tied again. The zombies' own strength was now turned against them.

Ken had gotten a glimpse into the old man's satchel while he worked. In there he saw another roll of wire rope, as well as duct tape and electrical tape; a crescent wrench with a reversible head, which would also act as a pipe wrench; and a Leatherman multi-tool. And that was just the top layer of stuff. Farther inside was a battered leather journal, full of drawings and schematics, notes and ideas.

The baseball bat was still lodged in place between the bottom of the door and the top of the stairwell, and Ken was pretty sure all their bases were covered.

Except for the water.

When the survivors climbing down had panicked and had dropped the garbage bags full of toilet water, Ken hadn't been too worried. Julius had assured him that the machine shop wasn't far from the water tower. Plus, Ken knew the old man had a way to gather humidity out of thin air.

He peeled his shirt away from his skin and closed his eyes, wishing that whatever had reanimated all these corpses had also taken away their voices. They sounded like old people suffering in a hospital. Like his great grandmother, groaning from all the bed sores and arthritis. She had begged for euthanasia, but state law at the time had prohibited it.

Her begging for death sounded just like the zombie pleas from outside.

Idly, he began scratching at the faux-leather cover of the driver's seat. His thumbnail, hard from use and broken in spots, didn't make much headway through the material, but from the looks of things, he had all day.

If I can get through, I can take some of the seat stuffing and fill my ears with it.

From his earlier tours of the bus, Ken had decided that this was the best-maintained school bus in the history of school buses. Not one seat or seatback had a single hole in it. All the nuts and bolts were tight. Everything worked like it was supposed to. It was an older bus, which kind of explained it; on the school district's shoestring budget, it was paramount to keep everything in working order.

There was also no air conditioning.

So, they left the windows open just a touch, which let the heat out, but also made the moaning twice as loud as it had been when everything was closed up tight. Ken looked around outside, and for a second, the faces, all the sorrowful, pale faces begging to be let in because they just hurt so much, blurred as if he were still turning his head.

They all looked like his great grandmother. Her ragged breathing, her sunken-in face.

"Mmm," he said, just to get a feel for it. If *they* were moaning, maybe *he* could do it, too. Yeah. And if *he* kept on moaning, maybe everybody else would start moaning, too, and they could all moan together. And maybe the zombies outside would think, "Hey, there's just more of us in there," and go away. It was a matter of timing, really. And *maybe*, if they were going to moan together, they could just be together and moan for real. All it would take was a quick jerk on the—

"Hey, you all right over there?"

Ken looked up into Kelly's eyes and gave her a wan smile. "I'm peachy." When he said that, his nail popped through the covering on the seat. "See?" He dug out a piece of foam and held it up. "Earplugs."

"Yeah, well I hope you've been busy thinking of something. We need to get out of here before someone loses it."

Ken tittered for a second before clearing his throat.

"Quite."

"Hey!" St. John shouted, alarmed by something he was seeing outside. The former cop pointed. "Is that one of them?"

Ken and Kelly stood, looking in the direction that St. John was pointing. They saw a Dog loping toward them on all fours. Grime and grease and gore streaked its coat, as if the monster had just torn its way out of someone's nightmare.

The Dog threw its head back and howled, luring the zombies away from the bus into a funnel formed by wreckage.

"Bottleneck," Julius commented as everyone stared out through the glass.

Only able to squeeze two or three at a time through the wreckage, the zombies wedged themselves in at the Dog, who stood and roared and swiped talons at their necks. Two swings of each mighty claw was all it took to decommission each zombie, and for the next ten minutes, the Dog busily removed heads from stalks, like a macabre meat thresher.

Every once in a while, a zombie would come flying out of the funnel, knocked back by one of the Dog's powerful kicks.

"I'm not sure I believe what I'm seeing," Ken said. "Somebody pinch me—ow!"

"You said."

"Kelly!"

Julius waved them off. "Get a room, you two. I think he's done."

The gory Dog climbed its way over the mountain of corpses, sniffing the air. It approached the bus slowly, sniffing at the ground and the windows around the entire vehicle. It stopped at the shredded tire and cocked its head.

Three more times, it went around the bus, smelling everything.

"What's it doing?" someone asked.

"Hey!" the man with the hook hand yelled out as the Dog passed his side of the bus. He clanked his metal pincher on the glass to get the thing's attention. "Hey, help us!"

The Dog glanced at him, but then continued his final round. With a grunt, the thing launched itself onto the hood of the bus, sniffing the windshield, the windshield wipers, the gasket around the glass.

Then it lifted its leg.

"Is it...?" Julius asked.

A yellow stream hit the window and ran down, coating the glass and wipers.

"It is," Ken said.

Chuffing once in pleasure, the gory Dog hopped off the bus and loped away.

"This day," Ken said, "just does not stop."

Kelly wrinkled her nose. "Was it marking its territory, or...? I'm not sure if that's gross, or what."

"It's gross," Ken said.

Julius hit Ken's shoulder, pointing to the back window of the bus. "Check it out. Another one?"

Indeed, a new Dog stalked toward them, looking around and sniffing.

"How many of these things are there?" Kelly said.

The new Dog sniffed the row of cars leading up to the bus, slinking from one vehicle to the next. The hackles on the back of its neck were up, and its nose kept twitching.

"That thing is on the hunt," Julius said.

The new Dog suddenly looked up at the bus and perked its ears. It moved straight toward them, its gaze moving back and forth as it sniffed everything. It stood tall to look in the windows, and the people shied back. Then the beast's head whipped around and suddenly it was running for the front of the bus.

It leapt up onto the hood and sniffed the yellow splashes, clearly excited by its discovery.

"Oh, shit," Ken said.

Everyone turned to look, forgetting the heat of the day, forgetting that they were stranded on a bus in the middle of a zombie-infested hellhole.

The gory Dog from before sprang up out of hiding in front of the bus and wrapped furry arms around the newcomer, then sprang backwards with his prey. The creatures turned in the air, and the newcomer landed on his head in a perfect suplex. Disoriented, the Dog wobbled to his feet.

Then the gory Dog was on him, punching and clawing. Blood arced up and splattered on the windshield, and Ken scrambled for the wiper switch so they could see.

By the time the blood was clear, the gory Dog had its jaws clamped down on the other Dog's throat, and both of them were snarling and jerking. They ripped apart from each other, and the gory Dog held a bit of gristle in its teeth.

The other Dog fell, holding its throat, and the victor fell on it, rending and ripping with its claws, eviscerating its fallen prey, making sure it would not come back to plague him.

Outside the bus, the gory Dog rose up and looked in on a wide-eyed Ken. In fact, all the survivors on the bus were staring at the animal with the same mix of revulsion and awe.

Lowering his head, the Dog slowed its breathing and relaxed. The Change happened, fur and extra body mass sloughing off and flowing from his pores in a thick river of ectoplasmic goo. He gritted his teeth as bones rearranged themselves into a more human frame.

There, in front of the bus stood Alpha McLoughlin. He raised a hand in a wave.

"Hey, in there," he said. "You're Ken, right? I'm... well, I guess I'm just Mac."

"Hey," Ken said in a small voice. "How are things?"

"Bad. Things are bad. You should know there isn't another rescue mission coming. I think I'm it, and you can see how my bosses took that news." He kicked the messy corpse of the other Dog. "So wherever you're headed, I'd like to help. I bring a unique skill set to the table."

"We just saw you kill your enemy with your own piss," Julius said. "Damn skippy, you've got a skill set."

Ken nodded at the Alpha Dog. "Okay. All in favor?"

The bus nearly shook with the volume of the "Aye" that came back.

Giving Mac a thumbs-up, Ken smiled. "Mazel tov, it's a Dog."

THIRTY-ONE

DONOVAN'S EYES TICKED back and forth between the picture-in-picture squares on the touchscreen marked Sigma 23 and Alpha McLoughlin.

The Alpha had just got done urinating on the windshield of a bus. *Sigma 23, Sigma 23.*

Donovan tried to remember which one was Sigma 23. He hoped to God it wasn't Theta Kaiser's. Theta Kaiser had enough reason to be infuriated.

It was very clear that McLoughlin was baiting the more inexperienced Dog with the scent of his piss. The old Alpha was leading the Sigma by its nose—right into a trap.

"Territorial, isn't he?" asked Summer Chan, watching over Donovan's shoulder as McLoughlin tore the other Dog apart.

Every time Chan talked about the Dogs, she sounded like some creepily enthusiastic nature photographer engrossed in an epic battle between two maned lions.

"He is," Donovan said through gritted teeth.

The Sigma fell down in a puddle of his own blood and then stared blankly along the same plane as the concrete. Donovan could see the rubble onscreen, and in it, barely discernible, bodies, just pale shapes.

Then the darkness of death spread through the twenty-third Sigma's brain and onto the screen.

"You should have sent more than one," Summer Chan said, almost startling the neurotech.

Donovan put a fist to his mouth to think. Then suddenly he rolled his chair around Summer Chan and started pulling the white instruction manuals off the shelf of Dr. Crispin's Wall.

)

Kaiser heard the guard let someone into Kennel 1. He didn't get up from his bed. The hormone deprivation was making him feel neutered. But he also sensed that the feeling was slowly going away.

For the last half hour he had been lying there, staring down the nearest corridor and listening to the shouts coming from somewhere else in the obedience school that Crispin had built underground.

The shouts, at their faintest, sounded like Kaiser's old Master barking commands. The warren of tunnels echoed with memories. He hated the smell of it down here. The musty stink of the underground, the faint ammonia of old fear-saturated piss.

Footsteps fell sharply as someone approached the Theta Dog's kennel. Sharp, professional shoes.

"Donovan," Kaiser said before he could even see the man—before the man could even see him.

The footsteps paused, but only briefly. Then Donovan finished his march and stood in front of Kaiser's cell, hands folded behind his back.

"Attention!"

"Hmph," Kaiser said, like a dog letting out a cocky chuff.

"Theta Kaiser—up!"

The Theta Dog still hadn't looked in Donovan's direction, still hadn't even moved from his bed. "Didn't you hear, Doc? They promoted me to Epsilon."

Donovan glanced down the hallway connecting this cellblock to Kennel 2. He could hear the voices of the quarantined down there. Could hear that loud immigrant, his insolent mouth.

He turned his attention back to the matter at hand.

"Theta Kaiser, I seem to remember promising that your imprisonment would be only temporary."

Kaiser took his time before answering. "I never remember promises, Doc. No point."

"We have a problem."

"The Alpha Dog?"

"No." Donovan said it too quickly, almost cutting the Theta off. "No, the Alpha Dog is no longer a threat."

Kaiser didn't respond, and Donovan was hoping his lie had taken seed.

"Our problem is the quarantined."

Donovan knew Theta Kaiser could hear the people, begging for their lives on the other side of Crispin's lair. *Those people* in Kennel 2.

"I need you to take care of them."

"Ah. So it turns out you're just like him."

The neurotech frowned. "Who? The Alpha?"

"You know, Dr. Donovan, if you're asking me to kill somebody for you, come at me point-blank. Don't dance around it with some sorry euphemism like 'put them down.' That's what the old man used to do."

Donovan now understood who he was talking about. He said nothing and glanced once more toward the other kennel.

That loudmouth in quarantine was hollering for *cerveza* and beer as if they were two separate things—as if he hoped to gain more from some unsuspecting fool.

Donovan flinched when he turned back around, finding Kaiser suddenly standing at the bars of his cage. The Dog stared him down like a captive panther stalking a child at the zoo.

"Say it," Kaiser urged him. "Order me to kill them for—"

"You need to know that I can terminate you at any second," Donovan interrupted, suddenly spouting off at the mouth again. He let it happen this time, still surprised at what was coming out of himself, but trusting the fervor to get him what he was after. "All I have to do is flash the right signal to the camera inside your brain, and my assistant back at Command will see it on the monitor, and then she'll push a little red button. And then do you know what will happen, Theta Kaiser?"

Donovan, hands still folded behind his back, got right up in Kaiser's face at the bars.

"I'll tell you what will happen. The same thing that happened to Theta Dunne. The same thing that happened to Alpha McLoughlin. Now, look: you are going to march right down to the quarantine, and you're going to kill every single last one of those people. For me. Is that clear?"

Kaiser gauged Donovan's eyes and Donovan did everything he could not to look away or seem surprised by his own words. He had come on strong and now he only had to sustain it.

"Yes, sir," Kaiser said with a smug smile.

Donovan nodded and stepped up to the card scanner and numpad. He released the Dog from his cage, and Kaiser marched right out into the hall and down the corridor, unwittingly granting Donovan a chance to lag behind and try to calm his trembling hand.

In the corridor to Kennel 2, Kaiser stopped at one of the doors. He let himself into the room.

"Kaiser, heel," Donovan said. He knew from reading some of the manuals that Crispin had instilled in the Dogs basic voice-activated commands. Good old-fashioned Pavlovian conditioning, with a pain response triggered by any kind of disobedience.

Kaiser didn't heel.

The room looked to Donovan like a space for physical education, except for the far bank of cupboards, which looked more suited to a classroom where nurses taught CPR.

Kaiser opened one of the cupboards and a body fell out. Some kind of no-bite dummy. A number was stenciled on its chest with a Greek Sigma preceding it.

Kaiser threw the dummy across the floor and pulled out more fake bodies stenciled with names. Donovan noticed more than a few bite marks on the dummies the Theta was casting aside, but nothing compared to the last dummy he pulled out.

Most of its arm and torso had been gnawed off, and its throat had been ripped out so that the head flopped around. Donovan was not surprised to see the name stenciled on the doll's chest.

"The point you're making is moot," said the neurotech. "Let's get on with it, shall we?"

Kaiser set the doll lovingly back into the empty cupboard and propped it up in a sitting position. Its head hung down. "'Lo, Doc," he said in a quiet voice.

Then, of his own volition, Kaiser left, and as Donovan went after him, he glimpsed one of the dummies on the floor, noticed the prominent name on its chest:

MCLOUGHLIN

The dummy looked as if teeth had never touched it.

)

"Aw, look," Jorge said as Kaiser and Donovan entered the cell block of Kennel 2. "Isn't it cute? I remember when *my* mommy would take me to the humane society. Or is this more like a mommy-daughter outing to the zoo?"

Kaiser headed for Jorge's cell first.

Jorge's eyes grew much wider, but he held his ground.

Donovan glanced at the two other cells, which held the man with cancer and a teenaged girl respectively. He looked away before either of them could make eye contact.

He was glad the loudmouth would be first.

Kaiser stepped right up to Jorge's bars and said, "I'll save you till last. So you can watch." And then the Dog turned and ran his fingers along the bars as he walked to the next cell.

The teenager curled up in her corner, sobbing hysterically—screaming. Donovan covered his ears. He would do anything to stop that fucking screaming!

Kaiser walked slower past her cage, still running his finger along the bars while he grinned at her and tracked her with his eyes.

"Hey, *puto*," Jorge said, pressing his head between the bars as far as it would go, trying to see down the cellblock toward the Theta. "You're really going to pick on a girl? You're that much of a carpet wetter?"

Kaiser didn't let Jorge's insults distract him. He crept past the wailing teenager's cage to the next one.

Donovan kept his hands held tightly behind his back, feeling his palms grow sweaty.

"Hey!" Jorge shouted at Kaiser over the girl's crying. "I bet your mom was a mangy bitch! You know what that makes you?"

Kaiser stopped at the cancer man's cell and grinned in at the living skeleton staring back.

"Please," the man said, almost wheezing. "Please don't."

Donovan felt a brief stab of vindication. Back at the quarantine, this cancer man had showed a complacent disregard for death. And for life. Now he was begging to be spared.

"Open the cell, Doc," Kaiser said without taking his eyes off the man.

Jorge started outright screaming and hurling insults and obscenities at the Dog, trying his best to earn the first bite.

"Mangy stray! Mom's not the lady, but the tramp!"

Donovan almost turned and walked out of the kennel—he couldn't handle the noise. It was giving him a headache.

"Doctor!"

Donovan suddenly was moving forward, as if compelled by his own Pavlovian conditioning, and he couldn't believe he was reacting so quickly to Kaiser's command. He took out the keycard that Jaden had made for him, and he slid it in the card reader, then punched in a security code on the pad.

The lock clicked and the barred door opened. Kaiser pushed through it and walked inside.

"Please," the dying man said, holding up a hand and cowering back on his bed. "Please!"

Theta Kaiser punched him in the throat and stopped his pitiful cries. Kaiser then grabbed the gurgling man by the neck and bashed his head against the concrete wall again and again. After a few dull smacks, the man's scalp left a smattering of blood, and then another, and then a splat, but Kaiser kept going until the blood was flinging everywhere each time he slammed the head forward and yanked it back, throwing red cast-off stains all over, even across Kaiser's face.

The bone began to crack.

With each strike of meat against rock, Kaiser twitched, and somewhere hidden in the cries from the other cells, he could hear Crispin shouting from somewhere far away—*"No, Kaiser! Bad!"* He could taste a phantom of a cloth-and-plastic doll, could feel his Master's hand striking him each time he bit down and worried at the thing.

The twinge emitted by the Pavlovian chip felt eerily like Crispin's punitive hand.

"Stop it," Donovan said. He had managed a whisper. Certainly not loud enough to be heard over the loudmouth idiot and the shrieking caged bird.

Kaiser just kept bashing the man's skull, and twitching each time like a broken record, bashing until there was practically no hard structure left beneath the cancer man's scalp.

"Stop it!" Donovan yelled. "Stop!"

Jorge kept yelling himself hoarse, and Donovan just couldn't take it anymore. He stalked right up to the immigrant's cell, pulled the gun he had taken from Crispin's office, and from the force and pressure and absentmindedness of shouting "Shut the fuck up!" he accidentally tightened his finger on the trigger.

The gunshot was deafening in the enclosed space.

Everyone fell silent, except for the girl, who whimpered quietly on her bed.

Donovan, shaking with adrenaline, noticed the gaping wound on the side of Jorge's head. Slowly, dazed, Jorge reached up and felt his face. He pulled his hand away and looked at his fingers, which were smudged black from the powder burn the bullet had left along his cheek.

He didn't seem to feel or notice the bite it had taken out of the back of his ear.

The smell of cordite was thick and oppressive in Donovan's nose. "Shut up," he said, swinging the gun over to point at the girl. "Just... stop."

He spotted Kaiser from the corner of his eye and whirled around. The Dog was now moving down the kennel to the girl's cell. He stopped and grinned in at her, and she started wailing again at the sight of his manic bloody face.

"Kaiser," Donovan said, "that's..."

He couldn't finish the thought. He had to close his mouth and swallow, or else vomit up the rest of the words. The taste of acid burning the back of his throat reminded him too much of the taste of Dr. Crispin's death.

Kaiser wasn't listening anyway.

The Theta growled at the girl, and she screamed.

"Kaiser, stop!"

The Dog slammed against the bars and roared—and then stumbled back as yet another gunshot rang out in Kennel 2.

"I said stop!" Donovan shouted, gun still smoking in his hand.

Kaiser hunched over and grabbed at his thigh where the bullet had gone in. He was panting and sweating, and some of the sweat ran pink with the cancer man's blood.

Donovan could see the bullet hole in the Dog's flesh, and realized his mistake a second too late—Kaiser wouldn't be able to heal rapidly in the absence of the hormone overflow.

But then the wound started to spit out the bullet.

Kaiser picked out the slug and let it drop to the concrete. The wound seemed to stop healing after that, but it wasn't bleeding as badly as it should have been, and Donovan now had no doubt that it would heal faster than any normal man's wound, even without hormone therapy.

Something had changed.

Theta Kaiser looked up at Donovan, grinning, grimacing, sweating from the pain. He climbed to his feet and, towering over Donovan, took a step toward him.

"Don't," Donovan said, sticking the gun in the Dog's face. "One little wave into the camera," he said. "Remember that."

Kaiser wiped the blood off his chin. Still grinning, he said, "Yep, just like him." Then he turned around and started hobbling back toward his cage in Kennel 1.

)

Donovan stood at the door to Command, staring down into a little cooler full of ice. Crispin's eyeball stared back up at him from a plastic bag.

He hated touching it. Hated it even more that the eye seemed to always be watching him.

Donovan fished out the bag and opened it. He used the plastic like a glove as he held Crispin's eye up to the retinal scan. The door to Command clicked open.

Donovan took the cooler inside.

Summer Chan immediately jumped up from a stack of instruction manuals she had been leafing through at her desk. She took the cooler from Donovan and immediately moved to put the eye in the little personal refrigerator.

Donovan stepped up to the manual that Chan had left open on her blotter. Using a cutaway of a Dog's skull, the left page illustrated how one branch of the Pavlovian implant monitored brain-activity patterns in the left-prefrontal cortex, specifically the parts related to aggressive cognitions and effects.

"Have you found it yet?" Donovan asked, turning a page.

Chan shut the refrigerator and said, "Nothing's caught my eye."

Donovan cursed and threw the manual, then turned to the screens. Sitting on the cot in his cell, the Theta Dog was looking down on the head of the doctor who was currently patching up the gunshot wound in his leg.

At least Donovan had been able to control Kaiser with bullets and threats. But he knew that con would only work for so long.

THIRTY-TWO

"HOLY JESUS," KEN SAID, taking a test step on his newly-wrapped ankle. "And right after he turned you guys around, he died?"

Mac nodded, now looking fully human, dressed in a pair of sweatpants he'd gone out and found on their way to the machine shop. "Crispin was killed," he said, putting down a box of water jugs harder than he had to. "He was gutted by my new third-in-command."

"A lot of that going around," Kelly said, standing from wrapping Ken's ankle and dusting her hands together. "I guess there isn't going to be a better time to tell you, Ken."

He turned to her. "I guess not. Thank you for not making me ask again."

Catching Julius's eye, Kelly tilted her head away. The old man put down his sack of canned food and herded the group of survivors away. "Right over here, folks. Let me show you to your new living quarters."

The pastor huffed after the group, already speaking words of comfort to people afraid for their families on the island.

"North Regional was a great place," Kelly said. "But if you knew the way in and out, and you weren't afraid of dying, you could ruin everything. For everybody." She looked up at Ken. "Did you know Jimmy had a girlfriend?"

He stood up straighter. He'd never considered the thought that his red-headed lieutenant would have somebody.

"Me, neither," Kelly said. "She was a little brunette number. Apparently, when Jimmy went to the island with the Dogs without her, she had some kind of breakdown or something." Kelly shook her head. "Before, when everybody was in line to get on the radio, she was convinced he was dead. So while all eyes were topside, she went downstairs and made her deal with the devil."

"What a bitch," Mac said.

"Did she ever talk to the pastor?" Ken asked.

Kelly wrinkled her nose. "The pastor is kind of an a-hole."

"Been my experience."

"Anyway. She didn't take it so well that, one, we repelled the zombies and, two, Jimmy was actually still alive. So while you were off getting the bus, in a fit of guilt-induced depression, she lit herself on fire."

"On fire," Ken said.

"In the quarters. Yeah. Londy and Clint were on the way down from the roof when they smelled the smoke—"

"And they tried to put her out," Ken said, sitting back down.

"—and they tried to put her out, yes. They didn't make it. And they also had the other two nines."

"That settles it," Ken said. "Next time we raid a drugstore, I'm looking for anti-depressants."

"She's dead," Kelly said.

"I meant for *me*."

Mac snorted a laugh. Ken and Kelly both looked over at him. "I'm sorry," he said. "I don't think I meant to laugh."

"Everybody's settled in upstairs," Julius said, wiping his hands on a rag. "How are we getting along down here?"

"We're okay, I think," Ken said. "This is quite a place you have here, Julius."

The old man looked embarrassed. "Aw, shucks. This old place ain't nothing."

He turned, taking the shop in as if seeing it with new eyes. Thick wooden workbenches with nicked and scarred tops lined one side of the room; the wall above was painted a light blue and stenciled with red outlines where tools hung. A great many of them were still in place; only three or four red shapes stood out. Along the adjacent wall, opposite the great roll-up door, stood red and black toolboxes. Near the wall opposite the workbenches were a hydraulic press, a pipe bender, a drill press, and a hose press. On the wall itself were rows and rows of bins, full of parts.

"It's very clean," Mac said.

"Yeah, well. Two months ago, the bank was all set to foreclose on me, and I made the place up nice to attract buyers."

"Did you find one?" Kelly asked.

Julius turned back to them, a smile on his face and tears standing in his eyes. "Nope. And then I didn't need one."

Ken whistled. "Imagine what we could do to that bus if we had power here."

Julius raised an eyebrow. "You want power? We can have power. The place next door has an emergency generator."

Kelly perked up. "We could have light! And music."

"That would be nice," Ken agreed. "Some long-lost creature comforts to take everyone's minds off the new regime on the island. What about the noise? Do you think we'll attract too many visitors?"

Mac shook his head. "No. While you were being tended to, I was scouting around. The buildings on this whole block are all close together. We need to go anywhere, we can head away by rooftop. So maybe the more visitors at the front door, the better. Concentrate them here—"

"And you know where they all are," Ken finished. "That's not bad." He leaned back onto a large covered object behind his stool. "So, if we have all of this at our disposal, what are we going to do?"

Julius stuffed the rag in his back pocket. "What do you mean?"

Ken ran his hands through his hair. "We can't just sit all comfy and pretty here while shit's going all crazy over there. We have families to put back together. Maybe the island is nice, even with a crazy dictator. But from what Mac has said, it's not the place for us."

He stood, testing his ankle again.

"So, the question remains. What are we going to do?"

Mac looked at Ken and raised his eyebrows. "How many men do you have who can shoot? Or, I guess, would be willing to?"

Jerking a thumb upwards, Ken said, "Every father up there will pull the trigger. That's how they made it to North Regional."

"Different," Mac said. "That was all dead people they were shooting at. Now they'll have live ones shooting back. And the Dogs."

Ken thought about going toe-to-toe with one of the beasts. "Okay, so a full-frontal assault is out."

"We need to get over there first," Mac said. "The marina is our gateway. Unfortunately, they know this. The entire perimeter of the island is lined with sonar arrays. They have radar. They have cameras. The security chief is very thorough."

"You know him pretty well?" Kelly asked.

Mac smiled. "Yeah. He was the first person I talked to that wasn't a scientist after I became a Dog. If I could find a way to talk to him..."

"We have a radio," Julius said. "Maybe if you called—"

"No. That's no good. If I know Donovan, and I can say that I do now, he's taken up residence in Dr. Crispin's old offices. Before all this, Crispin had linked all the radio and comms to his computer, recorded twenty-four seven."

Kelly slumped against the hydraulic press. "So if you make a call, even if you get to talk to..."

"Jaden," Mac said.

"To Jaden, Donovan will know what's coming."

"And he'll be ready, with or without Jaden. He's already got the Sigma Dogs at his beck and call, and I don't think it'll be too much longer before the Theta Dogs come around."

Mac stopped talking, taking in the lost looks on their faces. "Right. There are five ranks. I was the Alpha. Samson was my Beta. Kaiser was the new Epsilon. There were five other Thetas, but Dunne is dead. And there were six Sigmas, one for each Theta. Now there is one less."

"The Dog at the bus?" Ken said.

"Yeah. So, here's what I think. I can talk to Jaden. I *can*. I just have to word things so he'll understand what I mean and Donovan won't. And if we make it across the water, I can draw the Dogs away, I think."

"I'm already brimming with confidence," Julius said.

Mac waved his hand. "I know. These are just the quick and dirty details. The big thing will be getting a boat over there large enough so that all the survivors will fit. Not just your group; there was another group we picked up before we found you guys. And there's island staff who might want to leave.

"The original quarantine area isn't far from the pier. Then again, neither are the Dog barracks. And about half of the survivors were being moved from normal quarantine to someplace else, someplace underground. I bet it's the Kennel, but we need intel."

"How about a diversion?" Ken said. "There are enough of us that we could take two boats."

Mac snapped his fingers. "That might be what we're looking for. We take two boats out of the marina. We can run one right at the pier and trick the security team to concentrate on it."

"While we run another one up to the back of the island, all nice and quiet-like," Julius said. "How far will we be from the quarantine area? And the underground?"

"Not far, really," Mac said, shaking his head. "We'll have to be quiet about it, because the island isn't that big. If the security team gets an inkling that they're shooting at the wrong thing, it won't take them long to get turned around and aimed at something else."

"We're going to need guns," Ken said. "And ammo. And gas."

Mac laughed and slapped Ken's shoulder. "Those are just the little details. The big picture stuff, like two boats? That's what we need to focus on now."

Julius stood. "All right, commandos. I'm going to take one of the men from upstairs and get some wiring from next door before it gets too late and too dark."

Kelly watched the older man amble away. "He really is a genius. Too bad about his shop, though."

Ken laughed. "Are you kidding? If the end of the world hadn't come along, he might have lost everything. He's too old to start over."

"Let me see that map," Mac said. He took the folded-up paper from Ken's outstretched hand, then walked over and smoothed it out on the workbench. He rummaged around in the bins for a moment, then came back with four nails. With a hammer, Mac fastened the map to the workbench.

"Marker," he said.

Once Ken passed that over, too, Mac had the cap in his teeth and was drawing a shape on the workbench. "This is the island. We can plan our assault like so..."

He squinted. The marker stopped moving.

"Well. There is one thing we probably have to handle first..."

THIRTY-THREE

"WE SHOULD NOT be doing this," Lucy said. She was very aware of Jaden's presence at her back. Her eyes flicked to his reflection in the monitor in front of her, where he was staring right back. "If I get caught..."

"You're doing it for a good cause," Jaden said.

"This is blackmail," Pat chimed in. He was tied to a chair, and as Jaden turned to face him, Pat's eyes went right to the 9mm in the security chief's hand.

"Pat," Jaden said in a soft voice, yet it carried to both of the IT techs. "She's doing this to help *you*. Remember when I said I would figure out who was stealing the morphine?"

Pat nodded, his sweaty bangs falling down over the pale skin of his face. Jaden reached out and brushed the hair aside with the barrel of the gun.

"Imagine my surprise, the day we relaxed the guard on the med tent, when IT Pat comes slinking in, looking for a fix. Now, I'm not going to judge you. The end of the world as we know it has put a strain on all of us. But there are people who need that morphine. So, Lucy here is going to do whatever I ask her to. Lord knows why, but she's sweet on you. She doesn't want to give me any reason to put you in a condition where you'll *need* the morphine, Pat, which is the only way you're going to get it. Do I make myself clear?"

Shaking and sweating, Pat nodded.

"Good. Have you found anything yet, Lucy?"

Her fingers clacked on the keyboard. "Not yet. The encryption is one thing. Whatever's encrypted, we can get right past that. But the Command server, it's just not on this network." She moved her mouse around, clicking from box to box. "It's not on any network I'm connected to."

"Are you connected to all of them?"

She rounded on him. "Duh."

"Lucy..." Pat said.

Turning back to the monitor, she blew out a breath of air, resolving to get better taste in men. "I'm going to need a drink if... hold on. There's something. Huh."

Jaden went to one knee next to her. "What'd you find?"

"Well there's one computer that's on the regular island network, and the MAC address matches our files for Dr. Crispin's personal tower. But it's not in his office; there's only one computer in there, and it's this one." She pointed to a listing on the screen. "So, unless this is in his living quarters..."

"Check it," Jaden said.

Lucy tossed her mane of dark hair and cracked her knuckles. "I need some Mountain Dew. And some Jack to drown it in."

She clicked on the icon for the lone computer, and a prompt came up for a username and password. "Of course," she said, reaching into her shirt pocket for a small flash drive. It was black with a yellow skull-and-crossbones motif. "A WPA key has a forty-eight bit initialization vector key. That makes a possible five hundred trillion combinations, did you know that?"

"Yes," Pat said, rather sullenly.

Jaden ignored him. "So what does that mean to me?"

Pat's head came up. "It'll take hours for any hacker tool to eat through that kind of encryption. You get that, cop? You're going to be in here with us for hours. Someone is going to notice me and Lucy aren't around."

Jaden smiled, showing a mouthful of teeth, and Pat decided he probably should have just kept quiet.

"When they come looking, little junkie, you want to be the one who explains what's going on here? I don't have as much a problem with it as you might think."

"Shut *up*, Pat," Lucy said. The computer pinged, and she clapped her hands. "We're in!"

"Hours," Jaden said.

Pat looked confused. "How did you...?"

Lucy petted the thumb drive sticking out of the computer. "This little baby is what got me noticed in the first place. I knew when I wrote it, it would either get me into college or jail."

Jaden leaned forward. "What's on the computer?"

She wrinkled her nose. "Looks like this was his entertainment center for when he was working. It's full of old-man music. London Symphony Orchestra, Govi, Al Di Meola. What is this stuff?"

She clicked on a file called "Race with Devil on Spanish Highway," and cringed at the sounds of an entire band playing something at breakneck speed, instruments playing notes together that sounded almost impossible to her Top 40-trained ears.

"Old man music," Jaden said. "What else?"

"It'll take a while to sort through everything," Lucy replied. "The computer has a single five-hundred-gig drive; that's a lot of files to sift through by hand. What are we even looking for?"

Jaden paced, hands behind his back, the 9mm still clenched in his fist. He wasn't easily rattled, but tech bullshit got right under his skin. His first reaction was usually to see how much a computer liked a bullet through the CPU.

"I can narrow the search by excluding music files," she said.

"Do that. I'll be right back. You two stay in here. Do *not* fuck with me on this."

He walked out of the room swiftly, and the IT people exchanged looks. Pat opened his mouth to speak, but Lucy put her hand up.

"Just... save it."

❜

Jaden slipped his 9mm into its holster as he walked to the IT center. Pat might have been a junkie, but he was right. Sooner or later, they would be missed. He had to defuse the situation before it became an issue.

He opened the door to the IT lab, and Carmen, the department head, looked up from a circuit board she was soldering. Her light-brown hair had started to go grey over the past month, and he idly wondered if it was because she had run out of dye.

"Mr. Jaden! What brings you around these parts?"

He cleared his throat. "I just wanted you to know, I've enlisted the assistance of Pat and Lucy in a sensitive matter."

Carmen's dark eyes widened. "Is that so? May I ask what it is?"

Jaden made a face and put his hands on his hips. "Well, I suppose you might hear something about it eventually. They do, after all, work for you." He looked around the room, drumming his fingers on his belt. "Where's the other Lucy?"

"Oh, her. She's out with the maintenance crew, lending a hand with something Dr. Donovan wanted set up. I don't even know *what*, but I know she's terminating fiber optic connections for a batch of video feeds."

Nodding, Jaden cleared his throat again. "Well, make sure this conversation stays between us. And if Lucy gets to wondering where her co-workers are—"

"Don't worry," Carmen said. "They're running errands for me."

"Excellent. Here's the thing: we've been receiving a series of encrypted communications over the radio. None of the comms guys are cryptanalysts, but Winchester suggested to me that Lucy was good at that kind of thing."

"Very good," Carmen cut in, nodding.

"Well, she's working on it. Pat's helping her."

Carmen snorted. "Whatever Pat's doing, he isn't *helping*. But," she put her hands up, "if she wants him there, I'm not going to argue. Keeps him out of my hair."

Jaden smiled. "Thank you." He had more to say, but was cut off by the blaring PA system.

"Jaden to Radio. Mr. Jaden, report to Radio."

Carmen put her finger to her lips. "Maybe more coded stuff?"

"Maybe," Jaden said, leaving the IT lab. He had no earthly idea what it was, but it couldn't be good. He broke into a jog and was at the Communications door in minutes.

"What is it?" he asked Winchester.

The comms man turned, an odd look on his face. He held up a headset. "It's Alpha McLoughlin, sir. It's for you."

❧

"Is he ever coming back?" Pat said. As if in response, the door opened and Jaden strode in.

"Any luck?" he asked.

"Lots," Lucy said, turning the monitor so he could see. "It looks like Crispy kept a video log. The files go back years and years."

Jaden looked at the screen. "All I have to do to get these to work is double-click on them?"

"Yes."

He tilted his head at the door. "Get out. Take Pat with you. Say nothing." To punctuate this last point, he put the 9mm on the desk next to the keyboard.

"We are so gone," Pat said as Lucy untied him. They left the room, closing the door behind them. Jaden got up and locked it, then sat before the computer and put on a pair of headphones.

He clicked the first video. It was old, old enough that Crispin still had color in his hair.

Have I known him that long?

"Great strides in the experiment," Crispin was saying. *"I had some interaction today with them. They call me Master, but... I feel like their father—"*

Stopping the video, Jaden clenched his teeth and went to the top of the screen, reversing the sorting order. The newest video was now on top, and the cursor hovered over the file for a moment. The date stamp was the day of Crispin's murder.

Jaden clicked on it and sat back.

An image of Crispin appeared, his hair now totally grey. *"Picking up from an hour ago. Where was I? I think... yes. I refused to believe it at first, but I believe it is finally time to come clean. With my first son, I have made a mistake. The obedience training focused too heavily on negative reinforcement. With the others, that worked fine. But he's not like them. Theta Kaiser—excuse me—Epsilon Kaiser's only reward system is pain. He is an aberration, and I don't know what to do with him now. Especially now, when the whole world has changed.*

"I must say, however, that Alpha McLoughlin has risen to the challenge estimably. I bred the Dogs to be man's protectors, but McLoughlin... he has turned out to be man's best—"

Jaden almost flinched when someone knocked on the door. He blew out a breath, realizing the knock had come from the video. On-screen, Crispin spun his chair around, asking who was there. A man's voice answered.

Switching from the chair in front of his private tower to the chair at the Command console, Crispin hit the door release so the door would open.

Grimacing, Jaden had already guessed who would be standing there, in this video created the day the project director died.

)

Donovan stood in Command, clutching the sides of his head. He was surrounded by piles of manuals, the shelves on the wall almost totally empty.

"That code is somewhere," Donovan said to the empty room. "I know you're in here. You have to be in here somewhere, and I will find you, Mr. Terminate."

He turned and poured coffee into a white mug he'd found in Crispin's locker. It said WORLD'S BEST DAD. Donovan made a face. Crispin had never mentioned any children.

After downing the coffee, Donovan slammed the mug on the counter. As he did so, a smudge on the inside cover of a manual caught his eye.

Smudges mean use, he thought.

He squinted and picked up the book.

THIRTY-FOUR

KEN LOOKED AT THE TOP of Mac's now-shaved head, squinting. "So the first part of this here brain surgery, where we remove a delicate microchip thingy from inside your skull, involves a *chainsaw?*"

Julius shrugged, tightening the screws on the improvised head brace. "It's his skull. He ought to know."

The pastor, in the corner of the workshop, sat on an overturned milk crate, praying.

"Trust me," Mac said. "It sounds odd, but a hole saw just isn't going to cut it. Even a big one. I heal too fast. We already talked about this."

Ken nodded. "I know, I know. It's just, I'm having a little trouble wrapping my head around the idea, now that I have a chainsaw in my hand. And, you know, we're about to pop your head open like a tuna can."

"It's his skull," Julius repeated.

"I would like to register with everybody present, I am... uncomfortable with this part," Ken said. "Pastor, you still praying?"

The pastor, head down, nodded.

"Okay. No bets. If you have any, I don't want to know."

That said, Ken pulled his goggles down and yanked the starter rope on the yellow chainsaw. It roared to life on the second try, and he squeezed down on the throttle, making it scream. He inched the whirring teeth down to the Alpha Dog's skull.

"Are you sure about the painkillers?" he said, pulling back.

"Just do it, will you?" Mac shouted. "Hurry up, before I sweat the ink away."

Kelly scampered over and offered a leather belt for Mac to bite down on.

He said, "Fold it in half, please."

She did, and he took it into his mouth with a grateful half-smile.

Holding his breath, Ken came down with the chainsaw, hitting the thick, black ink marker that circumscribed the Dog's skull. He angled the blade, and the stench of burning skin filled the workshop. The teeth bit into bone, and the chainsaw tried to pull away.

"You're lucky I'm a construction worker," Ken said. "If I were a real brain surgeon, that probably would have broken my forearm."

Mac bit down on the belt, and Ken thought he heard a growl over the whine of the chainsaw.

"Right. More cutting."

True to his word, the bone in Mac's skull had already formed small tendrils, repairing itself. The skin was healing even faster than that. Ken saw it and grimaced, trying to cut faster.

"Pull," Ken said.

Kelly and Julius ran to the stepstool he was standing on and dragged it slowly around to Mac's right side. Ken continued cutting and couldn't help but think of winters during high school, when he'd tried his hand at ice sculpturing only to fail miserably.

Oh God, oh God.

Do not *think of this as just another test.*

He worked the chainsaw around, straining to see clearly through the pink mist that filled the air between him and Mac's head. He thought that he probably should have worn a mask over his nose and mouth too.

"Pull."

As they moved around to the front, Ken looked down and caught Mac's eye, immediately wishing he had not. The Alpha Dog's face was red and streaming with sweat and blood. The cords in his neck stood out, and his lips pulled back to show teeth embedded deep in the leather belt. But the eyes... even though the surgery was his own idea, Mac's eyes held murder in them.

Ken ran the chainsaw across the Dog's forehead, blocking his face out with the body of the saw. He blew out a breath.

"Pull."

As they maneuvered him around to Mac's left side, he continued the cut, and then rushed over to the beginning of it again, where the skin and bone had made significant progress.

"Okay. Let's just lift the hood, see what you have under there."

With an obscene cracking sound, the top of the skull came free to Ken's unyielding pressure; Kelly leaned forward with a sharp blade and sliced through the meninges, the membranes insulating the fleshy convolutions of the brain.

"Julius, you got the Dremel tool ready?"

The old man ran over with a small hand-held blue instrument. He clicked the button on the side and it whirred to life. As planned, he ran it around the top and bottom of the cut, holding the bone back on its journey to self-repair.

Mac spit out the belt. "Okay. There are two chips we're interested in. They're very close together. The one on the right—"

"Your right?"

"The one on *my* right is the Pavlovian chip. The other one is kind of important. That one lets me change whenever I feel like it. So don't touch it. Without that chip, I'll be far less effective."

"They're connected," Ken said, clearing his nose off to one side. The wet dust from Julius's continuous bone grinding was starting to become an issue. "Is there a fan in here?"

The pastor stopped praying and came over with a square yard of sheet metal. He waved it back and forth. "How's that?"

"Peachy," Ken said. "Mac, they're connected."

"I heard you. I'm just... you'll have to try to get one out without disturbing the other. Are you up to it?"

Ken made a face. "Kind of late to back out now, isn't it?"

Wiping the sweat from his face, he leaned back and took a deep, cleansing breath. He gripped the needlenose pliers in his steady right hand and leaned back in, but then immediately leaned back out.

"Just do it," Julius said. "Don't worry about hurting him. The brain processes pain signals, but it won't feel any."

"Not comforting," Ken said.

"Come on," Mac said. "Do you want the girl to do it?"

"Say no," Kelly said.

Ken leaned back in and rested the handle of the pliers on the ring of bone. He edged the tip under one corner of the Pavlovian chip. He pulled, ever so slightly, and the corner lifted off the surface, pulling a small bit of gold wire out of a fold of brain.

"Whatever you're doing, keep doing it," Mac said. "I felt something there."

"Still not comforting."

Ken pulled a touch more, freeing a larger web of gold wire from Mac's brain. "These fingers go everywhere," he said.

"Don't worry about the stuff coming to the chip," Mac replied. "Without it, they're just stuff. The chip is what needs to come out."

Blowing out a slow, shaky breath, Ken pulled more on the Pavlovian chip. It was almost all up, and he smiled. "Okay, I think this is... this is it!"

He pulled the last bit free, but it didn't come on its own. A corner of the other chip came with it. "Holy shit!"

"What happened?" Mac barked.

The pastor stopped waving the sheet metal and put his hand out. "You can't undo anything, son. Just pass it over and we'll get rid of the damned thing."

"Holy shit," Ken said, dropping the Pavlovian chip in the pastor's waiting hand.

The man of the cloth held it up to his face. "Such a small thing for so much trouble." He leaned over it. "Well, it's just best that it's—"

Crack!

The Pavlovian chip exploded, and the pastor reeled back, a hole in his hand and a hole in the side of his face. He fell, his one good eye rolling in its socket.

"I think... I think..."

"Holy shit!" Ken yelled again.

"I think I'm hurt," the pastor said, then fell over.

"Close my fucking head!"

Dropping the needlenose pliers, Ken and Julius pushed the flap of skull and scalp back into place.

"The keeper," Julius said.

Ken blinked and turned, grabbing at a corkscrew on a wire hanger. He turned the tool into the top of the flap of scalp, then suspended it from the ceiling.

"Try not to move for a while," Julius said on the way past. He knelt down by the pastor. "When your skull is more or less together, we'll take the keeper out."

"I know that," Mac said. "Why are you still talking to me? Help that man!"

Julius stood up, pulling the handkerchief from his back pocket. "Ain't no helping him now."

THIRTY-FIVE

DONOVAN HIT THE ENTER key with a triumphant "Hah!" and bounced in his seat as the McLoughlin window on the big touchscreen went completely, irrevocably black. He sat back in the Command chair, fingers laced behind his head, a smug look of bliss on his face. His Cupid's bow mouth was pursed as if he were about to receive a kiss.

"I did it. I found it." He leaned forward, slapping his hands on the open manual. "I found it right *here!*" He giggled, feeling high on his own accomplishments. And why shouldn't he? Wasn't he the one who followed the clues? Going from ink smudge to chocolate stain, tracing Dr. Crispin's progress through the manuals until he came to the one labeled MISC. PROTOCOLS IV. Who knew the Dog termination code would be in such an innocuous volume? Nobody could have.

But he'd found it.

Donovan stood, stretching his shoulders and back. He felt much better, even with the increasing stiffness from hours spent hunched over the piles and piles of technical manuals in Command. The stiffness was okay now because he had done it.

And he had done it without the help of that Summer Chan, insufferable as she was. Others might see her as aloof, but Donovan knew the truth about her. She didn't think anybody was good enough to fill Dr. Crispin's shoes. Every time he'd fumbled a line of Command syntax, or had to look again at a reference volume, he had felt the sting of her disdain. Quite acutely.

He shook his head. No, instead of letting that woman bring him down in his moment of conquest, he would use this opportunity to let people know how good he was. But who? Not Holly. Though he enjoyed the company of the engineer when she wasn't incessantly talking, she wasn't the right kind of audience for this particular piece of good news.

Striding over to the wide and multi-buttoned phone on the Command console, Donovan picked up the handset and tapped the 0 key.

"Get me Kaiser's cell," he told the comms officer.

A moment later, the sulkily defiant voice of the prisoner Dog came over the line, a bit crackly from a poor connection in the Kennel's speakerphone system. *"What the hell do you want now?"*

"I have good news, Kaiser."

"Yeah?"

Donovan felt as if he were smiling so hard, his cheekbones would surely burst under the pressure. "The Alpha is dead. I enacted the final solution on his Pavlovian chip."

For a moment, the line was silent, and Donovan was almost certain the connection had been severed. The smile on his face slipped a notch when he realized the mistake he'd made.

Kaiser already believed the Alpha to be dead.

"You know what this means?" Kaiser finally replied, a grin evident in his voice. *"It means there needs to be a new Alpha."*

"I'm not sure what you—"

"We need to hold a tournament. I've been robbed of my opportunity to take out the old Alpha. So, if I have to beat in the brains of every other Dog to take the top spot, so be it."

Donovan stared at the handset, unsure of what to say. Removing people from his path, from his ascendancy to his rightful place as ruler, that was one thing. A tournament, which almost surely meant gladiatorial-style combat, was something else entirely. It would be vastly entertaining.

"You there, Doc?"

The project director hung up the phone.

)

An hour later, Donovan sat in Crispin's old office, chewing on his knuckles and staring at the silver sword. He'd gone in there to listen to some music, perhaps unwind a little bit while he thought about Kaiser's idea, but when he went to open the audio folder, the first thing that caught his eye made him catch his breath.

Radio Call, 1730.

It was date-stamped the day before. He clicked on it and was shocked to hear McLoughlin's voice, then even more surprised to hear Jaden respond.

As soon as he recovered from his initial reaction, Donovan grabbed a pad of paper and restarted the file. He scribbled madly as he listened.

He then sat for forty-five minutes, biting his fist and trying to decide what to do. Even though the Alpha was taken care of, his fellow refugees might decide to try this ludicrous plan without him. Or maybe even *because* of him, because of his death.

Donovan stood and tucked the pad of paper into the breast pocket of his long lab coat. He couldn't think here, in Crispin's office. He did better in Command.

On the way, Lucas Jaden came alongside him and fell in step. "Dr. Donovan, sir."

The project director struggled to keep his face neutral.

"Sir, can we talk?"

"Yes, of course," Donovan said, keeping his face forward but casting furtive glances at the security man, moving only his eyes.

Jaden stopped walking. "Somewhere private."

Donovan paused, wondering what Jaden had to say.

"It's a matter of island security," Jaden said, and Donovan nodded.

Maybe he's going to turn on McLoughlin's group after all?

Or maybe it's something about the dead?

"Sir, perhaps we could go to Command? It's very private."

"Yes, of course."

"Good," Jaden said, walking toward the secure building. "Walk with me, sir. The breach in security runs high, higher than you would believe."

A thought floated in Donovan's head as they walked; how had Jaden cast his vote? When Crispin had polled the island personnel on whether to send the Dogs on a rescue mission, how had he cast his vote? Donovan couldn't remember.

They came to the entrance into Command, and Jaden gestured to the retinal scan. "Sir."

Donovan fought it, but he knew the deer in the headlights look had just come over his face.

"Sir?"

"Sorry," Donovan said, scrambling to collect his thoughts. The little red cooler was hidden, and there was no way he would just pull it out in front of Jaden. He shivered, thinking of what was in the cooler, and how it looked when he opened it, as if Crispin were staring—

Shaking this image out of his head, Donovan stepped up to the retinal scanner. He knew that *Jaden* knew that everything in Command was tailored to suit Dr. Crispin. But what other choice did he have? He couldn't even do this simple task quite right: Dr. Crispin had stood a head taller than Donovan, so the new project director had to balance on his tiptoes to reach the retinal scan.

He let it flash across his eyes, once horizontally, once vertically. The lights under the scanner flashed red, and he made a show of sighing and doing it again.

"It's not working," Donovan said, slapping the side of the metal box as if that might help.

Then he was thrust face-first into the wall, his forehead bouncing off the bottom edge of the scanner.

Jaden's rough hand held him there by the back of the neck. Donovan opened his mouth to yell, but stopped when a hard, metal circle touched him behind the right ear. He went up on his tiptoes again, trying to get away from the cold ring.

The hand left the back of his neck to pat him down, quickly and efficiently. Jaden confiscated Donovan's gun, and the project director's hope of getting out of this alive fell sharply. The barrel in the back of his head never moved.

"I could cry out," Donovan said, his lips brushing the cool metal of the scanner panel.

Jaden laughed, a harsh sound in the lonely hallway. "You go ahead and do that. And, sure, someone might come along. And they might even kill me. But..." He moved the gun in a rotating motion. "Your brains will be all over the retinal scan before you've finished yelling. What's your percentage in that?"

The frisk was repeated, this time more thoroughly. "Where is it?" Jaden asked, his voice raspy and close to Donovan's left ear.

"Wh-where's what?"

"Have you forgotten what it is I do around here? People lie to me on a daily basis. I would be a pretty shitty head of security if I couldn't tell when I was being lied to." Pressure from the gun increased. "Or when I'm being stalled while you think of a good lie. So don't. Where is Crispin's eyeball?"

"It fell apart."

Donovan felt the click of metal-on-metal as Jaden pulled the hammer back on the gun.

"Honest to God! I swear! Do you know how quickly the retina deteriorates? Once the eye is removed from the skull?"

"Doctor," Jaden said, his voice no longer menacing, which was somehow worse. "I know all about what happens to eyes outside of the skull."

Donovan's mind whirled. Could he fool this man? Could he lead him toward the Dogs somehow and entrap him? The Sigmas accepted Donovan as Master, and they wouldn't let this treachery stand.

"I'm really considering making this easy on myself," Jaden said, shattering Donovan's train of thought. "I don't even have to make any noise by pulling the trigger. I have a knife on my belt that would fit nicely between the C5 and C6 vertebrae. Or is it the C6 and C7? I may forget at the last moment and just paralyze you instead of killing you. Head on a stick. Either way, I know the eye's around here somewhere. You were headed right this way when I found you."

"Fine," Donovan spat. "Fine! But you'll have to unhand me."

Jaden smirked at that, but stepped back, keeping the 9mm trained on Donovan. The doctor went around to the maintenance panel and popped it open, revealing the red cooler.

"Scan it," Jaden said.

Donovan held the eyeball up, and the scan illuminated it from the inside, a cool blue glow that made the doctor feel sick.

As they stepped into Command, Jaden immediately noticed the black square on the big screen.

"Why is McLoughlin's screen blank?"

Donovan looked down, and Jaden stepped closer, the 9mm leveled at the doctor's navel. "You son of a bitch."

Eyes rolling all the way up to track the gun, Donovan saw the tip of Jaden's finger whiten as it tightened against the trigger. The gun didn't make its one note, though. Instead, Jaden tilted his head at the Command station.

"Show me," he said.

Stiff-legged, Donovan walked over to the big screen and motioned with his fingertip to one side, sliding McLoughlin's black square away. He expanded his thumb and forefinger over Hayte's screen, zooming in. The Theta was in the barracks, talking to Rose and playing cards.

"This... this is, ah, from here we can either take direct actions, using the Dog as a puppet, or..."

Donovan thought furiously. Was Jaden trying to take over? Already? That was totally, completely *unfair*.

"... or, through a series of commands, we can adjust the Dog's neuro-chemical impulses to alter his actions, or reactions." He thought about calling one of the Dogs to Command to end this treachery once and for all, but Jaden would see him do it. The security man wasn't stupid. And he now had two guns. And that knife.

Donovan typed in a string of code designed to increase Hayte's heartbeat. "See, just this one thing, that will alter the outcome of his game. Watch how his focus changes."

Jaden stepped closer to the large monitor, and Donovan lunged sideways, whacking the security chief's gun hand with his clipboard. Jaden turned, and Donovan was on him, hands wrapped around his neck. As they fell, Dr. Crispin's sentimental coffee mug came with them, shattering next to Jaden's startled face.

But his surprise didn't last long. He swung a brutal elbow down across Donovan's forearms, and the neurotech let go. With an easy sweep, the security man reversed their positions. He leaned down, keeping his right forearms across Donovan's throat.

"Thank you, Doctor. I didn't really want to kill you. I just wanted to make you suffer. But since you're giving me this wonderful excuse..."

"Radio," Donovan croaked out. "Attack plan."

Eyes wide, Jaden sat up, and Donovan's hand swung up in tandem, bringing the broken handle of the WORLD'S BEST DAD cup with it. The triangular shard on the business end stuck into the security chief's neck.

Everything stopped.

Jaden's eyes got even wider.

Donovan pulled the handle away and blood spritzed all over his face.

Something in the neurotech snapped. He jabbed the shard into Jaden's neck again, over and over, and the blood kept coming, spurting out with the failing action of Jaden's heart and the force of Donovan's thrusts. Sprays and squirts flooded the director's cheeks and forehead; he could taste its coppery, salty tang. He grinned, getting the blood on his teeth.

The shard went in one last time and the force of it broke the triangular piece off in the flesh.

He pushed Jaden away, and the security man fell backwards, trying to hold the ruins of his neck, hands twitching and feet kicking. His face had gone grey, and his eyes rolled up to meet Donovan's. His lips moved, but there was no sound.

Donovan got up on his knees. "What?" He put his ear closer to Jaden's mouth.

"Fuck yourself," the man said, and his chest rumbled as he gurgled out his last wet breath.

Donovan fell back, sitting in the expanding puddle of blood that he—*he* had released from Jaden's throat. The project director wiped a shaky hand across his face, smearing the blood.

He did it. Not Kaiser. Not one of the Sigmas. *He* did it. He'd never been in a real fight before. And he had survived.

"Where Crispin failed," he whispered, "I have persevered."

He got to his feet, slipping in the blood, and then stood up straight, hands still shaking. Everything seemed so clear. Every detail in his vision was crystal clear.

So clear!

He picked up the handset and dialed 0. When the comms officer picked up, Donovan smiled.

"Tell Kaiser—hah! Tell him he'll get his competition."

THIRTY-SIX

KEN RAN DOWN THE AISLE of the supermarket, his cart full. "That's the toy train set. Kelly's got the road emergency kit. Is that everything?"

Julius stood in the aisle intersection, reading his list, one finger in the air. "Blowtorches?"

Ken stopped running. "I thought you had one?"

"*One.* We need two more."

Ken turned back, then looked down at the cart and left it where it stood. He caught a glimpse of Mac standing at the front doors of the store, a tire iron in each hand. Even if he couldn't turn into a werewolf or whatever on command anymore, he was still a big, scary dude with Special Forces training, and Ken was glad he was there.

Kelly passed by with her cart full. "That's the road emergency kit, all the CO2 canisters I could find, and all the shotgun shells and ammunition they had under the counter. We don't even have guns that will fire some of this stuff, Julius."

He nodded, checking off items on his list. "What about the chlorine tablets?"

"Um..."

He pointed back down the aisle she had come from.

Running up with a blowtorch in each hand, Ken whistled. "This is it?"

"Light bulbs and the five-gallon jugs?"

Ken turned back, and Mac laughed.

"You are running them ragged, old man."

Julius cocked his head. "Teach 'em to read a list right the first time."

Ken and Kelly made more trips. Water filters. Mason jars. Nails. Leather belts. When finally Julius folded the list and stuck it in his pocket, the tired pair looked over their haul. "How are we going to get all this back to the shop?"

Mac laughed again. "Trips. Lots of trips."

For the rest of the day, Ken, Kelly, and a handful of volunteers trekked from the store to the shop, with Mac "riding shotgun" each time. They encountered small knots of the dead, but the noisemaker Julius had set up across the street from the shop's big roll-up door kept them there, away from the survivors' access to the rooftops.

On the last trip, Ken came down a fire-escape ladder to find Mac down on one knee, surrounded by a quartet of laid-out zombies. The tire irons were on the street, and Mac looked as if he was having trouble standing. Ken rushed over.

"You all right, man? Did one of those things—"

"I'm fine," Mac said, heaving himself to his feet. He walked to the tire irons and picked them up. "Let's just hit the road already. We got more trips to make for food, now that all of Julius's toys are gathered."

He turned away and jogged slowly down the street. Ken watched him go, eyeing him up and down, looking for blood. He waved Kelly down, and she and Ken ran after the old Alpha Dog.

"What happened?" Kelly said.

Ken shrugged. "He was down when I got to him. He looks bad."

Thuds from ahead drew their attention, and Ken poured on a burst of speed. His hand fell to his beltline, where a police baton hung. They had decided, for these runs, silence was crucial: no guns, no unintentional noisemakers.

Ken drew his baton and laid into the zombies on Mac's unprotected side. The Alpha Dog was doing well, but he was slowing. Kelly caught a glimpse of darkened material on his side, and she didn't think it was sweat.

Snapping out her Maxam collapsible baton, Kelly swung and knocked away a zombie approaching from Ken's blind side. "Back to back," she said.

Mac stepped away. "You two go back to back," he replied, grunting and swinging the tire irons with deadly effect. Kelly saw the web of black iron he wove around himself and urged Ken a little farther away.

The trio made quick work of the knot of walking corpses. Preparing to move on, Mac fell to one knee again. His bald and newly-healed head was pouring sweat. Ken stepped over to help him up, but the Alpha Dog snarled and waved him off.

Hands up and backing away, Ken said, "Fine. Fine, whatever. Whenever you're ready."

Once inside the store, Mac closed the security gate and chained them shut. He collapsed in a heap there, waving Ken and Kelly on.

Kelly stepped forward, but Ken stopped her, shaking his head. "We have to fill these bags. People got to eat."

Pulling on her arm gently, he guided Kelly away from the reclining Dog.

She pulled her arm away. "I know that. But he could be really badly hurt. You macho boys don't like to fess up to shit like that."

Ken turned to her. "He could have been bitten," he said in a low voice. "You've seen him go at it when the zombies get close. He's used to a melee fight when he's got teeth and claws and fur. Don't get me wrong, he scares me plenty. But he's not as fast as he's used to being, and yet he still throws himself at them anyway."

She thought back to the stain on his shirt and frowned. "I don't know. Maybe. When we get back, I don't care how scary he is, we're checking him over."

Ken raised his eyebrows and put cans of soup in his duffel bag. "I'll stand with you for it. But if he takes it into his head that he doesn't want to get checked…"

Shoulders stiff, Kelly turned away and started filling her bag with pre-prepared dry meals. Ken put his hand out, but stopped himself from touching her. Instead, he put more cans in the bag.

His two-way squawked, and he jumped. "Jesus. Forgot that thing was there." He picked it off his belt and hit the XMIT button. "Yo."

"Yo? Is that how they taught you to use a radio?" Julius sounded either amused or annoyed. Sometimes the two were the same.

"Is that how *who* taught me? What do you need?"

"You and Kels are loading up on horrid foodstuffs. So get antacid. Lots of it. And if you forget my Cheez Whiz, I'll let Mac use the chainsaw on you."

Kelly raised her eyebrows. "You going to tell him?"

"Tell him what?" Ken said. "We don't know anything, so what do I tell him?"

Shrugging, she kicked her bag away and moved down the aisle.

"Thank you, very helpful," he called after her. Into the radio, Ken said, "When we get back, we got to have a talk with Mac. Maybe, um, check him."

The radio stayed silent.

"Did you get that?"

"I got it. Talk later."

Ken put the radio on his belt and loaded his bag. "It's so easy. We'll talk later." Grabbing his bag, he walked to the end of the aisle and looked at the meat section. What hadn't been ransacked had rotted, so he moved on to the snack section.

Hard cheeses and salamis should be okay, shouldn't they?

Not if the Dog's been bit.

Half an hour later, Ken and Kelly were back at the entrance. Mac was standing, leaning on the security gate and looking pale. "What took you guys so long? I've run out of ways to have this thumb up my ass while I wait for you two."

Ken hefted Kelly's bag onto her shoulders, then lifted his own. "Underachiever. You were in the military. Should be used to 'hurry up and wait' by now."

Mac laughed, and it turned into a cough. He cleared his throat. "Can we get out of here now?"

Peering out, Mac pronounced the way clear and opened the safety gate. The supply-laden pair rushed out, and he closed the gate behind them, wrapping the chain around the handles but not locking it.

"I hate that lock," Ken said. "I always feel like I won't be able to open it when I really need to."

"Ditto," said Mac. "Let's go."

He jogged off, still moving as quickly as he had been, but no longer carrying himself with the easy athletic grace. Now he reminded Ken more of himself, a lumbering bear, using momentum more than agility to keep himself going. He and Kelly kept up, and the road was relatively clear. There were only three or four knots of zombies about.

"Not that I'm complaining," Ken said, "but this time of year, this place is usually jammed with tourists. Where the hell *is* everybody?"

"That sounds enough like complaining to me," Kelly said, breezing along next to him. "Shut it."

Mac snorted out a laugh and jumped for the fire escape ladder, catching the bottom rung and pulling it down. He waved the civilians forward.

At the top, Ken looked down to see Mac following, but slowly. The big man's cheeks expanded as he blew out huge breaths, just forcing himself up the black iron ladder. He kept shaking his head to clear his eyes of sweat, and his grey shirt was several shades darker than before. And as grateful as Mac had acted when Julius presented him with a pair of boots, Ken was ready to bet the footwear felt as if it were cast from concrete.

"Problem?" Mac said, looking up.

"Nope," Ken said, and then he hurried to the top.

)

He and Kelly stood in the pantry over the machine shop, unloading the bags. She still hadn't said much to him, other than "Move," or "Move." He got the hint.

Julius appeared in the doorway. "We got stuff to talk about. You mean Mac?"

"Yeah," Ken said, stacking cans of beef stew on the shelves. "He's acting funny. Been moving like he's hurt, but he doesn't say anything. Sweating, slowing down. And he... he..."

Julius turned.

"He's right there."

Mac stood in the kitchen, his face pale. He'd stopped sweating, his skin looking cold and clammy instead. One corner of his upper lip twitched, sending his face in and out of a sneer. And he stared at Ken.

"Hold on, big guy," Ken said, putting his hands up. "We're just worried about you."

Taking a faltering step forward, Mac put his hands up too. Coming from anybody else, the gesture might have been a funny mirror to what Ken was doing; but coming from Mac, it looked as if he were contemplating murder. Again.

A rumble started deep in his chest, and his lips peeled back to reveal pale red teeth.

"Oh, shit," Ken said.

Mac took another step and started bleeding from his nose. His eyes rolled back, and he fell over, blood coming from everywhere; his eyes, his nose, his ears, even his fingernails.

Julius ran over, straightening the Dog out on the floor. He pulled a wallet out of his back pocket and stuck it between the Dog's teeth. "Help me get this shirt off."

213

Ken jumped forward, grabbing the Dog's shirt collar and pulling it apart. The material split and he tore the shirt away. He and Kelly pulled Mac's arms out of the sleeves, and Julius snapped on a flashlight.

There was no bite.

Not a single unhealed wound.

"Well, now what?" Julius said.

Ken just sat down and stared. For some reason he couldn't even shrug.

THIRTY-SEVEN

"OH, *NO!*" KAISER YELLED, laughing as Theta Rose tumbled away across the concrete floor of the sparring cage, clutching at his arm as it flopped at his side. "You're so brittle. Not enough milk?"

Rose staggered to his feet, panting. His short, dark-brown hair lay plastered to his scalp. He backed away, keeping an eye on Kaiser. Rose was the third Theta to be rushed into the cage; Kristos and Landis had fallen to Kaiser in a matter of seconds. The fights had all started the same way: human Dogs facing off. Neither of the previous Theta Dogs had lasted long enough to even start the Change.

Knowing he was the exception, Rose grinned, not sure whether to be happy about his achievement. The way Kaiser had manhandled the others... maybe Rose would be lucky to get off with a broken forearm and dislocated shoulder.

We'll see how much Dog he really is, then.

The cameras set up on the enlarged posts of the sparring cage whirred, capturing the fight from every conceivable angle. Donovan had a ringside seat, and he was happy in the knowledge that if he missed anything, he'd be able to play it back later, in full color, full stereo sound.

Grunting in pain, Theta Rose dropped to all fours and made himself change. The pain was something new this time, a red agony that re-sounded in his broken bone and loose shoulder joint. As he'd hoped, the radical movement of bones and tissues inside his body had snapped the limb into place, and the increased flow of hormones and everything *else* had kick-started his healing processes.

He rose to his full, shaggy height, his yellow eyes glistening. Rose glared at Kaiser, who had yet to change. Snapping his teeth and chuffing, Rose moved carefully to the side. He feinted in and then back, gauging Kaiser's reaction to attacks in full Dog form.

The Epsilon seemed more amused than anything else.

That thought triggered a rush of rage in Theta Rose, and the thin veneer of humanity boiled away. He snarled and spit, charging Kaiser, claws out and ready to rend and tear.

Kaiser leapt neatly to one side, landing on his hands and rolling back to his feet. He jumped backwards, spinning and kicking, landing a powerful blow to the small of Rose's back. The Theta Dog lurched forward and, spurred by his own momentum and the added impetus of Kaiser's foot, collided headfirst with one of the iron I-beams surrounding the sparring cage.

Blood covered Rose's furry face in crimson sheets, blinding him even as his skin stitched itself together. He wiped the curtain of red away in time to see Kaiser pushing through the last stage of the Change.

A pair of emotions chased each other through Rose's brain. The first, pride in having forced Kaiser further than either Kristos or Landis. The second, fear of the very same thing: fear of escalating the fight.

The spike of adrenaline bumped something in his system, and he threw himself headlong at Kaiser, more carefully than before. It worked against him. The Epsilon was faster in full Dog form, and when Rose pulled his punch, Kaiser was there and ready.

Sharp nails dug furrows up Rose's chest, and he yelped when the talons hung up on his collarbone. Kaiser lifted up on the bone, pulling Rose onto his clawed toes. With his left foot, Kaiser kicked up, raking his lesser opponent along the inside of the left thigh.

Rose fought to get away, realizing his femoral artery had been cut. Even in full Change, there would be a moment where he would just keep losing blood, temporarily weakened until the artery healed.

Kaiser's double hammer-fist came down on the side of Rose's head, and the Dog fell.

Turning in place, Kaiser lifted his snout to the air and howled, clawing at the sky in triumph. In the stands, Donovan stood, clapping. Holly Randall, sitting beside him, looked up and cringed at the sheen in the neurotechnician's eyes. The look was a cross between religious fervor and the glaze of a lunatic.

She realized what she had just been thinking and it struck her as horribly, horribly unfunny. So she laughed. Donovan looked down at her and she laughed harder, pointing at Kaiser. Nodding, Donovan clapped harder and shouted.

Holly's laughter turned into yelling sobs, and no one noticed. Not even her.

)

One hour and several hormone boosters later, Kaiser sat cross-legged in the sparring cage, waiting for the final Theta Dog. Though the last opponent was smaller in stature, Hayte made up for his lack of size in determination and willpower. Kaiser respected that.

Hayte walked out to the sparring cage wearing only a loincloth and a bandana, moving in a short stutter-step, leaning forward and back as he chanted and beat a small drum with the flat of his hand. At the door of the cage, he stopped coming forward and instead skipped around in a circle. His chanting came to a crescendo, then halted altogether. He put the drum to the side and addressed Kaiser.

"I have made a Song to my ancestors. This one," he said, holding his fist to his chest, "this one wears the shoes of the Monster Slayer."

He stepped into the cage.

Kaiser slapped his thighs and stood. He towered over the native, even more so when the smaller man crouched in his curious stance. It was nothing like any of the Dogs had seen in training. A small twinge of fear fluttered in Kaiser's belly.

This one. This will be the one.

Without words, Kaiser launched an attack, striking out with his right hand. Hayte weaved deftly back. Not far enough to change his balance, but far enough to avoid contact. His hands floated around his waist, half-fists that never stopped moving. Flat black eyes threw Kaiser's stare back at him, reflected.

Hayte's foot shuffled forward, and Kaiser ducked down. When he did, Hayte's hand lashed out, the hard ridge of his palm chopping across the end of Kaiser's chin.

Kaiser stumbled back a couple of steps. He blinked. "Not bad, chief. Kind of an east-meets-west thing you've got going there, huh?"

He leapt up, kicking out. Hayte fell back, rolling to his butt, then brought his hands up to catch the axe-kick that Kaiser brought down.

The same karate chop struck the side of Kaiser's knee, and then he was stumbling free of the native's grasp.

Slowly, keeping his gaze pinned to Kaiser, Hayte came to his feet. He took a deep breath, and again began to circle in that curious, crouching stance.

Kaiser circled with him, hobbling. The pain eased slowly, and he grimaced. If not for his Dog physiology, he would have had a bad wheel for the foreseeable future. As it was, his system was having a hard time keeping up. He had grown stronger, but not strong enough.

Not yet.

The Epsilon's right elbow shot out, sweeping past Hayte's face as the native swayed out of the way. The elbow swung back, and as the native moved again, Kaiser's left hand darted after him, landing a thudding blow to Hayte's midsection. Air exploded out of the Theta's mouth, and he took a step back.

Never blinking.

Kaiser feinted again, but pain erupted in his left foot as Hayte's hard heel came down on his instep. The bigger Dog hopped back, only to find himself up against the new I-beam. Hayte's leaping knee caught Kaiser in the solar plexus, followed by a forearm across his temple.

Fighting the blackness, Kaiser threw himself away from the cage, snarling and grunting. Hayte turned and stalked after him. The eerie stillness emanating from the native made the flutter of fear that Kaiser had felt earlier now spread its wings. A tic appeared at the corner of his eye. He'd been right to respect Hayte.

Yes, he will be the one.

Kaiser threw a looping punch, one that Hayte sidestepped, slipping around the bigger Dog as smoothly as a shadow. His arm snaked under Kaiser's, a foot in the back of his knee, and the Epsilon found himself suddenly kneeling in front of Hayte, trapped in a half nelson.

Hayte caught his other hand to lock in the hold, and then leaned down to look into Kaiser's face.

"I've always known, Kaiser. You were never a man who *became* a wolf. The procedure... it only brought out the real you."

Kaiser began to laugh, and a spark of alarm flashed across the native's eyes. It was too late. Kaiser's snout had already begun to grow, and he leaned his neck back, the pliant cartilage and bones ready for the Change, allowing greater flexibility. Teeth snapped on Hayte's gut, and Kaiser dug in.

Hayte let go, beating down on the crown of Kaiser's head, but, again, it was too late: the Change had started, and the Epsilon had a good hold on him.

Head thrown back, Hayte tried to change too, but Kaiser's growing snout and elongated teeth took a firmer hold on his midsection, and all Hayte could think of was pain.

Kaiser stood, lifting Hayte into the air by his stomach. He reached up and gripped the sides of the native's head, then let go with his teeth. Grunting and growling laughter, the fully-formed Dog twisted and pulled until Hayte's neck popped free from his body.

The stands went quiet. Donovan threw his drink over the cage and started cheering. The rest of the island staff clapped, but more than one face was streaked with tears.

The beaten Theta Dogs all lowered their heads.

Kaiser had won. He'd beaten them.

All of them.

Donovan stood and yelled at the security guard. "Open it. Open it, already! I want to congratulate my new Alpha!"

The guard extended a shaking hand and unlocked the gate. Donovan ran over and yanked the door open. He approached Kaiser, arms open, singing praises.

"Beautiful! Magnificent! Oh my God, I have never seen such a display in my life!" Donovan turned to the crowd. "Ladies and gentlemen! I give to you, your new Alpha!"

He began to clap, but a growl from behind him stopped him cold. Crazy, but it felt as if Crispin's eye were ogling his back.

"Alpha?" Kaiser grunted, darkly amused. Then he roared. "I am the *Omega!*"

He dashed forward, seizing Donovan by the neck and hip, lifting the neurotechnician over his head.

Kaiser brought Donovan down hard across his knee. A sharp crack rang out, and the seats began to empty as everyone went running. Pointing a clawed hand, Kaiser beckoned the watching Theta and Sigma Dogs.

"Change."

Obliging their new Alpha and Master, their new Omega, the Dogs put themselves through it again, their bodies reconfiguring in painful, unnatural ways, bones and cartilage popping, muscles and connective tissues stretching, tearing, then healing. One of them vomited from the pressure on his stomach.

Then the seven Dogs entered the cage to stand with their new leader. His excitement spread to them, infectious, a thing that had only ever happened with McLoughlin; their shoulders began to heave up and down in time with his. They snapped at each other and paced.

Kaiser barked. He pointed again, this time at the prone and still very much alive form of Donovan.

"Feast," he said.

And they did.

THIRTY-EIGHT

KEN SAT ON THE ROOFTOP, looking down at the mass of shuffling humanity below and popping plastic wrapping bubbles. As far as pastimes went, it would never beat baseball, but it was something to do. Though they hadn't been there for that long, he already liked the shop better than North Regional. The tools and workbench made him feel more at home, and the accommodations above the shop were set up for people living, not people working, like back at the offices.

"I can't believe you're still up here," Kelly said from behind him. "How much of that bubble wrap do you have left, mister?"

He half-turned to look over his shoulder. "What are you offering for it?"

She laughed. "Oh, *ho*. So that's what it's come to. The death of romance at the end of the world."

Ken patted the ledge next to him, and she sat down.

"Sorry about before," she said. "I just feel bad. Mac just got here, and he does so much. Nobody asked him for anything."

He nodded. "I know. It's all right. Shitty times all around, right? How's it going downstairs?"

Kelly snorted. "Julius is still running around, setting things up and keeping everyone else out. I don't get what he's doing, but he seems to have a plan."

Tearing his piece of bubble wrap in half, Ken gave her the good part.

"Thank you," she said. "I hate these things. We're not going anywhere for a little while. I don't see why Julius doesn't turn off the noisemaker."

It was Ken's turn to laugh. "The old man has his eccentricities. He told me he couldn't sleep without the sound now. Did everybody get something to eat?"

"Everybody that wanted something. People are taking this hard. First the pastor, and now Mac looks so sick."

Ken rolled up the bubble wrap and twisted it with both hands, setting off a string of rapid-fire pops. "I'll be back. I think I'm going to give Julius a hand. Will you be here for a while?"

Kelly stood, handing the plastic back. "No. I have some stuff to do too. Mac asked me to put lampblack on all our metal stuff. And there's quite a bit of metal stuff. He's down there now, all pale, with your .44 in the vise."

Raising his eyebrows, Ken stood with her. "Well then, I guess I'd better get down there."

Julius was sitting on a stool, rolling an open jar over and over in his hands.

"Is that gasoline?" Ken asked.

"It is. And over there is a pile of nails soaking in it." Julius eyed the jar. "Hand me some, will you? About two dozen. No, don't count them out."

He held the jar out, and Ken dropped the nails into its mouth. "What is this?"

Julius set the jar on the bench and picked up a white plastic bottle. "Hold on. Don't want to try to do this while I'm talking." He poured a dark-purple powder into a plastic cup and put a cap on it. He put the cup into the bottle with the nails and screwed the lid on tight.

"What is that?"

"Low-income nail bomb," Mac said from the other side of the workshop. His head, freshly shaved at sunup, already looked like a crew cut instead. He looked bigger, too. More heavily muscled. "Man's been making things that go boom all morning. Without mistakes. I'm starting to think he wasn't going to just let this place default to the bank." His words were pleasant enough, but he sounded brusque, almost rude.

Lips twisted in a stiff smile, Julius put the small jar with a dozen others just like it. On the shelf above them sat a pile of gleaming CO_2

cartridges. "I've always wanted to go down swinging. Maybe I've seen *Butch Cassidy and the Sundance Kid* too many times."

"They didn't know they were going down," Mac said. Then he clapped his hands. "Ken. Come look at this." He pulled the .44 out of the vise. "Try that."

Ken took hold of the gun. "It's lighter."

Mac shook his head. "It's more balanced. I've seen how you hold it, so I adjusted the grips. The trigger pull is better, too."

Looking up at Mac, Ken smiled. "Thanks. Let's just hope I don't need to pull the trigger that much, yeah?"

"This is it," Julius said. "All the party favors are put together. Thermite's ready, torches are tested."

Ken whistled. "And the boat?"

"The boats are good to go," Mac said. "Good thing you remembered where the military convoy went down. The .50 cal is mounted and ready to go. Plenty of ammo."

"Thanks, Mac. Since you're all done, I guess I'll get out of your hair. Um, never mind."

Ken walked away, feeling Mac's eyes on his back and cursing himself for his stupid choice of words. He went upstairs and stopped in the kitchen. His stomach rumbled and he realized he hadn't even eaten yet. There was some macaroni and cheese left on the stove, so he grabbed a bowl and spoon and dug in.

As he ate, he was vaguely aware of voices from other parts of the living quarters. They got closer, and he wished he'd taken his bowl to the roof to eat. Conversation hadn't been his thing lately.

"Here he is now," Kelly said. "Ken, this is Teddy. He'll be driving the decoy boat."

Ken looked up into a tired set of eyes sunken into a narrow face. "Sit down."

Teddy sat, his thin wrists banging the table as he did. Ken winced, but the pale-faced man hadn't seemed to register the pain. "What kind of—"

"Before we talk about the plan," Ken said, "I have to ask, are you sure you want to do this? The boat is going to draw a lot of fire, and will probably get sunk. No one can guarantee you'll make it out of the drink alive."

Teddy laughed, and it was turning into a dry, rattling cough that shook his thin chest. "I might be all right with that. Unless you think there's a plucky HMO that's hiding out somewhere in the city, I don't think I have much time left."

"Drowning—"

"Save it," Teddy said. "I'm not going to drown. I've decided, and I talked to Julius about some preparations already. I'm not coming here to ask you. I'm telling you."

Ken picked his spoon back up. "Thank you. I think."

"Now. What kind of timetable are we looking at here? I've got places to be and people to look forward to."

)

Later, Ken was back on the roof and feeling deflated. On the one hand, having someone volunteer to drive the decoy boat was great. Really, really great. He hadn't felt like handing out a death sentence. On the other hand, the reality of the situation came home again. He wished Jorge were there. Lightening the situation. Even if it was with a fart joke.

He smiled. Jorge. Even at his worst, he'd always been able to make Ken laugh.

He stared out over the sea of dead, thinking. It had been, what, three months before the outbreak? He wasn't even sure about the date anymore, but that sounded right. He and Jorge had been late, incredibly late to work because of Jorge's screwball antics...

"Come on, it'll only be a couple of minutes," Jorge had said. "In and out, boom. On the way to work. What could go wrong?"

Ken sighed and pulled the truck into the minimart's parking lot.

"That's the spirit," Jorge said. "I'll keep 'em in the cooler, and we'll have brewskis two seconds after we knock off. Set the weekend off right. Isn't that a plan?"

"It's a plan. Go get the beer already."

Jorge unbuckled and hopped out of the truck.

"And no cheap shit!" Ken yelled after him. Jorge answered with a middle finger over his head.

Not a minute after Jorge went into the store, he was followed by two other men; a young black man in a hooded sweatshirt and jeans, and an older Latino in a three-quarter-length denim jacket.

Feeling like a racist, Ken shut off the truck and went inside, too.

He went straight to the back and grabbed Jorge's elbow. "Come on. Get your beer already."

"What the hell, man?"

Ken dragged him to the front.

"Let's go."

Shaking his head, Jorge paid his bill and they left the store. "What was that about?"

Ken shrugged, walking them to the side. "I don't know. I just got a bad feeling about those guys that went in after you."

"Bro," Jorge said.

"I'm sorry. They looked..."

"Brown?"

"Shifty, I was going to say." Ken slapped Jorge's shoulder. "You know me better than that."

"Yassuh, bwana," Jorge said.

"Hey! You take that shit back."

Jorge put the six-pack down. "Make me, Grand Wizard."

Ken put his hands up.

"Ah, that's how it is, maricon. *Bad enough I got to put up with the racist attitudes of the fat cats we build shit for, now you too?"*

"I'm not—"

Jorge pushed him.

Ken stepped back.

Jorge pushed him again.

"Well?" he said.

Ken tackled him.

They rolled on the hard asphalt of the parking lot, their jackets taking most of the damage, but it was still asphalt. Jorge punched Ken in the side, short jabs, until Ken kneed Jorge in the balls.

His air came out in a rush and he fell to the side. His jacket hiked up, and Ken saw something that was irresistible.

Yanking as hard as he could, he picked Jorge up by the elastic band of his underwear.

"Ah, shit!" Jorge yelled out, and Ken dropped him.

The door to the minimart sprang open, and the two shady men ran out, automatics in their hands. Jorge and Ken watched them hop into a beat-up Lincoln and peel out of the parking lot.

They laughed for ten minutes after.

"You all right up here?"

Kelly sidled up next to Ken and bumped his head with her shoulder.

"I think so," he said. "Just remembering stuff. Psyching up. Big night."

Kelly reached down and gripped his hand. "I feel really good about this; the plan. Mac is amazing, and you, sir, are fearless. My big Webelo."

Ken felt his face heat up. He really never should have told anyone he was in the Scouts. "Well," he said, "I wouldn't say fearless, exactly, but—"

She shut him up with a kiss. It lingered, and then it grew deeper, and then they were holding each other as if they were the only two people left in the world.

)

Ken came downstairs into the darkened workshop and found Mac sitting alone in the shadows. "You all right in here?"

Mac grunted. "Not sure anymore. Look at this."

He lifted his shirt, showing Ken a gash on his side, something from the day before. Ken remembered, it was from squeezing by a piece of sheet metal as they ran back to the store for last-minute stuff.

"That's, uh..."

"Not healed yet," Mac said. "Worries me that it hasn't healed up yet." He shook his head. "That's not all that worries me. I been... different. Snappy. Harsh. I wasn't like that before. Not my nature."

Ken put his hands in his pockets. "You *are* a lot less cuddly now that it's out. What do you think your nature is?"

"I don't know. The full moon is coming. The Dog in me will be out again. So maybe it's just that time of the month."

Ken laughed, and Mac smiled. "Go on, get out of here," he said. "This is my locker-room time."

Waving and still chuckling, Ken left.

Alone in the dark, Mac dropped his smile.

What do you think your nature is?

A loaded question, and Mac tried not to think about it too much. What kind of person kills his best friend? Even if he was tricked into the cage, even if he had the best of intentions, he should have known Donovan was full of it.

And Samson. He'd just *charged*. He had to have been in control of himself, or it would have been a total beast attack. Instead, he was sloppy. He had left openings, even in Dog form. *He had left openings.*

And Mac had taken advantage of them.

He had tasted his best friend's blood in his mouth, had tasted the chemical tang of Sam's inexplicable hatred for him. And he had to wonder, had he spit it out? Or had the hatred gotten into his blood now, too?

THIRTY-NINE

"COME ON!" KAISER YELLED, his voice booming out into the falling night. "Let's see some *blood!*"

The humans in the sparring cage stepped away from each other, fully illuminated in the halogen lighting. The weepy IT Lucy and a girl in black biker leathers were both panting from their wrestling match. But Kaiser didn't want a wrestling match. He wanted the rich, coppery smell of blood. Wanted that to be the atmosphere he breathed to sustain himself.

And he wanted it *now*.

Shayna, the girl in the leathers, stepped back and doffed her jacket. "Sorry, girl. Going to have to hit you now."

"Please," Lucy said. "Please don't."

"You want to die? He'll kill us! You're more than welcome to hit me back."

Shayna stepped forward and dug a fist deep into Lucy's midsection. The girl *whoofed* and doubled over from the blow, rocking back on her heels before stumbling away. She retched and coughed, finally puking up water and rice.

"Yes!" Kaiser yelled. He picked up a curiously long thigh bone and threw it. "Fetch," he said. Holly Randall, naked and on all fours, crawled after it. The gravel bit into her hands and knees, and she winced as she moved.

In the sparring cage, Shayna circled Lucy, fists up. "You going to make it look good, or what?"

Lucy looked up from her vomit and bared her teeth. "Bitch!"

"More like it," Shayna said, and Lucy charged.

Shayna hit her with two quick jabs, then rocked her gut again with another uppercut. Lucy fell sideways, and Shayna stepped away. On the ground, Lucy yelled and picked herself up, still retching, charging at Shayna again.

The girl in black sidestepped, snapping a kick into Lucy's face. The IT girl went down, eyes rolled back in her head.

"Emotional content," Shayna told her. "Not anger."

The crowd roared, a mixture of yelling Dogs and frightened humans. Kaiser had made no distinction between survivors and island staff. They were all his playthings now.

Sigma 37 stood, bowing low before Kaiser. "Should the loser die, Alph—"

Kaiser backhanded him. "The Alpha was a mutt. If you call me anything, it will be Omega."

From his knees, Sigma 37 nodded. "Yes, sir. Should the loser die, Omega Kaiser?"

"No. She will be taken to the Kennel for breeding stock. Or entertainment." He noticed Holly at his knee, head down and bone on the ground.

"You're not wagging your tail," he said.

Face burning, Holly moved her backside back and forth.

Smiling, Kaiser grabbed the bone and threw it again. "Fetch." He leaned forward. "Who's next, 37?"

Sigma 37 raised his face. "The construction worker and the youth. They hurt Sigma 19 yesterday."

Kaiser grunted. The humans had been pressed into service, removing the door to Command, since the eye that Donovan had so thoughtfully left for him had deteriorated to the point where the retinal scan no longer recognized it. The two humans, whether through sheer clumsiness or spite, had dropped the heavy door on Sigma 19's leg, shattering his femur.

"Bring them out."

37 ran off to collect the gladiators. Holly dropped the thigh bone at Kaiser's feet; it was wet with her slobber.

The Omega reached out and patted her head. "Good girl."

Jorge looked out at the crowd. "There are so many of us, and only eight of them. Why don't we just bum-rush them?"

Jimmy shook his head fast, making his red hair fly around his face. "You go first, dawg."

"Don't call me that," Jorge said.

"You two," Sigma 37 interrupted. "You're next."

Jimmy dropped his head into his hands. "Ah, Ken. Should have listened to you."

Jorge stood. "Forget about it, kid. We'll just put on a show for them and figure something out."

37 grabbed Jorge's shoulder and pushed him forward. "Go!"

He and Jimmy marched out to the sparring cage, greeted by the howling Dogs and the cheering and crying crowd of human beings. Jorge caught Marie's face in the stands and waved to her.

When she saw him, she instantly burst into hysterics.

Pushed from behind, the pair of men stumbled into the lighted cage and squared off.

"Okay," Jorge said. "See this shit on my ear? Hit me there. It's a gunshot wound. It'll bleed a lot, make it look good."

Jimmy swung, a haymaker right that landed flush in Jorge's face, sending him spinning away.

He looked up at the redhead kid, dazed. "What...?"

Dancing forward, Jimmy kicked out, laying his foot across the same spot on Jorge's cheekbone.

"It's like that, huh?"

Jorge yelled, charging at Jimmy.

The younger man dipped down, and Jorge jumped over him. He landed on the other side and just kept running, leaving Jimmy behind. Jorge hit the fence and started climbing.

"Hey!" Jimmy said.

He sprinted over and grabbed Jorge by the back of his pants. The kid pulled so hard that the snap button popped open and the seat of Jorge's jeans sagged, showing off his buttocks to the crowd.

"Get off!" Jimmy said, yanking harder.

There was a loud ripping sound, and at first everyone suspected it was a seam bursting on Jorge's pants. But then suddenly Jimmy was staggering away, gagging and fanning his face, and the source of the sound became clear.

"¡Frijoles, frijoles!" Jorge exclaimed, wagging his butt in the air. Several people in the crowd erupted with laughter.

Jimmy, recovering, came back around and pulled Jorge off of the fence. His bare butt hit the ground hard, and then the kid kicked him in the ribs before dancing back.

"¡Ah, pinche joto!" Jorge yelled, rising slowly. "Let me get up at least! Making me look bad in front of my gir—"

Jimmy hopped forward, landing a sidekick on Jorge's shoulder, sending him flat on his back once more. He moaned and farted again, and everyone laughed.

"This is terrible," Kaiser said. "37! Equalize things."

Sigma 37 nodded and snatched up a folding chair, running for the cage door. He opened it and threw the chair in. Jimmy turned at the clatter, and Jorge dove at him, headbutting him in the crotch. Jimmy fell over, and Jorge pounced. He managed to give the kid a noogie, rubbing off some of the young man's red hair with his knuckles.

With an up-kick, Jimmy threw Jorge back.

They rose and circled each other. Feinting with his hands, Jimmy closed the gap and threw a knee into Jorge's gut, then grabbed his waistband and threw him down. Landing on his face, Jorge retched and rolled.

Jimmy stood over him and hit him three times in the face. Jorge tried to turtle up, but Jimmy wasn't having it. He moved back and started kicking him again.

Flailing his arms, Jorge caught one of the redhead's feet and pushed him away. Getting clumsily to his feet, Jorge staggered back. He stepped on the folding chair and looked down. Jimmy charged, but suddenly Jorge had the chair and was swinging it around. It caught Jimmy in the mouth.

"Foreign object!" he yelled as the redhead went down. The Dogs roared again, their bloodlust up. Jorge looked over at Marie.

A clutching hand on his leg brought him back to the cage, and he raised the chair again, bringing the flat of it down on Jimmy's back. The redhead flattened against the ground and rolled off his bloody face, and Jorge threw the chair down. He planted the sole of his shoe on Jimmy's chest and tilted his head back, screaming and beating his chest.

Jimmy grabbed his foot and twisted, sending Jorge off-balance. The kid rose up, fists raised and teeth bared. He fell on Jorge, who sat up and swung his elbow out. Jimmy's jaw cracked against it, and he fell onto Jorge, out cold.

Pushing the unconscious kid off of him, Jorge got to his feet and swayed for a second as the Dogs cheered and the humans clapped.

Sigma 37 started yelling, "Kill! Kill! Kill!"

Soon all the Dogs were yelling it.

Kaiser got to his feet and faced the crowd, raising his arms with the chant. When all the humans were yelling too, the Omega Dog turned back and put out his fist, thumb down.

Jorge knew what that meant. He looked at the redhead and back at Kaiser. Then shook his head.

Kaiser popped his neck and pointed. "Kill!"

Jorge crossed his arms.

Turning, Kaiser stalked through the crowd, sniffing. Unsure what was happening, Jorge uncrossed his arms and walked to the fence, locking his fingers in it.

What's he doing?

With a growl, the Omega leapt forward and grabbed Marie's hair, pulling her up out of her seat. "Quiet!"

The chanting stopped immediately.

"This one has your stink all over her," Kaiser said. He started walking forward, dragging Marie behind as if she were a sack of flour. She sobbed and yelled, stumbling just to keep up. Kaiser walked down to the cage and held up a finger. He gritted his teeth, and the fingernail there grew yellow and extended.

He held it to the soft spot under Marie's throat and grinned at Jorge.

"*Kill*," he hissed.

Jorge rocked back. He looked from Marie to Jimmy, stepping from foot to foot.

"Holy shit, sir!"

Kaiser turned to see one of the human sentries waving.

Boat!" he yelled. "Boat!"

Growl rumbling in his chest, Kaiser threw Marie to the ground and stepped over her. "How'd it get so close?" He climbed the outside of the sparring cage to see out over the dark ocean.

The Omega Dog grinned as one of the island's spotlights exposed the little fishing boat, bobbing in the waves. *Idiots. Approaching out in the open. This ought to be a piece of cake.*

From the side, another security man ran up. "Sir, there is a message about this, sir."

Kaiser dropped down from the fence and grabbed the man by the neck. "Speak."

"Sir," the security man choked out, "Dr. Donovan told us to watch for a boat at the pier, and then another at the east end. This one's a decoy, sir."

Snarling, Kaiser threw him down too. "Nobody tells me anything. Take the security team to the east end and blow that thing away!"

The uniformed guard ran off, yelling into his radio as he went. Kaiser climbed back to the top of the cage and sat, watching. The security force gathered as they ran, until all of them were on the eastern tip of the island. Several spotlights set the sea alight.

The guards lined the boat up in their sights and opened fire. Kaiser smiled as the sound came to him. It wasn't like wetwork, where everything was up close and personal, but he enjoyed shooting at things. And people. The oncoming boat sustained a hail of fire, soaking in the bullets.

Howling like animals, even in human form, the Dogs arrived behind security, taking over with their own firepower as the guards reloaded.

Somehow the fusillade had done enough damage that the boat went dead in the water. Dogs and security forces alike continued to pound the vessel with their semi-automatics.

Kaiser thought he saw somebody move behind the big silver steering wheel.

I wonder if he's going to surrend—

He was thrown off his perch atop the fence as the boat exploded into a giant fireball.

FORTY

"HOW'S IT GOING, JULIUS?" Ken said into the radio. He could hear gunfire outside the sailboat. A lot of it.

"Looks good. They just opened fire on the second decoy."

Kelly put out her fist, and Ken bumped it.

"Kick ass. How many of them?"

A moment passed. *"It looks like all of them. Uniformed and not. I'm guessing those are the Dogs?"*

"Looks like you were right, Mac," Ken said. "They knew about the decoy." He looked out over the prow, catching a last glimpse of Julius's fishing boat bumping against the side of the pier as his own boat rounded the dark edge of the island.

Three boats. Subterfuge had never been Ken's strong suit, but planning this raid with Mac had opened up a door for him. With his knowledge of how buildings were put together, with enough time, he could probably find a way into most places. Especially now, when the end of all things had put a stop to fancy security systems.

"What?" Kelly asked, noting the look on his face.

Ken shook his head. "Nothing. Or maybe everything. It's weird, you know? We spent all this time, building barricades and reinforcing doors and whatever. Demolishing stairwells. All to keep the zombies out. And now it's us, trying to get in. Moving around security forces. Creeping up. It's like *we're* the zombies."

Kelly grimaced. "Now there's something to kill the mood."

An explosion rocked them all. Ken and Kelly looked up in horror at the fireball coming over the silhouette of trees and structures on the island. "What was that? Do they have rockets?"

"That was Teddy," Mac said, his voice rough. His condition had gotten worse as night fell and he grew hairier and hairier, his teeth sharper and sharper. "He told you he didn't want to drown."

Ken's reply was cut off by their sailboat thumping against something.

"That'll be us," Mac growled.

"Julius, come in," Ken said into the radio.

"*Yo.*"

"Hah. We're headed in. Don't blow your cover if you don't need to. Keep ready though, you hear?"

"Ten-four, Mr. Bishop. Kick ass."

"We better move soon," Mac said. "Won't be long before the moon is up."

Kelly turned to look at him. "What are you talking about? The moon *is* up." She pointed, and Mac's bleary eyes followed her finger to the sky.

"Where did the time go?" he asked, and slumped over in his seat.

Ken put out his arm and caught Kelly as she ran to the Dog. "Leave him be. He'll feel better after the Change. At least, he thinks so. Come on, give him space. I don't want to see this part again." He grimaced at the memory of Samson's Change, and the healing gunshot wound in his face. He pulled Kelly to the stairs.

They went down into the hold, where twelve men and women sat in the dark, shotguns and rifles between their knees.

"All right," Ken said. "Everybody knows their parts. This is about stealth. Everybody's seen the Dogs before, right?"

There was a murmur of mutual assent.

"Good. So no freaking out if you see one now. Especially our Dog. Do not mess up and shoot him. Without Mac..." He shook his head. "*Anyway.* All of us need to make it through. If one of our groups fails, the whole thing fails. The lives of every man, woman, and child on the island and in this boat are depending on you." He smiled. "So don't get me killed, huh?"

There was dry laughter at this, and Ken smiled. He hadn't expected to knock them dead anyhow.

A shape blocked the entrance to the hold. Ken turned and saw the hulking form there. "Mac?"

Kelly went halfway up the stairs. "Come on, I'll guide you down. *Hey!*"

The bestial shape was gone, and Kelly with it. Ken ran to the stairs, shouting out.

He tripped over Kelly.

She lay prone in front of the door, breathing but playing dead. And as he fell, the god-awful smell hit him. One of his childhood friends had had this old dog, with maggots in its flesh where a foxtail had drilled a hole in its hide. This smell now was way worse.

Ken looked up at Mac and gasped.

The Alpha Dog stood on deck, powerful legs apart, claws extended, teeth bared in a feral show. But there was nothing of Mac in those eyes. Ken saw into the twin pits of black rage in Mac's face and recoiled. The Dog was covered in oozing sores, and the wound on his side had opened, gaping horribly from being stretched during the Change.

"What is it?" a voice said from behind him, and Mac leapt. He cleared Ken's body and collided with the wall of the sailboat.

"Get back!" Ken shouted. He swung his shotgun by the barrel, hoping to stun the Dog until he got ahold of himself. They couldn't afford to have Mac either out of commission or out of his mind.

The shock of the impact vibrated all the way to Ken's shoulders, and he looked, expecting to at least see the Alpha Dog staggered.

Instead, he found himself staring again into those empty black eyes.

The Dog threw back its head and howled, the sound of it carrying over the entire island.

Ken dove and grabbed Kelly, pushing her through the hatch and closing it. As he began to dog it shut, a fist the size of a frying pan collided with his side, and he went flying to the handrail.

"*You have incoming*," Julius said over the radio.

Mac threw open the door to the hold and dove into the darkness below.

)

Hunt. Feed. Mate?

Movement in the hold excited the old Alpha Dog, his senses coming alive with the hunt. Figures scurried before him like mice fleeing a housecat. One of them struggled with a box by the door, flicking the light switch.

The rapidly dwindling cognitive centers in Mac's brain registered that they'd disabled the lights to keep a low profile on the approach.

Snarling, he charged the one at the light switch, jumping and slashing. The man opened up from shoulder to hip, spilling hot blood and greasy entrails. Burying his snout in the open wound, Mac tore and pulled, nuzzling around for the best parts.

It all tasted the same to him.

Tasted... familiar.

Like...

Samson, he thought, but couldn't remember why.

Didn't care.

Three more people ran behind him, headed for the stairs. They were fast, and he only had time to snap his teeth at one, catching a tiny amount of flesh.

Grunting, he went back to his meal.

Kelly and two other women came out of the hold as Ken was rousing himself.

"He's lost it!" Kelly said, winded. "Mac's gone!"

She was answered by the heavy *whump-whump-whump* of the .50 cal they'd mounted on Julius's fishing boat. Looking out, she saw the old man had powered away from the pier and was firing on a multitude of shaggy beasts, all running down the beach toward their sailboat, toward the sound of Mac's howl.

"Oh, shit." From her messenger bag, Kelly pulled out a double-handful of mason jars. "Give it to them!" she shouted.

Three of the jars went hurling overhead, arcing out into the night. One of them hit a Dog's shoulder and bounced away, the other two landing on the rocky shore. When the glass and plastic broke, the gas fumes and potassium permanganate reacted, turning into little fireballs that shot iron nails everywhere.

If the Dogs even noticed, they didn't show it.

One of the smaller Dogs went flying sideways as Julius's skill with the .50 cal improved. Two of the smaller ones peeled off, heading for the water. And for Julius. The rest of them powered on toward the sailboat.

"Ken, get up!" Kelly yelled, and the door to the hold burst open. Mac stood there, covered in gore. Catching sight of Ken and Kelly, he stepped forward. Then he stopped, lifting his snout into the air. His head snapped around, and he saw the rest of the Dogs coming.

A growl born of frustration loosed itself from Mac's chest, and he launched himself over the handrail into the ocean, just as five other Dogs came aboard. There was a loud splash, and he was gone.

Ken pointed his shotgun up, and it was swatted out of his hands. Contemptuously.

A scream cut through the night, and the lead Dog looked out over the water toward the fishing boat. A pair of howls came up and he gave an answering bark.

"Julius," Ken whispered.

FORTY-ONE

"KEN BISHOP," Sigma 37 said. "Remove your shirt." The Dog stood in front of a roaring fire, a pair of needlenose pliers in one hand and a sadistic smile on his face. Working as Kaiser's Sigma had prepared him well for the Omega Dog's eventual rule.

Squaring his shoulders, Ken returned the Dog's glare and set his jaw out.

37 pulled a long piece of metal out of the fire. "Have it your way then. Hah. I should swap these around so they read BK." With deft movements, he rearranged the entwined wire hangers so that the loose ends formed Ken's initials. "If you don't take your shirt off, I'll put this on your face. See how much your lady friend likes you after that."

Sigma 37 raised the brand, and Ken could feel the heat coming off the glowing metal.

"You've got until the count of... one."

Resigned, Ken shrugged out of his long-sleeved flannel shirt and tee.

"Good idea," Sigma 37 said. "Wouldn't want to catch that Grizzly Adams on fire. Hold still. You're going to feel a little pinch. And then it will burn like hell, hah."

He jammed the glowing brand into Ken's right shoulder, and the hiss of cooling metal and burning flesh wasn't quite loud enough to cover the strangled sounds coming from Ken's throat. His face went red, and sweat sprang from his forehead and chest. Droplets fell on the haft of the brand, sizzling.

"There we are. That wasn't such a chore, now was it?"

Ken breathed fast, like a locomotive getting up to speed. "I'm going to make you eat one of those."

"We live in the land of opportunity," 37 said. "I'll make sure the boss gives you yours. Next!"

Ken was herded off by the uniformed security force, who had taken to wearing balaclavas. He stared loathingly at the man, knowing that he himself couldn't do this to survivors.

A familiar yell caught his ear, and he turned to see Jorge being pushed back and forth between a pair of shirtless steroid freaks with MORITURI TE SALUTAMUS tattooed across their backs.

Jorge looked terrible, like he had been through a blender, and Ken wondered whom he'd had to fight. He waved, whistling through his teeth to get Jorge's attention. The Latino troublemaker saw it and waved back.

Kaiser also saw it.

Ken slowed his walk. "Hey, I know that guy," he said to the security guard. "Come on, I just want to say hello."

The guard prodded Ken with the barrel of his SPAS-12; the automatic shotgun was cold against Ken's skin and he realized how hot he was.

The guard said, "Keep walking, dead man."

"Just a minute, you shit."

The black stock of the shotgun jabbed down, catching Ken on the shin. "I said move, dirt bag."

Ken straightened, his blue eyes glaring into the guard's. The shotgun came up under his chin.

"It's okay," Ken said. "I'm just remembering your eyes. For later."

"You don't have a later. Sit here."

The guard pointed a black-gloved hand at a folding chair. Ken sat and was handcuffed to a handrail. The guard walked off, and Ken had nothing else to do but watch the gladiatorial matches as they unfolded in the sparring cage.

He saw Kelly, sitting quite a ways down from him, looking as if she might be ill as she stared down at her feet. He called her name, but she didn't seem to hear him over the sound of the crowd.

A deathmatch had just ended, a vicious knife fight between a short, stocky Latino with MT branded into each shoulder, and a fatter curly-headed man branded with HA. The bigger man was down, bleeding out into the dirt. MT discarded his knife and stepped away.

The Dogs all yelled their approval. A fat man stood by the cage in a white coat, spattered with red. He was shifting from foot to foot and was wet, as if he had just showered. With him was a pair of thin nurses, one of each gender.

Meet the medical staff, Ken thought.

The masked guard opened the cage, and the fat, wet looking doctor, with a peculiar rolling gait, jogged to the bleeding man's side. Ken couldn't make sense of the way the physician moved.

A woman in black leather leaned forward in her seat behind Ken. "One time, he was too slow to see if the other guy could continue. One of the Sigma Dogs broke his shinbone."

Ken looked back. "This is disgusting."

She raised her eyebrows. "Yeah. It's also your life for the foreseeable future, so nut up."

A guard came to get her, and she stood, holding out her wrist. He unlocked the handcuffs, and she slid her leather jacket off, revealing the initial S on her shoulder.

"Just one name?" Ken asked as the guard led her away.

"All I need, sugar."

The nurses and heavy doctor dragged the curly-haired HA out of the arena, and the guard pushed the girl with only one name in to take HA's place.

The Sigmas began to chant.

"Shay-NA! Shay-NA!"

Ken watched in horror as the girl, Shayna, raised her fists. The insides of both arms were bruised and covered in scabbed-over cuts.

The next one into the arena was a slightly older man, with a wrinkled forehead and a receding hairline. His shoulder bore a TS, and he must have flinched when they'd branded him, because the outline of the letters was warped and dragged out. The guard pushed TS in, and he fell to his knees.

"I can't do this anymore."

Shayna kicked out, catching TS in the ribcage.

"Fuck you, Todd. You didn't have a problem killing Scott. Try me, shithead."

Something ugly peeked through Todd's eyes. "You know how long I've worked in human resources?"

"Go to hell, that's how long." Shayna jumped, scissoring her legs, driving another kick into Todd's ribcage as he stood. He staggered back, hands out to block the punches she threw next. He caught one of them, twisting her wrist. She gritted her teeth as the scabs split and blood ran down her forearm.

She brought a knee up, missing him entirely.

The Dogs gasped.

Then the leg came back down, catching the side of Todd's knee.

"I knew it!" one of the guards yelled behind Ken. "Bitch don't miss."

Todd went down, losing his grip on Shayna. She tried to back away, but he flung himself from his knees, wrapping his arms around her hips. They fell to the ground, but he held on, and she pounded at his temples with the sides of her fists.

Todd let go and curled into a ball, wrapping his arms around his head. Shayna stood, and the cage door opened. One of the Sigma Dogs threw in a machete.

"Oh, shit," Ken whispered.

Ignoring the blade, Shayna walked around Todd, kicking him over and over. He writhed with it, trying to avoid the blows, but she was too fast for him. Desperate, he swung out both legs and caught her ankles. Shayna fell.

Todd jumped up, hobbling for all he was worth toward the machete. Shayna was up right after him, limping on her left ankle. He grabbed the blade and turned, swinging. She leaned back and the machete whistled past her. Shayna's hands shot out, catching Todd's wrist, keeping the weapon at his off-side so that his arm was crossed over his body.

She brought up a deft elbow and nailed Todd's nose. He dropped the machete into her waiting hand and staggered back. Shayna raised the blade.

"Kill! Kill!" the Dogs chanted.

Omega Kaiser stood, fist out, and the crowd stilled. Sneering, he put out his thumb and pointed it down.

"Sorry, Todd," Shayna said. "Them's the breaks."

With a two-handed swipe, she opened the front of Todd's neck and swayed back to avoid the spray. The Dogs went crazy, and the human crowd applauded, their eyes full of fear as they looked out through frozen, smiling faces.

The guard brought Shayna back to her seat and allowed her to put her jacket back on. "That's how you make it through," she said to Ken as she was being handcuffed to the handrail. "You want to live, you do it one minute at a time."

Stepping forward to uncuff Ken, the guard grunted a laugh under his mask. "Listen to the girl, big boy. You're next."

He led Ken to the cage door as Todd's corpse was being dragged out, leaving a bloody trail on the concrete.

With the end of his shotgun, the guard prodded Ken inside. Rolling his shoulders, the burly construction worker readied himself for whatever was next.

Another curly-haired man, obviously Todd's brother, was being led to the cage. OA was burned into his shoulder.

Kaiser stood and shouted, "Halt!"

The guard stopped, and OA breathed a sigh of relief.

"The loudmouth one instead," Kaiser ordered, and Ken's stomach fell. "Since he failed to kill for us yesterday, let him fight his friend."

Ken paced in the cage as the guard took OA back to the stands and retrieved Jorge. He could see his friend's mouth moving the whole way to the cage, and he couldn't help but laugh. Even now, Jorge was being an ass.

The guard pushed Jorge in and the gate slammed shut behind him. He looked into the stands and his face drained of all its humor. Marie was sitting next to Kaiser, her tear-streaked face looking down at him.

"*Este perro malo*," Jorge said. "I'm going to kick his ass for this."

"I'm not fighting you," Ken announced. He turned to the stands. "I'm not fighting!"

"Fight or die!" Kaiser yelled back.

Ken shook his head.

Jorge took a step toward him. "Come on, bro. He'll kill you. And me. And Marie, too."

Crossing his arms, Ken shook his head again.

"Jesus Christ, you're going to get us killed, for what? We fought before, *vato*. Don't tell me you don't remember."

Ken closed his eyes. His lips moved as if he were praying.

"Jorge!" Marie screamed from the stands. He looked, and Kaiser was holding her throat.

"Mama said knock you out," Jorge said, and he lunged forward, burying his fist in Ken's stomach. The bigger man doubled over, but stood back up fast. His face was red, but his eyes were still closed, his lips still moving.

"Ah, you pigheaded *gringo maricón*, do you want us dead?" He swung again, hooking a punch into his friend's side. Ken stepped back, and his hands came down, but his eyes stayed shut.

"Shit!" Jorge yelled, hitting him again. "All those times I took the blame for something you did, and this is how you repay me?" He hit Ken again in the stomach. "Remember when you bashed up her Mustang? Divorce wasn't even final yet, and not only that, but you steal her dog! And you make me hide it?!" He hit Ken again, then kicked him in the shins.

Ken wasn't budging. His eyes were still closed. Jorge swung and hit him in the face.

"You said I was drunk!"

Eyes flying open, Ken stepped back. "You *were* drunk!"

Jorge flew forward. *"But I didn't steal the dog!"* He hit Ken again, connecting on the side of his neck. Ken staggered back, and Jorge kicked him in the crotch.

The Dogs were laughing, yelling, enjoying the show. Kaiser had let go of Marie's neck and was sitting back, a bright and sunny smile on his face.

Jorge bowed and Ken tackled him to the ground.

"Goddammit, Jorge! I'm not going to fight you!"

Jorge laughed as they grappled. "What are we doing now?"

He rolled, straining to the left, but Ken fought him down. Jorge tried again, then again, and when Ken pushed back for the third time, Jorge switched his pressure and rolled them on the ground.

"This is getting boring," Kaiser said. "37! Make it interesting again."

Sigma 37 got up and ran to a trashcan full of weapons. He tossed aside someone's old prosthetic hook and then reached in again and pulled out a Bowie knife. "This ought to do it."

The other Dogs roared as they saw the blade, and Sigma 37 opened the cage door.

"Bring me the other girlfriend," Kaiser said to the guard. "Maybe the big one needs an incentive, too."

The guard ran over and uncuffed Kelly, who looked up at him with completely red eyes.

"What?" he said, and she started bleeding from everywhere. Hemorrhaging, shaking, she flung out her arms. The handcuffs dangling from her wrist caught the guard across the eyes and he fell.

Kelly shook, bleeding from her pores, her eyes, her nose, her ears. Her quick, jittery movements flung red droplets everywhere. In people's faces. In people's mouths. And then suddenly she stopped.

The crowd around her tried to get away and wipe off the blood that had gotten on them, but some of them were handcuffed to the handrail and couldn't go anywhere.

Kelly's head snapped up, and she hissed.

"What the hell is that?" Kaiser yelled.

Kelly leapt at the guard, knocking his hands out of the way and clamping her teeth down on his face. She yanked back, pulling the balaclava away. Red immediately began to run; it wasn't just cloth pulling away from his cheek.

Screams rang out, and Kelly stood, running from person to person, sinking her nails and teeth into each one, tearing out throats and eyeballs. Those who tried to run fell first; those who tried to fight back failed.

It was an abattoir.

Kaiser stood and pushed Marie away from him, into the crowd. He reached down and grabbed the collar of a naked, blonde Asian woman, then brought her up to his face and yelled.

"Why is this spreading so fast?"

Summer Chan, more fascinated than anything else, tilted her head. "Was she bitten?"

"She was on the boat when the Mutt went berserk, but—"

Finally, Chan showed some concern. "Oh, Jesus. We have no idea what being inside a Dog, especially the Alpha Dog, has done to the virus."

The screams started again, and Kaiser dropped the naked intern. Everyone Kelly had killed was getting back up, pouring blood and spraying it everywhere. And screaming. Not moaning—screaming. He kicked out at a security guard.

"Why the hell didn't you screen these people? Never mind. Dogs! Sic 'em!"

Howling as a pack, the Dogs instantly fell to all fours and changed. The Thetas were done first, bounding up the stairs with the Sigmas following close behind.

Their earlier encounters with the dead hadn't prepared the Dogs for this new strain. Even as the Dogs waded in, they were greeted by three walking dead apiece, moving fast and biting—always biting. And the holes they tore in the Dogs never healed.

"Time to go," Ken said, helping Jorge up from the concrete floor of the sparring cage. He grabbed the Bowie knife on the way to the exit.

The zombies had already swarmed past the Dogs and were starting to work on the crowd.

One came at Ken, and he lashed out with the big blade, nearly decapitating the monster.

He hefted the knife. "Where's Kaiser?"

The Omega Dog had covered ground quickly. As soon as he had seen the Dogs being swarmed and bitten, he had run for Command. He knew what would happen to them soon, and was not about to let it happen.

Flipping open the notepad by the keyboard, he half-wished he had dragged the Chan bitch with him. She would be so much better at this.

One by one on the touchscreen, Kaiser brought up the Dogs' video feeds and typed in the termination code. Hunting and pecking, he kept looking up at the big screen as the squares went black, one by one.

"Thank God for copy and paste," he muttered.

He looked up at Rose's screen and stopped dead. *He* was there. The Mutt. The old Alpha Dog. His fur was wet and matted from his swim in the sea, and water droplets flew with the blood as he tore into the crowd.

McLoughlin had gotten bigger, somehow, and he was rending everyone who crossed his path limb from limb. He caught sight of Jorge and Ken and took after them.

"Come on, Rose," Kaiser said. "You haven't been bitten yet, so come on!"

The Mutt stopped chasing after the loudmouth and the lumberjack, and turned to Rose. Kaiser felt the empty black eyes staring *through* the other Dog, right at him.

McLoughlin charged at Rose then, launching himself, jaws open. A second later, the picture spun crazily, showing sky and headless Dog and then sky again before going black.

FORTY-TWO

OMEGA KAISER STRIPPED off his shirt as he walked down the corridor. He caught a glimpse of himself in a darkened office window and stopped.

"Idiot," he said. "Child."

You get what you want, after all this time, and it isn't until you're about to lose it that you realize...

He kicked off his canvas shoes and undid the buttons on his BDUs. Stepping out of them, he leaned his forehead on the window and stared into his own eyes. Killer's eyes. He'd wanted to be a leader, but he hadn't been able to put the killer away. Couldn't achieve that balance that the Mutt—

No. McLoughlin.

He couldn't achieve the balance McLoughlin had achieved. The Alpha had been feared, but he'd been respected. He had inspired instead of coerced. Kaiser smirked at himself in the glass.

"Learn something new every day."

He straightened up and walked out of Command. Outside, bright halogen lights illuminated something that might have been what Hell looked like. The ground was awash with corpses spilling blood and entrails, and the entire gladiator seating section was now peopled by screaming, bleeding zombie upgrades. Screaming as if just the act of existing caused them pain.

The large shaggy lumps of his Dogs spotted the landscape.

Baring his teeth, Kaiser cursed himself again. He laughed once, a harsh sound; he had been right to call himself the Omega Dog.

"McLoughlin!" he shouted. He had no clear idea whether the former Alpha remembered his old name, or whether he would even respond. There was only one way to find out.

He shouted again, the word twisting into a scream at the end. A couple of shamblers came his way, and he reached out to them, gripping their heads and twisting, one at a time.

"Where are you?!"

He looked around. The lumps of meat on the ground were wriggling, trying to get up on the remains of their stunted limbs. Most of them were missing from the chest down.

The Alpha has feasted.

Kaiser heard it and stopped: the sound was both a howl and a moan, as if somehow the old Alpha Dog's throat was producing two notes at the same time. Kaiser looked around, squinting through the dark smoke of a recently-started fire. In the drifting smudges, he saw him.

McLoughlin waited in the sparring cage.

"Perfect," Kaiser said. He dropped to all fours and arched his back, staring up at the full moon. The Change rippled over his body, taking him faster than it ever had before. Faster than he had ever seen any of the other Dogs do it.

Except for McLoughlin.

The Dog replaced the man, and Kaiser looked into the sparring cage with yellow eyes full of hate. Black, dead pits stared back at him. The two beasts stood immobile, each reaching out with that extra sense the Dogs had, probing the other. As they did, Kaiser and McLoughlin flinched back.

There was something wrong with both of them now.

Running, Kaiser made for the sparring cage door, tearing through it. It bounced off the I-beam of the cage and slammed shut behind him. The Dogs paced inside, eyeing each other. There was no growling, no snapping. No shows of dominance. Just two animals, waiting for the perfect moment.

When it came, nothing else mattered.

The Dogs rushed at each other like freight trains on the same track. They crashed together, clawing and punching, kneeing and stomping. The Alpha snapped his jaws at Kaiser's throat, forcing him to pull back.

McLoughlin continued to bite, his teeth gnashing together in the air as Kaiser moved away.

The Omega Dog reached up and clamped a hand around McLoughlin's snout and pulled their faces close. His other hand came across McLoughlin's cheek like a missile, breaking the bones in his jaw and snout, scattering teeth.

Unleashing another dual-note howl, the Alpha staggered back, sneezing dark brown blood and shaking his shaggy head. The golden fur from healthier days was now matted with gore and mud, and patches of it were missing completely. The skin beneath was oozing something. Not quite blood, not quite pus.

Kaiser knew that biting this diseased creature, this vector, would be the death of him.

He rushed forward, swiping a clawed hand at McLoughlin's stomach as the Alpha howled. Four gashes opened in his midsection, and dark blood poured from the wounds, but Kaiser was not rewarded with a gush of entrails.

Laughing, the Alpha brought his fists down on Kaiser's head and shoulder. The Omega buckled and knelt on the hard concrete, immediately lashing out with his own fists, hammering the side of McLoughlin's knee.

The Alpha wasn't healing quite right. The slashes in his stomach gaped and suppurated.

Kaiser hit him again and leapt away, catching the Alpha's face with the talons on his feet. McLoughlin fell, and Kaiser landed half a dozen yards away, crouching to see what was coming next. A savage light came into his eyes as the Alpha got up. The damaged knee wouldn't completely support his weight, and his snout was still crooked and mushy and all out of sorts.

Roaring, Kaiser charged again.

McLoughlin reached out, stumbling after Kaiser's streaking form, missing and falling again as the Omega's claws tore the muscles loose from his thighs. The Alpha went down, pounding the concrete in frustration.

Kaiser landed heavily on McLoughlin and began tearing away, flaying skin and muscle from his back with black claws.

The Alpha turned, swiping with his own talons and removing a hunk of Kaiser's chest. With a bark of glee, McLoughlin threw himself after the discarded meat, forcing it between his broken teeth. He swallowed and shuddered, immediately feeling the effects.

Kaiser watched as the bent and broken snout straightened with the muffled crunching sound of moving cartilage. Small black points emerged from the Dog's gums. Not quite full teeth, but they were making a comeback.

All the Alpha needed was more fuel.

More meat.

He turned to Kaiser, still favoring his injured knee, and then lurched after him, jaws snapping. The Omega Dog backed off, slashing out to keep the Alpha at bay. The savage bloodlust from just minutes before had turned cold, an icy weight in Kaiser's gut as the implications became clear.

Not only would a bite from this monster turn him into the same thing, but the meat would restore his adversary as well.

Keeping low, Kaiser darted in and away, striking at McLoughlin's leg again, claws seeking out tendons and cartilage. The parts Kaiser knew took the longest to repair. Each time in, the Alpha clawed down at the faster Omega. Each time, Kaiser bounded away with a different set of wounds.

He feinted and McLoughlin dove down, hoping to catch him. Holding back a split second, Kaiser got a clear shot at the back of McLoughlin's neck.

He took it.

A touch of cold at his knee was all the warning he got, and then Alpha McLoughlin's teeth were wrapped around Kaiser's calf. The bigger Dog wrenched his head back, removing a large chunk of muscle and gulping it down.

Kaiser staggered back, eyes wide in horror. He glanced at his wound, which was itching like it normally would, but it was not closing. A smear of brown at the edge of the gash caught his eye, and he knew that was it. He was done.

Bounding in, Kaiser attacked. With no further need to hold his teeth back or dodge McLoughlin's, everything had changed.

The Dogs tore at each other. Kaiser bit and slashed, howling as one of McLoughlin's eyes burst under his claws. The Alpha sunk his teeth into Kaiser's shoulder haunch, then pulled back. The Omega stumbled away, screaming, but then dove in again, breaking McLoughlin's ribs. Hairy arms wrapped around him, and both Dogs fell to the ground.

McLoughlin jumped up, catching Kaiser's right leg in both hands and biting at the knee. Twisting, wrenching, biting, McLoughlin split Kaiser's leg in two. He bounded away, the lower part of the leg in his teeth, mad joy dancing in his one good eye. Greedily, McLoughlin cleaned the shinbone of meat and went back for more.

Kaiser's hand swatted out but the Alpha caught the wrist in his teeth, which had long grown in, black and white fangs crowding his gums. He crunched down and the hand fell away from Kaiser's arm.

The other hand came across, swiping at McLoughlin's throat. It left gashes behind, but no blood flowed from the wound. Instead, it bubbled out slowly, like a gravy. Undaunted, the Omega stabbed McLoughlin's chest over and over, sinking his claws in and tearing the muscle away.

As if he didn't feel a thing, the Alpha began chewing on Kaiser's middle, gnawing through his stomach and organs until his teeth closed on backbone. Shaking his head violently, McLoughlin worried at Kaiser's spine. The Omega fought, slashing at McLoughlin and trying to drive himself away with his feet. A sharp snap filled the air, and the Omega Dog's kicking legs went still.

McLoughlin dragged Kaiser's lower half away, snacking on the meat there. Kaiser screamed at the uncaring moon.

Licking his chops and almost fully healed, McLoughlin came back for more. Kaiser beat at him with his stump of an arm until the bigger Dog caught the Omega's bicep and plucked the limb straight from the socket as easily as dismembering a fly. Kaiser screamed again, but not in agony; his Dog system had shut down pain receptors long before.

He screamed in frustration.

Stripping the meat from the arm, the Alpha kept his new eye on Kaiser's, making sure the other Dog saw how much he was enjoying his hot meal. Then he dug his head into Kaiser's middle, feasting on glistening organs.

Kaiser tried to pull himself away with his good arm, and the Alpha rose. He paused over Kaiser's neck, and the black, black eyes rolled up to look into Kaiser's.

Then his mouth sprouted a silver blade and vomited thick blood.

Looking up past McLoughlin, Kaiser saw Ken standing there, pulling Crispin's sword out of the Alpha's neck. The big infected Dog went to turn, but Ken swung the blade. It sliced through McLoughlin's cheekbone, almost removing the top of the head, exposing the cavity of his mouth, his lower teeth. His tongue wagged as his sinuses gurgled and sucked, then began to pour out that same dark-brown sludge the Alpha had for blood.

Ken pulled the blade out and swung again, this time cleaving through the Alpha's neck.

The body fell and the head bounced away. It landed sideways, staring in a silent snarl at Kaiser and Ken Bishop. Ken kicked it with his boot, and it went flying, colliding with an I-beam with a loud *kerrang!*

He stood over Kaiser, sword in hand.

Kaiser couldn't draw in breath; his solar plexus was shredded and torn and useless. His voice came out in a sad croak from the back of his throat. "K-kill... me," the Omega Dog said.

Ken considered it. He thought he should just leave this bastard for everything he'd done, for all the pain he had caused. For turning regular people into animals.

"Kill me!"

"The messed up thing is," Ken said through gritted teeth, "before this, I would have never met you. But seeing what you've done, I don't have to know you to know that you're a monster."

Sparks on concrete.

The heat drained out of Ken's face.

"New world. Maybe we're all monsters now."

Looking down at Kaiser, Ken gripped the handle of the sword in both hands and raised it up.

FORTY-THREE

"JORGE!" KEN YELLED OUT. He had been wandering the island compound for an hour. After seeing the mess in and around the sparring cage, he branched off to check the other buildings. The first had been the Dog barracks. On his way out, there was one uniformed zombie, a fast one that was oozing blood.

Ken took it out with an easy swing of the sword. He cleaned the blade with the leaves of a tree, wondering what the hell a weapon like this was doing in a high-tech facility, but grateful for it anyway.

He called out for Jorge, but kept thinking of Kelly. He had been busy wrestling with his friend when she had turned, and he hadn't known about it until she had come rushing out of the shadows at him earlier. Hurling herself forward, she had impaled herself on the silver blade. Unable to look at her face, Ken had dragged her around by the sword until he'd picked up one of the guard's discarded shotguns.

Come on, Jorge. Don't do this to me.

The fire had spread from the medical tent to the original quarantine area, making things hard to see, even with the bright lights. He had seen people running back and forth, fighting off the half-zombies dragging themselves around. But no sign of Jorge.

Before Ken's team had started the island assault, Mac had told him about the yacht that the Dogs had used on their rescue attempts; where the keys were, and how to start it. Ken had half a mind to just head for the pier and start the yacht up, then leave it running while he sought out his friend. Speed up the getaway. But Ken didn't want any overzealous survivors taking off without him.

Not until he had found Jorge, one way or the other.

A tightness in his arm got his attention. There was blood there, coming from a thin cut he hadn't noticed. Ken frowned. The way the new zombies had been flinging blood everywhere, he was amazed he hadn't gotten any on him.

Getting closer to the fire, he put the sword down and reached around to his back. He drew the Bowie knife he'd picked up in the sparring cage and put it into the fire. He turned and put his hands to his face, forming a megaphone.

"Jorge!"

The yell echoed out over the island. But it brought nothing back.

Who else could he call for?

Kelly? Dead.

Julius? Dead.

He thought about Jimmy, but then immediately had an even better idea.

"Marie!" Ken yelled. He'd seen her in the stands, and hadn't seen her since.

Ken waited until the blade of the Bowie knife was a dull red color, then pulled it from the fire.

"Here goes nothing."

He pressed the back of the blade to the cut, sealing it off. The searing sound reminded him of the Sigma Dog who had branded him, the one with the 37 tattooed on his forehead. He pulled the knife away, looking at the angry red welt raised there.

Picking the sword up, Ken turned to see a shape hurtling at him. He raised both blades and—it was Marie.

"Is you! Is you!" She was breathless, panting and unable to speak. He lowered the blades and she stepped forward, grabbing his elbow. "This way."

"Is it Jorge? Is he all right?"

Shaking her head, Marie dragged him to a covered alcove, batting fronds out of the way.

"Marie! Is Jorge okay?!"

She shook her head again. "You come."

Exasperated, Ken went with her until they came to a wooden door. She knocked and it opened. Jorge's shining face looked out. "Oh, hey! You found him!"

"Jesus Christ," Ken said, stepping up and grabbing Jorge. For the first time since the car wreck, since the whole world had started to die, he hugged his friend. "Why didn't she just tell me you were okay?"

Jorge pounded Ken's back. "Let me breathe! Dummy. Her English sucks, remember?"

They separated, laughing, and Marie looked mad.

"*Todo esta tranquilo*," he said to her. Then to Ken, "We've been taking turns looking for you. We got a couple of people here; they haven't been bitten or anything. Just one of the covered walkways collapsed and knocked them out."

Ken nodded. "All right. Let's get to the pier. Mac told me how to operate the boat. Let's get the hell *out* of here."

Jorge shrugged. "You sure about that? Seems to me an island is a nice enough place to call home. You know, as long as we get rid of the zombies and clean up the place. They got power here. Facilities. Hell, they even got a radio. Maybe we could figure out what things are like down in Mexico."

"Yeah, okay, but either way, we should try to gather whoever we can and..."

"And what?"

Ken smiled, a lopsided affair. "You know what? I think I'm done calling the shots for now." He tilted his head at Jorge. "What do *you* want to do?"

Jorge put his hand out, clasping Ken's shoulder. He looked his friend in the eyes and all the levity went out of his face. His breathing came slower, and his jaw set with determination.

"I want, with all my heart, to drink a beer."

Ken burst out laughing, leaning over and falling against the wall.

Jorge said, "What?" Then he was laughing, too.

"All right," Ken said, wiping the tears from his eyes. He put his hand out. "All right, *muchacho*. Let's go find ourselves some brew. But then we're going to talk about finding your kids."

"Okay," Jorge said, grabbing the offered handshake. "Just one condition."

"What's that?" Ken asked.

"*I'm* driving."

AUTHORS

THOM BRANNAN (est. 1976) has been a submariner, a nuclear operator, an electrician and now works on an offshore drilling platform. He lives in or around Austin, Texas, with his lovely wife, Kitty, a boy, a girl, a cat and a dog.

D.L. SNELL is an acclaimed novelist from the Pacific Northwest. Anthologies include Pocket Books' *Blood Lite* series, edited by best-selling author Kevin J. Anderson. Snell's first novel, *Roses of Blood on Barbwire Vines*, also attained critical acclaim from popular novelists such as *New York Times* bestselling author Jonathan Maberry. Visit his website at <u>dlsnell.com</u>.

Permuted Press

delivers the absolute best in **apocalyptic** fiction,
from **zombies** to **vampires** to **werewolves**
to **asteroids** to **nuclear bombs** to
the very **elements** themselves.

Why are so many readers turning to
Permuted Press?

Because we strive to make every book
we publish feel like an **event**, not
just pages thrown between a cover.

(And most importantly, we provide some
of the most fantastic, well written, horrifying
scenarios this side of an actual apocalypse.)

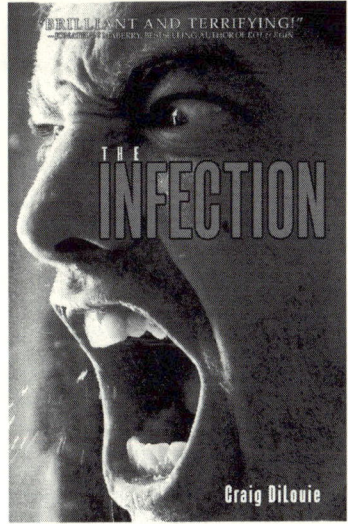

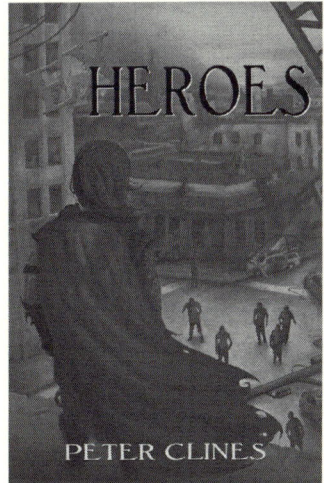

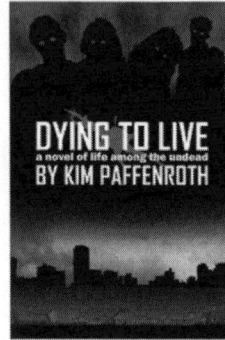

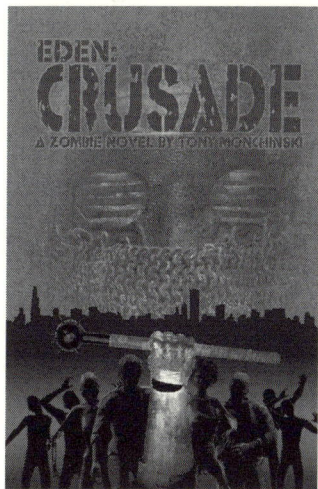

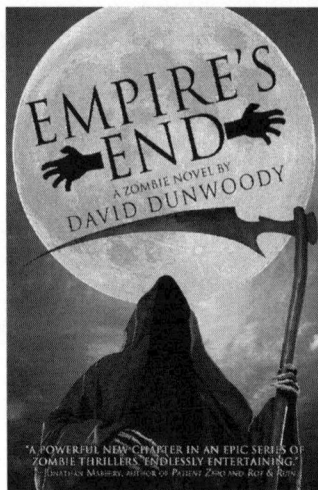

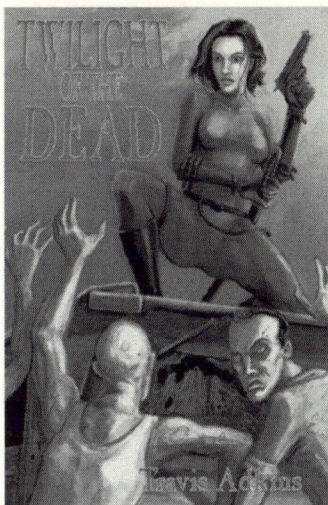

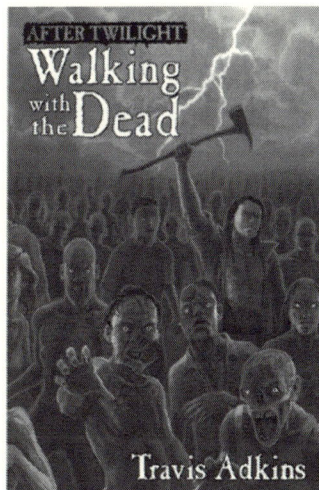

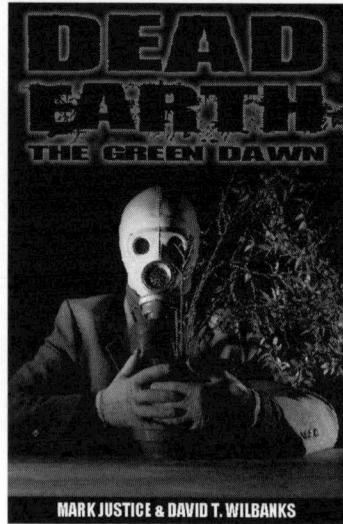

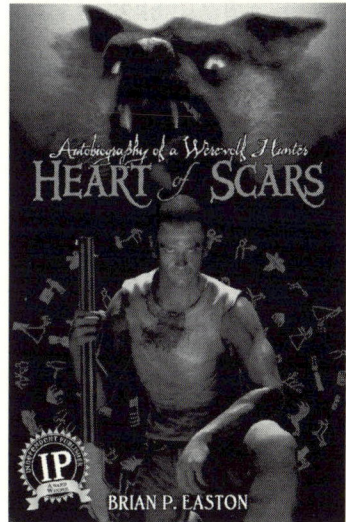

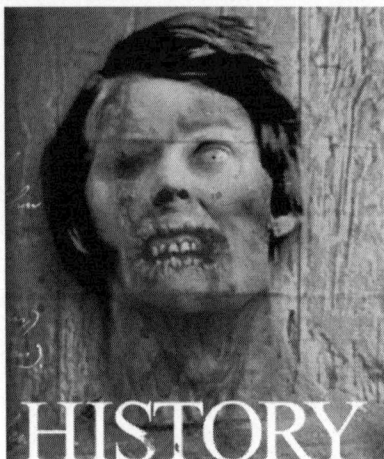

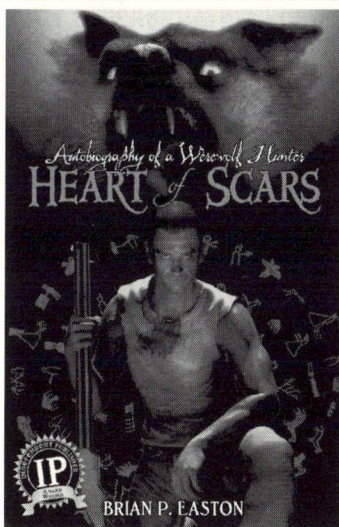

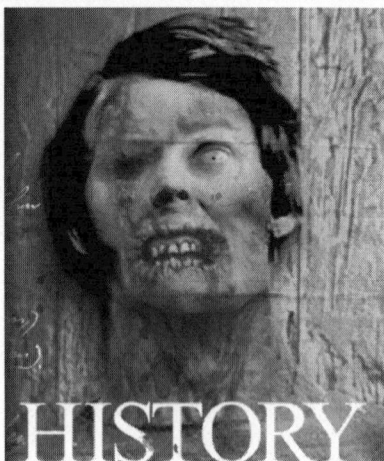

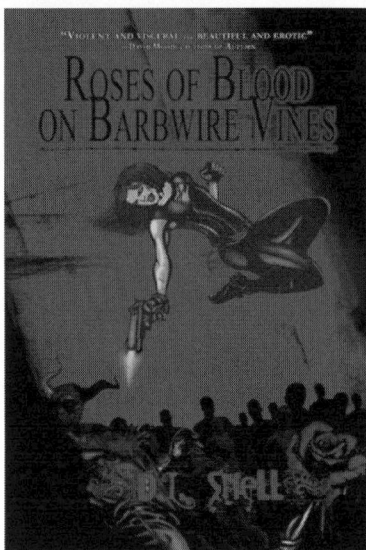

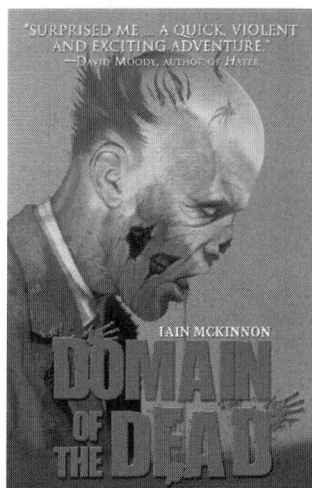

Printed in Great Britain
by Amazon.co.uk, Ltd.,
Marston Gate.